CHASING THE CAPTAIN

TERRY SHEPHERD

D1319116

RAMIREZ & CLARK

Indomitable female cops hot on the trail of justice (and maybe a little revenge), bad guys I loved to hate, an international conspiracy, a little romance, and one blazing action sequence after another kept the pages turning and me happily reading until the end. Can't wait to see what Jessica and the gang get up to in the next installment."

— KERRY SCHAFER, AUTHOR OF THE SHADOW VALLEY MANOR MYSTERY SERIES.

Buckle up! CHASING THE CAPTAIN is a breakneck ride crammed with tension, action, and kick-ass characters. The pages will flash by and when you finish, you'll want more. An excellent thriller.

— DP LYLE, AWARD-WINNING AUTHOR OF THE JAKE LONGLY AND CAIN/HARPER THRILLER SERIES.

Terry Shepherd's latest installment of the Jessica Ramirez series is packed with girl power action, nonstop suspense, and compelling characters that hit close to home. In CHASING THE CAPTAIN, we join Detective Ramirez and her colorful counterparts on a mission that runs as deep as her love for the job. As a lover of the unexpected, I was full-on floored with every turn of the page.

Shepherd is one of those rare authors who can bookend a masterful action scene with poetic prose, descriptive settings, and human emotion, leading readers to fall effortlessly into the diverse worlds he creates.

— KATE ANSLINGER, AUTHOR OF THE MCKENNA MYSTERIES

Terry Shepherd knows how to weave steamy romance into a popcorn thriller that grabs you from the opening scene. Jess and Michael finally come to terms with his drugged-up marriage proposal at the end of CHASING VEGA. And Alexandra Clark gets her own delectable love interest. Two couples trying to sort out their compartmentalized emotions as bullets fly and the bad guys seem to be everywhere. Just my kind of love story!

— MACKENZIE MASTERS, AUTHOR OF PLEASE HER AND PANDEMIC LOVE

With the same wit and cynicism only hard-working officers can have, Shepherd has brought back his best investigators, and you feel like these are people you know! And will cheer 'em on all the way..

Terry Shepherd's second thriller sends Jess and Ali to London and Moscow, chasing "the one who got away." Shepherd's layered plot flies like a ballistic missile. His inclusive cast is augmented by a resourceful mixed-race London DI and an MI6 director who guides one of the world's most sophisticated spy operations from a wheelchair. With CHASING THE CAPTAIN, Shep has conjured another winner, where heroes come in all shapes and sizes the twists and turns keep you turning the pages until the last secret is revealed.

For Colleen, who believed in it.
And for Traci, who lived it.

INTRODUCTION

What would happen if the technology we trust turned against us? And what if that betrayal was directed by someone bent on destroying all that we hold dear?

Jessica Ramirez stumbles into just such a scenario when her usual dogged pursuit of the truth takes her to London and Moscow in search of the one man who she couldn't catch in *Chasing Vega.*

Vladimir Prokofiev is the type of villain who bad people hire to implement their darkest vision. He's the kind of guy you want to see defeated in the most gruesome way possible.

When you open a Jessica Ramirez Thriller, you know that's where we're headed.

But like life itself, the real fun happens on the journey.

So, turn the page and let The Chase begin!

He could feel the reaper slicing through the last filaments of his consciousness. Letting go was warm, inviting, overpowering. He gulped three large breaths to press a last burst of oxygen toward his brain. The burner cell phone was in his fist. The text was ready to send. Could he remember the number?

The alley smelled of rotting produce, pot, and excrement. His impending demise there was a foregone conclusion. The gunshots puncturing his torso were draining the last drops of the ruby-red river of life from his body. Eluding his pursuers was one last miracle an uncaring universe provided. There were others in the thin passageway between a pair of crumbling buildings, a surreal stage where the last moments of his adventures would play out. The homeless congregation who sought shelter there was used to death. No one even looked up when he collapsed against the brick wall.

The oxygen did its work. A whisper from somewhere deep among his dying synapses repeated the ten digits, over and over. He couldn't feel his fingers. He could barely see the keyboard. He channeled the last of his survival instincts *toward pressing the green "send" key. His vision compressed into a single pinpoint of light. The only sense that remained was his ability to hear faint vibrations from a world that was slipping away. A soft conformational beep echoed into the encroaching shadows. Then came the darkness and surrender.*

AUTOMOTIVE PROVING GROUNDS
—ROCHESTER HILLS, MICHIGAN

Gary Sherman buckled his seatbelt and pressed the black, circular button that turned on the all-electric Hollister high-performance concept car. The earpiece inside of his helmet crackled to life. "If this baby passes the test, stock car racing will never be the same."

Gary chuckled. Self-driving vehicles were still controversial. The unions didn't like them because they eliminated jobs for dues-paying operators. The company lawyers didn't like them because they occasionally killed people.

But they were inevitable. GM had just announced an all-electric fleet by 2035. Tesla already had smart cars on the road. For Gary Sherman, chief design engineer for his company's forthcoming line of high-tech automobiles, the Hollister was the ultimate. The aerodynamic, all-electric competition cars that would wow the spectators at Daytona topping out at an average lap speed of 180 miles an hour, ran at full throttle for 500 miles and did it all without a human in control.

The marketing guys were already talking about how big

spenders could buy their way into the cockpit. "The ultimate theme park attraction," they called it.

None of that mattered to Gary. All he cared about was the engineering. He knew the thing would work. He was the guy who had designed it.

"Telemetry recording?" he called out to Nash Burton, his number two who sat in the crow's nest, a control tower at the center of the infield on the winding asphalt ribbon where every concept car had to pass muster.

"Recording and ready," Nash responded. "Light her up."

"Okay, Holly," Gary said to the brain that controlled the vehicle. "Run the race program. Seventy percent power."

A female voice with the hint of a Canadian accent answered, "Initiating race program. Seventy percent power."

Gary smiled. Somewhere up north, his ex-partner, Eve, would never know that he had duplicated her vocal timbre and programmed it into the artificial intelligence engine that translated millions of bytes of data into the rudimentary English language a customer could understand.

At the edge of the track, a light pole blinked the countdown routine Gary first memorized as a kid, hanging with his father at Detroit Dragway. When the green LED at the bottom flashed, the Hollister took off.

Zero to one hundred miles per hour in four-point-three seconds.

Gary felt the g-forces press his body against the bucket seat as Holly flexed her muscles. Electric motors didn't need transmissions. All they needed was some juice and something to focus their power in a productive direction.

The Hollister had both.

Holly whispered the speed and gravity multiples as she

took the first turn. Sensors tracked the way the tires grabbed the pavement, calculating the exact micro pressure where the rubber might lose its grip, keeping the power one-hundredth of a mile per hour below the failure point.

"The crowd at Daytona won't like how quiet Holly can be," Nash observed over the comms link. "People connect power with decibels."

The Hollister navigated the S-curves on the far side of the track, pressing shock absorbers and struts to the limit as the vehicle rocketed into the 27-degree-banked turn that flattened into the home stretch.

"Lap one," Holly whispered. "One hundred ninety-seven average miles per hour. Systems nominal."

The car was a blur as it passed by the twin five-hundred-gallon infield fuel tanks, between four thick concrete pylons and underneath the fly-over that creased the test track. Gary weaved his fingers behind his neck and imagined the diesel gas guzzlers that used the elevated stretch of road to test the capacity of the company's fleet of long-haul semi-trucks.

"We're getting this all on video, aren't we, Nash?" he said into the wireless microphone that was hidden in the sun visor. "This is history."

He could hear Nash trying to suppress a laugh. "What did Henry Ford say? 'If I gave my customers what they asked for, I would have invented a better horse?'"

"Hear that, Holly?" Gary said. "Nash called you a horse."

"Current motor capacity: 2,400 horsepower. Power at seventy percent," Holly responded. "Systems nominal."

"Take us there," Gary commanded. "One hundred percent power."

The Hollister instantly responded. Her passenger felt

another g-force event as the machine accelerated to maximum capacity.

Holly's reflexes were exponentially faster than the most agile human being. Gary's body swayed from side to side as the vehicle entered the S's for a second time and swung into the final banked curve.

"Predicted average lap speed: Two hundred three miles per hour," Holly purred. "Systems nominal."

"One more lap and we'll shut her down, Nash," Gary said, making a note on the aviation clipboard that was strapped to his knee.

There was technology for that job, but Gary still liked to do some things "Old School."

He addressed the brain that was the only thing that kept his titanium missile on wheels under control. "Holly, transmit lap data to the mainframe, please."

Gary knew the word "please" wasn't necessary. But he still felt affection for Eve and liked to think she would have appreciated the courtesy.

"Average lap speed, one-hundred ninety-seven point five three miles per hour. Systems nominal. Transmitting," Holly answered as the finish line, the gas tanks, and the pylons loomed. "Florida, here we come."

Holly spoke again. "System anomaly. Manual control recommended."

Gary took the wheel and applied the brakes. Holly responded. "Controls unresponsive. System anomaly. Attempting correction."

Nash's words were the last that Gary Sherman would hear. "Cut the master switch, Gary. You're drifting left."

Two seconds later, the Hollister cleaved the fuel tanks and disintegrated into a fiery inferno as it slammed into the concrete abutment at two hundred ten miles per hour.

ANDREWS AIR FORCE BASE—
MARYLAND

Darell Sisson and eighteen of his fellow state governors stood at the hangar entrance that was home to the four Boeing 757 jetliners painted with the distinctive blue and white colors that denoted "Air Force Two."

Despite a presidential plea for restraint, Sisson organized the trip to Brussels so he and his counterparts could meet with representatives of the Group of Three, a trio of oligopolists who virtually controlled the economic destinies of Russia, China, and India, and by proxy, over half of the world's economy.

Governor Sisson knew that in the twenty-first century, politicians were increasingly beholden to big business. The G8 Summit that was about to take place in the Belgian capital would be front-page news. But the three powerful men who pulled the puppet strings in the background guided the future destiny of the world.

The gubernatorial trip itself had supplanted the usual G8 pontifications on the television networks. It was unprecedented for state leaders to demand a very public meeting with these very private men.

The world watched as the president reluctantly waved an olive branch and offered Air Force Two as transportation.

What, Sisson wondered, was the delay?

———

IN THE COCKPIT OF USAF 80002, LT. COL. DONALD Babington cursed his luck. The pilot, tapped to shuttle the recalcitrant group across the Atlantic, noticed what he thought was a hairline crack in an aft exit door window. The chief master sergeant in charge of maintenance assured the colonel that the window was safe. But Don Babington wasn't a man to take chances.

"Transfer everything to eight triple-0 three," he told the NCO in charge of flight services. "We don't want these taxpayers to think we are casual about their safety."

The colonel himself descended the stairs and motioned to his passengers to surround him. "I apologize for the delay, gentlemen. We are dealing with a rare maintenance issue, much like the minor headaches you sometimes have when you fly commercial."

Babington pointed to 80002's gleaming twin. "Luckily, we have more than one Air Force Two and should be wheels-up in about twenty minutes. The jet stream is helping us today, so we should still arrive in Brussels on time."

There was a palpable groan from the governors, most of whom, Babington assumed, were more upset about the delay in getting their in-flight cocktails.

Major Kyle Padfield approached Babington. The former Thunderbird pilot was young but well qualified to fly the mission as a backup if need be. He was also resourceful.

"Excuse me, Colonel," he whispered. "I took the liberty of fully preparing and pre-flighting eight triple-0 three for you. If you'd like to do a walk around with me, she's ready to go now."

Babington grinned at his junior counterpart. Kids who made senior officers look good had bright futures in his air force.

"An update, gentlemen," he said to the passengers. "This is Major Kyle Padfield. He's a former flight leader with the Thunderbirds and one of the best officers in the Air Transport Command." The colonel pointed to aircraft 80003. "Thanks to his efficiency, we will board Air Force Two in ten minutes. Departure will be on time, as scheduled."

There was a smattering of cheers and applause, followed by directions from the flight service officer, guiding the governors to the backup aircraft.

"Great job, Major," Babington said. "Tell you what. Let's give these guys a treat and get you some stick time in triple-0 two. I'll approve a parallel take-off on nineteen left and right. Let's show them a little formation flying and you can have the chief do a pressure check on the window in the aft exit while you're airborne."

Padfield saluted with a grin, and the colonel shook his hand.

"I'll write up a commendation when I get back, Major."

———

"THE GROUP OF THREE UNDERESTIMATE THE economic power of the United States of America,"

Governor Darell Sisson said as he took his seat in the first row of the Air Force Two passenger cabin. "Their rumblings that we are a dying economy and a failed state are fighting words to this Southerner."

Sisson ignored the smirks from his fellow governors. Everyone knew he was about to announce a presidential run, and this trip was as much about showing Americans the size of his balls as it was about drawing imaginary lines in the shifting political sands.

The governor could hear the Pratt and Whitney PW2040 engines spin up to two-thirds power. He reflexively looked through the windows as eight triple-0 three began its take-off roll.

Babington's voice cut through the turbine noise on the PA system. "Gentlemen, if you'll look to the left side of the aircraft, you'll see Major Padfield at the controls of our original magic carpet. He's performing a maintenance test, and I thought you would enjoy a bird's-eye view of a Boeing 757 taking off."

———

Kyle Padfield still preferred the agility of a Thunderbird F-16 to the sluggish response of the lumbering 757 controls. But missions like this one got him one step closer to another promotion and to his holy grail: The left seat on Air Force One.

The major flew his heavy bird with military precision, exactly parallel to eight triple-0 three and the audience who watched him from within.

The two aircraft turned over Delaware, gently swinging east-northeast as Atlantic City passed on his port side.

"Air Force eight-zero-zero-zero-two from Air Force Two. Okay to break off and return to Andrews."

Padfield could hear the subtle approval in Colonel Babington's voice on the radio. "Thanks again, Major."

"Roger, Air Force Two," the Major responded. "Safe travels."

At that moment, the autopilot engaged, pointing the nose of the aircraft downward toward the ocean.

Padfield and his co-pilot knew the aircraft systems inside and out. As he barked commands and flipped switches, the 757's systems refused to respond.

"Mayday. Mayday. Mayday," Padfield said calmly into his headset. "Air Force eight-zero-zero-zero-two's flight controls unresponsive."

As the passengers on Air Force Two watched in horror, the giant aircraft nosedived toward the ocean, exploding into an orange kerosine mushroom cloud on impact.

NATIONAL TRANSPORTATION SAFETY BOARD—490 L'ENFANT PLAZA SW, WASHINGTON, DC

J osé Wodehouse didn't recognize the caller ID when it flashed on the aging Rolm telephone on what passed for his desk in the tiny analyst cubical at National Transportation Safety Board headquarters in Washington.

He almost didn't pick up. The newly minted analyst was feeling the pressure to update his superiors on two month-old investigations, the flight 80002 crash, and some odd accident on an automotive test track in Detroit.

The voice on the other end of the line was equally young and equally unfamiliar.

"Mr. Wodehouse?"

At twenty-four, José wasn't used to being called "Mr."

"This is Cameron Dunham at the NSA. I've been told that you are looking into the Air Force Two incident."

The visibility of José's work on that one went all the way to the White House. He wished a more seasoned analyst were on the case. "For better or worse, yes. How can I help you, Cameron?"

"I think I've found a connection between that accident and something that happened in Michigan."

This NSA kid must have the same enemies, José thought. "What have you got?"

"A hacker may have caused both events."

THE RIVER BEND MAXIMUM SECURITY PRISON—NASHVILLE, TENNESSEE

Detective Jessica Ramirez concluded that malfeasance was bathed in florescent lighting and smelled like industrial cleaning fluid.

This place was not dissimilar to the lock-up at the police department where she worked.

The fundamental difference was that they killed people here.

The execution they sent her to witness made no sense. A death sentence without a body. And a fish out of water from a small Illinois river town, ordered by a cruel chief to watch a man burn to death.

She would have preferred the Mississippi River crickets to this somber scene. The alleged perp's name was Vincent Culpado. They said he killed his wife.

Today he would walk his last mile.

Jess's years of training recorded the drill. Two of the eight guards marched ahead of him. Two more walked on either side of the prisoner, each supporting an arm in case he suddenly bolted.

Behind the condemned, another pair of uniforms flanked the prison warden.

Jess walked behind that trio with the final two guards bringing up the rear.

"What's she doing here?" a guard asked the warden.

"Her chief pulled some strings to get her on the inside for this thing. He must be one sadistic son of a bitch."

"Why her? Why allow an outsider to have intimate access to an execution?"

The warden shrugged. "She made the arrest ten years ago. They say it was her first day on the job without a training officer."

Jess could see the guard steal a glance at the shield and name tag on her chest.

"Detective Jessica Ramirez," he muttered. "They must really hate her back home."

TEN YEARS EARLIER - PALOMA, ILLINOIS

U nlike most of her colleagues, Jess had the hot sheet memorized. So, when the late model sedan rolled a stop sign ahead of her, she knew that whoever was inside was driving a stolen car.

The minute Jess turned on the light bar, he took off.

"Don't feel you have to save the world from someone who ran a stop sign, partner."

Alexandra Clark, another probie who was a classmate at the academy, pinched her seatbelt tight around her waist. Jess and Ali became fast friends and drew one another as partners after their field training officers failed to wash them out, despite their herculean efforts to do so.

Jess pressed the accelerator to the floor. "It's a stolen car, babe. Let's sing to him."

Ali powered up the yelping siren. "I think you became a cop just so you could get attention."

"I became a cop to piss off my father. I wanted to be a swimmer. He said, 'Get a job where you use your head and not your body.'"

"Well, use your head, then. Think about the other cars

that share this street, partner. You're cutting it a little close with some of these passes."

"'Get a job where you use your head and not your body,'" Jess repeated. "You'd think he was talking me out of being a hooker. Why do parents do that?"

The Latina spun the steering wheel counterclockwise to avoid a pedestrian. Ali held on to the dashboard for dear life. But the almost disinterested tenor of the conversation between the two might well have been happening in some bar.

"When I told my parents I was gay, all my dad said was, 'Well, Mona. I guess that means we don't get any grandchildren.' My mother hasn't spoken to me since. Lesbian couples have kids. We can be great moms!"

The subject vehicle sped up.

"Seventy in a thirty-five zone, Ali. What the hell did this guy do?"

Ali was still in the past. "I think there's some sort of universal rule that parents screw up their kids. I bet our perp was too short to drive the bumper cars in middle school."

She checked the safety on her Smith semi-auto as the Howzell's Ice Cream parlor sign as it flew by in her peripheral vision. "Hey! Salted caramel is on special today. My all time favorite. Let's get some on the way home."

Jess keyed the radio. Her voice was dead calm.

"Dispatch from 4-David-15. In pursuit of a 2009 Chevrolet Caprice, Illinois plate Mark David Uniform Three One Seven. Westbound on Collins Street, crossing Boyd Avenue."

An icy voice responded. "Ten-four, 4-David-15. The Captain orders you to continue pursuit only if you are not endangering lives."

The subject vehicle left a rubber trail as the driver

swerved around a slower car, nearly picking off a pedestrian.

"Endangering lives?" Ali said. "He's the guy endangering lives. I've got an idea. Why don't we just let the boys bag this shithead? It's day-one alone in the car for both of us. And it's almost 5 o'clock. If we kill somebody, we'll spend the next two weeks with internal affairs."

For the first time, Jess felt the adrenaline rush that would soon become an addiction.

"If we break off, partner, the boys will never let us live it down. This one isn't getting away."

Ali braced herself against the dashboard.

"Why do I feel like I will forever be the voice of reason you will never listen to?"

"Would you like me to drop you off at the next corner and take this guy down alone?"

"Of course not. If you get yourself killed on day one, at least I can tell your mother that I warned you to be sensible."

The Caprice hit a cyclist, tossing its rider into the air and over both vehicles like a rag doll. He landed unhurt, shaking his hands and cursing a blue streak.

Jess saw Ali assessing the damage. "That guy must be some sort of gymnast. He's barely got a bruise."

Jess kept her eyes on the perp vehicle. "I'm gonna bruise the moron who hit him in a moment." The bad guy swerved into another right turn. She was almost on top of him now. More cops fell in behind the cruiser.

Ali's head hit the ceiling as the vehicle sailed over a speed bump. "He's headed for the freeway, Jessica. If he gets there, we'll lose the bust to the state troopers."

"I know, I know," Jess said, impatience clouding her focus on what was ahead of her. "Get ready to run in case he bails."

Buildings and stoplights flew by the two cops like fence posts. The freeway overpass lay dead ahead.

Jess could see two state cop cars maneuvering into position. "We're running out of time, partner," Ali warned. What's the plan?"

Jess tightened her grip on the steering wheel. "I'm going to hit him with a pit maneuver."

"Jesus, Jessica. You are not certified yet."

"I saw it done as a ride-along."

"Not at eighty miles per hour. It's never been done."

"Then let's rewrite the book."

The radio came alive.

"4-David-15. Break off pursuit. State police will engage."

"See?" Ali said, "I told you so."

Jess floated to the right of the target and hit the gas. "I couldn't hear the radio. You were talking too loud." Jess knew her partner would bow to the inevitable.

She was in position. Gently nursing the car to the left, her front bumper caught the Chevy's right rear quarter panel. Ali was right. The book said Jess was going too fast on a road filled with other vehicles. She intended to rewrite the book.

The Caprice slid into a spin. Nearby vehicles swerved to avoid it. Even the cops behind Jess slowed a bit to take in the spectacle.

But Jess overcorrected, sending her own cruiser into a spin. A front wheel caught the edge of the curb, tossing the car and its occupants into the air. After a double horizontal flip, the car landed on its feet, just as if Jess had planned the whole thing.

She looked at her disheveled passenger. "That, my dear Alexandra, is how it's done."

The Caprice did a half dozen 360s, coming to rest nose

to nose with Jess and Ali's vehicle. Two state cop cars configured a *V* formation directly ahead of it.

In seconds, there would be dozens of boys in blue surrounding them.

Ali shook her head. "Something tells me I'll be forever pulling your chestnuts out of the fire. We better arrest this guy before someone else does."

Jess's partner stood behind the passenger door, her Glock pointed at the perp's windshield. Jess tried to look calm as she walked up to the driver's side window.

He rolled it down and put his hands onto the steering wheel, staring through the glass at the barrel of the gun she aimed at his head.

"My name is Vincent Raymond Culpado. I am wanted in Tennessee. I'm sorry if I caused you any trouble."

"Nobody was seriously hurt, Mr. Culpado. Keep your hands where I can see them, and don't move. Some more senior officers will arrive in a few moments to take credit for the arrest, and I will probably never see you again. Thank you for a thrilling first day on the job."

Culpado's eyes met Jess's, and she saw sadness and resignation. He studied her name tag. "Be careful what they tell you about all of this, Officer Ramirez. I didn't kill her."

6

PRESENT DAY - THE RIVER BEND
MAXIMUM SECURITY PRISON—
NASHVILLE, TENNESSEE

A dozen witnesses claimed to have seen Vincent Culpado push his wife off The John Seigenthaler Pedestrian Bridge and into the Cumberland River. The prosecution portrayed the accused as a jealous husband who murdered his spouse when he thought she was having an affair. No evidence of an assignation was ever discovered. The jury unanimously agreed that Vincent Culpado was guilty and recommended the death penalty.

Nobody was talking about how he escaped from prison. Those close to the District Attorney's office whispered that they hoped that Vincent Culpado would just disappear.

Jessica Ramirez screwed that one up for them.

The bust went down exactly as she had predicted.

Jess didn't get the credit.

Typical, she thought. Back then, the place was a bunch of barely caged animals, only slightly evolved from the ape culture where males dominated, and females were relegated to procreation.

Now, ten years later, Jess got the credit. Perhaps it was a punishment for catching someone everyone else didn't want to be caught.

She could smell the perspiration that drenched Culpado's body. A guard strapped a metal helmet that looked like early football head protection around his chin. The guard apologized that salt water was dripping from the sponge inside it and into the prisoner's eyes.

"This isn't your fault," Culpado said.

Jess recognized the calmness in his voice. It was disquieting.

They tightened the straps; electrode placements were double-checked. The prisoner was one with the thick oak chair that would usher him into eternity.

The extraction team left the death chamber, motioning for Jess to follow. The warden guided her to a viewing room, where the witnesses waited behind closed aluminum blinds. An old-style rotary telephone hung on the wall, a tool the lawyer could wield if he felt something about the process was awry.

The warden made the introductions.

"Ladies and gentlemen, this is Detective Jessica Ramirez, representing the arresting jurisdiction. Detective, this is Henry Morris, Mr. Culpado's attorney, Tony Eldridge of the *Nashville Tennessean Newspaper*, Officer Hanks, representing the Bureau of Prisons and Mr. and Mrs. Yates, the deceased's parents."

"Presumed deceased, Warden," Attorney Morris said. "This will be the first execution in Tennessee history where no body was ever found."

This stunned Jess. She knew of no case in modern times where a man was condemned to death without a body. She compartmentalized the thought.

Keep quiet, Jess. This isn't your battle to fight.

Mrs. Yates lit up.

"Many witnesses saw that man push my daughter to her death, Mr. Morris. I'm glad I can watch him pay for his crime."

The warden ignored her.

"I'll ask you all for silence during the proceedings, ladies and gentlemen. Officer Hanks is here to ensure that we all maintain decorum. The courts have spoken. They have approved you as witnesses to the execution. Our job is to carry out the sentence."

Tony Eldridge made a note of the quote. Jess knew it would be the "money line" in tomorrow's paper. She gave the reporter a nod of recognition, a silent thank-you for a Dropbox full of research on the Culpado case Eldridge had quietly shared with her weeks earlier.

The room stank of sweat and stale cologne. A lingering bouquet of puke added another uncomfortable layer of complexity to the air.

This was not a place where one came to be entertained.

The blinds rose. Vincent Culpado's eyes met Jessica's.

He was hyperventilating. A small speaker in the room crackled to life, and the witnesses could hear the voice of a guard.

"Vincent Raymond Culpado, you have been tried and convicted of the murder of Marie Yates-Culpado and sentenced to death by electrocution. May God have mercy on your soul."

The guard asked the prisoner if he had any last words.

"I have made many mistakes in my life. But I did not kill my wife. God, forgive me for my sins. I surrender myself to His will."

There was one last inspection of the chair and the terri-fied life form bound in its deadly embrace.

Then, Vincent Culpado sat alone, facing those whose

lives were so profoundly affected by the turn of events that brought everyone to this moment.

His eyes never left Jess's. She couldn't bring herself to look away.

Culpado's features morphed into a familiar face. Jess saw her own father sitting in that chair. How could that be? He died when the assassin destroyed the Ramirez family home. Was the post-traumatic stress of losing the one person Jess could never please, the one person whose life she could not save finally forcing its way into her consciousness?

She cursed Vega, the woman Jess battled to the death in the Colorado River. And she cursed the man they called "The Captain," the one who remained a mystery; the one who got away.

Jess thought about the vow she made on the day her family finally buried its patriarch.

Whatever happens, I will bring The Captain to justice.

The warden nodded. Somewhere, behind a two-way mirror at the edge of the death chamber, the anonymous cop who had drawn the short straw threw the switch.

The witnesses could hear the dynamos spin and vicariously felt the twin bolts of lightning that contracted every muscle in the prisoner's body at the same time.

Blood ran freely from Culpado's nostrils, darkening the stark-white prison jumpsuit in an ever-expanding scarlet stain. His body convulsed up and down like one large ice cube in a cocktail shaker. Small, gray, curling strands of smoke floated from beneath his headgear.

In her peripheral vision, Jess saw Mrs. Yates's face contort into terror. Despite the warden's warning, she screamed.

The tiny pulses of electricity that fired the synapses in

his brain amplified into infinity, erasing every memory, every emotion, every sign that a person named Vincent Raymond Culpado had ever existed.

HE'S DEAD

"**H**e's dead."

With two words, the doctor removed the stethoscope from the prisoner's chest. A guard lowered the blinds.

Mrs. Yates sobbed silently. Her husband held her hand. Officer Hanks was as stoic as Jess expected. The warden was nowhere to be found.

Culpado's lawyer put a hand on Jess's shoulder. "Are you all right, Detective?"

Cops are well inoculated against the stresses of police work. But Jess still couldn't hide a shudder. The attorney must have seen it.

His voice was kind. But she could sense a hint of revulsion in its timbre. "I've witnessed a dozen of these in my lifetime. You never get used to it."

Her own voice was calm. "Thanks. How do I get the hell out of this place?"

Jess silently cursed her chief and his sycophants, who had done everything they could to drum her out of the force over the last decade.

Damn you, testosterone simians. Time is relegating your attitudes to the anachronisms they always were. You can try to demoralize me, but you will never break me!

She left the viewing area, another layer of post-traumatic stress grotesquely welded into the searing tapestry of battle scars she knew would never fully heal.

THE MAN IN THE LIMO

I t's a common saying in the profession. "How I wish I could un-see what I've seen."

Detective Jessica Ramirez couldn't get the picture of Vincent Culpado's writhing body, her father's writhing body, out of her mind. Somehow, he maintained eye contact until the last second, perhaps trying to transmit some final message.

What was it?

That a jury sentenced him to death without finding a body didn't sit well. When Jess got into a mood like this, trouble almost always ensued.

She expected a taxi to collect her outside of the prison. The uniformed chauffeur beckoning her into the back seat of a black limousine was a surprise. He bowed. "A courtesy for the Detective."

Jess hesitated. At no time during this experience had anyone treated her with even a modicum of respect, let alone a shiny Lincoln.

"It's all right, Detective Ramirez," a deep voice said

from the dark depths of the limousine. "The Warden approves."

JESS' TRAINING COULD DECIPHER HEIGHT AND weight, even when the body was partially obscured by darkness and bent into a sitting position.

He was 5'9", around 200 pounds that Jess imagined was once prime beef. He had black hair with silver roots that belied the bottle it came from. Sagging flesh surrounded brown eyes. He was a high-mileage model. She guessed late 50s to early 60s. A perfectly tailored Brioni Vanquish suit with a neatly folded handkerchief and matching silk tie around the neck of a red and white striped silk shirt enhanced his features. A Rolex watch gleamed on his left wrist. A diamond onyx ring bulged on his right finger. Jess could hear a hint of New York in his accent.

"I'm Jack Crawford. Vince Culpado was my friend."

Jess's every sense was on high alert. She felt for the comfort of her service weapon. "Are you taking me to the airport?"

"Yes, ma'am. Vince's attorney told me you were here, and I wanted a few minutes to speak with you, alone."

Jess's eyes focused on the road ahead. The airport signs flashing by on the side of the interstate were a small consolation. "Mr. Culpado didn't seem to have many friends, Mr. Crawford."

"Call me Jack."

"Your name didn't pop up in any of the court documents I read, Jack."

"That's because someone in power wanted it that way."

Jess's stress level went down a notch. She was interested

but still cautious. This guy came out of nowhere. That's usually how the danger you don't see appears.

"Yes, Detective. We'll be at the airport soon, so I'll come straight to the point. I was the one who saw Marie with another man, and I told Vince about it. His attorney tried to get that into the record, but the DA convinced the court that I was a tainted witness."

"Why would he want to do that, Jack?"

"Like I said, Vincent Culpado was my friend."

"And why are you talking to me?"

"I want to hire you to investigate his murder."

If she were back home, she would have called for backup. The chauffeur kept his eyes on the road. Crawford did not appear to be armed. Jess kept her voice under control. "They executed your friend for killing his wife, Jack. Several layers of jurisprudence agreed he was guilty. What's to investigate?"

"Oh, the state may have pulled the switch, Detective, but Marie Yates made it happen."

"You seem to imply that Mrs. Culpado is still alive."

"I believe she is. And I want you to find her."

In the back of Jess's brain, a flash of insight began to emerge. "Trust your hunches," Ali always said. Was her sixth sense that Culpado was wrongly convicted on the money?

No, Jess. Not now. Think about this at the airport.

"I have a job, Jack. I'm a sworn peace officer in the State of Illinois. I'm already way outside of my jurisdiction, and there are a dozen reasons why it would be inappropriate for me to be a private investigator on a case where I was the cop who made the arrest."

Crawford glanced at his watch. He waved a hand at the driver to pick up the pace.

"I know a few things about you, Detective. I know you

believe in fair play. I know you sometimes color outside the lines. And I believe that, like me, this mess is eating away at your insides. You won't be sleeping well until you have a better sense of whether the man you saw electrocuted tonight really deserved to die. Nobody can tell you what to do on your own time. I'm just offering to pay your expenses and add to your retirement fund."

Crawford had her nailed. Somehow, he knew her story. Was it another of Chief O'Brien's sick attempts to trap her? "What's your interest, Jack? Why is this so important?"

"Vince helped me get started in the business. While he did okay, I did very well. I owe my fortune to Vince Culpado. And I owe it to him as a friend to avenge his murder."

Not with me, you don't. I have a job to do and my own father's murder to avenge. Engaging outside of my jurisdiction nearly got me killed. I'm going home to get some sleep and think things through.

"I'm not your girl, Jack. This is just another chapter that will populate the nightmares I already have. It sounds like you can hire the best of the best to chase this goose. I suggest you set a higher standard. If you need some recommendations, I know a few people."

"I already know who I want, and I'm looking at her," Crawford said. He pressed a business card into Jess's hand. "Think about it and call my cell if you decide you are interested. I have friends in high places who can smooth any bumps in the road you may have back in Illinois, and if you won't take my money, perhaps I can return the favor in another way."

Jess didn't like the sound of that at all. Her face must have telegraphed it because Crawford softened.

"Look, Detective, I'm nobody special. I just have the knack for building mutually beneficial relationships. And my business throws off enough cash flow that I can pursue whatever interests me. Right now, I'm deeply interested in finding out if Marie Yates-Culpado is alive. If she is, there has been a grave miscarriage of justice. That's a wrong that you, of all people, would want to see put right. If you see a thread I could follow, call me. And if you decide to chase this goose, I promise to make it worth your while, whatever the ultimate outcome might be."

The limo pulled up to BNA Departures with time to spare. The chauffeur opened the door.

"It's too bad you couldn't press the DA with the same intensity you've been pressing me, Jack. Mr. Culpado's death bothers me, too. But my life and work are back in Illinois, and that's where I'm headed."

Crawford smiled. "You're a good person, Detective. And I know you've worked off the clock and out of your jurisdiction before. Give it some thought."

How did Jack Crawford know that?

The door closed, and the limo glided away into the night. Jess had maybe another thirty minutes to put the man in the Brioni suit out of her mind and scan Dropbox for the flurry of documents that the reporter Eldridge shared.

There was nothing mentioned about this so-called best friend anywhere.

But in the middle of the sea of notes, there was an interesting name. Liyanna Evans. And an international phone number she didn't recognize.

It was just one sentence, an afterthought, out of context. In Jess's experience, that was often where you find the most interesting information. She called the number, and a woman answered.

"Liyanna Evans."

"Ms. Evans? I'm Jessica Ramirez. I'm a detective with

the Paloma, Illinois Police Department and have a crazy question for you."

The voice on the other end was a mixture of Scottish brogue and a language Jess couldn't place. "We're sisters in the craft, Detective Ramirez. I'm a Detective Inspector with Metropolitan Police in London. They call us 'DI's over here. Always glad to help a colleague."

"I have notes here from a newspaper reporter in Nashville, Tennessee, that tell me you think you saw a Marie Culpado in your neck of the woods, perhaps a decade ago. I know it's a long shot, but do you remember anything about it?"

There was a protected silence on the other end of the line. Jess could feel DI Evans flipping through her memory banks.

"Yeah. I remember. The murder story was a bit of a sensation over here, and her picture was fodder for Fleet Street. I could swear I saw her double boarding the tube at The Strand. Nobody on your side of the pond seemed to care."

Jess couldn't suppress a chuckle. "I'm not surprised. Not to get too graphic, DI Evans, but I just saw her husband fry for murder, and my cop sense is telling me the whole thing stinks. Did you dig any deeper?"

"That was ten years ago. I'm surprised I remember as much as I told you."

The gate agent was calling Jess's flight.

"Well, I had to ask. Sorry to bother you. If you think of anything else, can you save my cell number and call me?"

Jess imagined her colleague making a note of the Caller ID.

"Glad to. And my friends call me Lee."

"Thanks very much, Lee. I'm Jess. If I ever get to London, I'll buy you a Guinness."

"Stay safe, sister. And Cheerio, as we say."

Nothing about this case felt right. Jess's conventional cop instincts were screaming to stay as far away from Jack Crawford and the whole Culpado mess as she could.

She saved DI Evan's number to her contact list and boarded the plane. Jess's cop sense whispered that this wasn't the last time the name Vincent Culpado would cross her lips.

LONDON - DETECTIVE INSPECTOR LIYANNA EVANS

D etective Inspector Liyanna Evans couldn't remember what triggered her to chase down the backstory for Marie Culpado. Maybe it was the serendipity of reading about it in the tabloids. They plastered Marie's picture across page three. Of course, the rag made it more lurid than it turned out to be.

Until she received Jessica Ramirez's cryptic phone call, the London-based detective inspector had nearly forgotten about the body double she had noticed dashing into the carriage at the Strand Tube Station.

It was a story she had never shared with her Met colleagues. All new police constables struggle for credibility with their counterparts. Telling one of them she thought she had seen the supposedly dead American splashed across the tabloids was fodder for ridicule.

The one person she trusted was her partner, PC Zoe Doyle.

"You're half South African Zulu, half Scottish and a female," Zoe told her as they scanned the football jerseys on break at the Granberry's department store. "You had three strikes against you from day one."

Lee chuckled. "That's how I play cricket. This one looks like it will fit ya, Zoe."

She handed PC Doyle an Arsenal jersey, knowing that her partner was a Manchester United fan.

Zoe didn't say that Lee's same-sex preference was also a landmine. There were still many older cops who thought being gay was a step beyond the famous UK reserve.

"You know my 'team' preference, mate," Zoe said, tossing the shirt back into the bin and grabbing a Manchester United jersey. "And you've definitely learned how to move the levers. Few of us ladies make Detective Inspector in less than a decade. And you're not afraid to go your own way."

"This Yank detective rattled my cage, Zoe. The Culpado case still bothers me, too."

"You're not going to get involved in this, are you? It's as cold a case as they come."

"I did some cursory research on the web last night, partner. The Nashville paper's description of Culpado's electrocution gave me nightmares. I think a Crunchy bar and a visit to Belmarsh may be in order."

Zoe's eyebrows rose. "Not Harry Duggan!"

"If Marie, in fact, came to the UK, she would have needed documents. Harry was active back then. Perhaps his memory is better than mine."

Harry Duggan was serving Her Majesty's pleasure for forgery at HM Belmarsh. His specialty: false passports. The timeline Lee constructed would have put Marie Culpado right in the middle of Harry's prime.

Granberry's was a step down from the Marks & Spencer chain but could be a formidable competitor in the retail space, especially in London's less affluent areas.

100,000 square feet of commerce covered two stories, filled with everything from clothing and appliances to cakes and candies. And it was close to Belmarsh.

Zoe threw the Manchester United jersey over her shoulder. "I don't know, partner. It feels like you are tilting at windmills again. That's a great way to short circuit a career."

The two joined the end of a long queue at one of the check-out kiosks.

Lee frowned. "One thing I don't like about Granberry's is that they have too few of these. The queues are always massive, and they are located close to the exits. There is almost always lots of cash in the till since her patrons often have bad credit and trade in the 'coin of the realm.' They attract thieves like bees to honey."

Zoe touched Lee's arm. "Look at the low-life in the purse section. He has a partner checking out the jewelry." Zoe pointed to a short rat-faced Mediterranean-looking man inspecting the women's purse display to the left of the kiosk. To the right, a tall, unshaven Caucasian fondled the lingerie.

"Out of place," Zoe added. "Two odd sods."

Zoe pointed to a short rat-faced Mediterranean-looking man inspecting the women's purse display to the left of the kiosk. To the right, a tall, unshaven Caucasian fondled the lingerie.

"What triggered you?" her partner asked.

"The raincoats."

"Why?"

"It isn't raining."

Lee saw Zoe feel for the collapsible baton in her fanny pack. Moments like these made her wish they let more coppers carry guns.

On the other hand, Lee felt as if Zoe had just given her

a Christmas present. She rubbed her hands together, smiling like a child about to raid the biscuit box.

"Let's see what the tall boy is up to."

Lee took the Manchester United jersey from her partner's grasp and pulled it over her head. She was no longer the focused, plain-clothes police constable but now a flighty tosser. She stopped to touch some hanging outfits as she moved in the taller man's direction.

When Lee made eye contact, she perked up in surprise. "Dennis?" Her voice was loud, obnoxious, and got attention. "You have the nerve to make love to me and then don't call me?"

"I don't know you," he growled.

"How dare you, Dennis? You take me to dinner. You take me to bed. In the morning, you are gone. What way is that to treat a lady?"

"Shut up," he hissed.

Lee was getting close to him now, invading his personal space. "My mother warned me about your kind. 'Never fall in love with an Irishman,' she said. Did I listen? No. What a fool I was."

The man put a hand on Lee's chest, shoving her to the ground. A shotgun appeared from beneath the raincoat.

"Nobody moves and nobody gets hurt," he yelled. "Me and my pal over there have you all covered."

He nodded across the way, where Rat Face vaulted over the circular counter and into the kiosk. He produced a handgun and put it against the head of an associate. Lee watched Zoe slip closer to her target.

"It's payday, luv," Rat Face whispered. "Just put the pounds into this black bag, and we'll be on our way."

Lee didn't break character. She was on her feet and in subject number one's face.

"You should be ashamed of yourself, Dennis. You have a good job. That's why I went out with you."

The man in the raincoat put the barrel of the shotgun against her forehead. "I warn you, lassie. Get back, or I'll blow what little brains are in that empty melon all over the panty display."

Lee stepped back in horror. "You've changed, Dennis. What happened to the man I thought I loved? I believed in you. We were going to have a family, a future."

"I swear to you, woman, if you don't shut up."

Lee swept the shotgun away from her head with a forearm, smashing a fist into the suspect's face. Momentarily stunned, he loosened his grip on the weapon. Lee grabbed it, thrusting the butt between his eyes. He fell to the floor, the barrel of the shotgun now trained on his temple.

"Move a muscle, arse-hole, and I'll blow what little brains you may have in that empty melon all over the floor."

Lee saw Zoe clear the countertop and force Rat Face's gun hand into the air. The weapon discharged into the ceiling tiles as Zoe crushed her baton against the perp's windpipe. A moment later, the pistol was in her fist and Rat Face was writhing on the floor.

"Police officers," Lee announced. "Everything is under control. If one of you kind people would call 9-9-9, we'll take care of these gentlemen. And by the way, I'd like to pay for that Manchester United jersey and a Crunchy chocolate bar, please."

The place erupted in applause.

Lee had her suspect cuffed, face down on the tiles.

"You have skills, Detective," Zoe said.

Lee winked. "Let's take Harry a candy bar."

10

FBI HEADQUARTERS— WASHINGTON, DC

Terry Taylor, Associate Director of the Federal Bureau of Investigation, studied the single sentence text message, sent by a dying man in a dark alley. He imagined the scene playing out; the searing sting of the slugs entering the man's body, his strength draining from him in a trail of blood, and the sheer will it took to make sure the information he was sent to discover made it home, even if he didn't.

The Captain is Vladimir Prokofiev.

A cell phone screen scan lay atop the thick file, entitled simply, "Vega."

Taylor didn't like the feeling in the pit of his stomach. This one would cross into CIA territory, perhaps even the National Security Agency. It was a case he had hoped would stay closed and ice cold.

Now it was heating up.

A couple of phone calls had given him all the information he needed to decide. Prokofiev was reportedly in London. Perhaps Taylor could quietly hand this one off to a man he knew at MI6.

But this would have to stay below the radar.

Taylor punched a series of digits into his personal cell phone. The man answered in a single ring.

The associate director put on his most ingratiating voice, the one he used when he wanted to convince someone to do something that wasn't quite by the book.

"Tom Anastos, you old bugger. Is MI6's most talented agent keeping his nose clean these days?"

The voice on the other end of the line knew Taylor's act well. "Terry Taylor. We can dump the rubbish and cut to the chase. What is it you need?"

"Something that's right up your alley, old boy. But I'm hoping you can engage without having to tell your superiors about it just yet."

There was silence on the line as Taylor imagined Tom Anastos' mind calculating the trouble headed his way.

"Okay, Terry. What's the story?"

11

HM BELMARSH—LONDON, UK

L ee and Zoe met Harry Duggan in one of Belmarsh's interrogation rooms. If Marie Culpado needed documents, Duggan would likely be the man to provide them and might well provide a key to her whereabouts.

Harry's residency there was a little odd because the prison was usually home to more high-profile inmates. Jeffrey Archer and Julian Assange were among the more famous. Harry was just a forger. Even the UK prisons had a class system.

Incarceration had not changed Harry. He was still the same cheerful chap, arrested with a flat full of printing equipment and hundreds of counterfeit passports.

Lee allowed herself a smile as Harry Duggan inspected the two women. She knew he was pleased to have such handsome visitors.

"Well, hello, love. I would give you a proper hug, but they don't allow that kind of thing here. It's been a long time." Lee watched as Harry eyed her companion with evident delight. "Who is your beautiful friend?"

"This is PC Zoe Doyle, Harry. We wanted to ask you some questions about somebody who may have been one of your… clients."

Harry leaned back in the plastic chair, weaving his fingers behind his head and looking toward the ceiling.

"The business just isn't what it once was. Syrian passports are going for less than £200. One must sell many to maintain a lifestyle. I take their money. But I don't want to know anything about them."

Lee produced the picture she found online from a tabloid.

"This is what she looked like. It would have been ten years ago, an American, perhaps with a companion. Short, 5'2" tall. A little heavy, maybe 150 pounds. Brown hair."

Lee took a breath to give Harry time to process the information.

"Her distinguishing characteristics are a tattoo of a rose on her right shoulder and a noticeable scar on her chin from a childhood fall."

Harry closed his eyes as if he were flipping through a mental card file of clients.

"Tattoos are easy to hide. Tell me about her chest."

Lee caught Zoe's confused look and smiled.

"Harry fancies breasts, Zoe. Baps are the puzzle pieces he remembers."

Harry's features took on an expression of warm satisfaction.

"The old brain isn't what it used to be. But some things a man like me never forgets. There was one American, I remember. About the dimensions you describe, missy, right down to the scar. It was a long time ago, and I would have consigned her to the dustbin, but for that gorgeous balcony."

43

Lee searched her memory for that brief encounter in the Strand. It was an uncertain recollection now.

"If she's the one, Harry, what can you tell us about her?"

"There was a third party that did most of the work. There were two passports. A woman and a man. I never saw them in person. But that passport picture. Some things even close-ups can't hide."

"Can you tell us what names they used?" Lee asked.

Harry shook his head.

"No, missy. But I can tell you this. I saved a copy of that picture. The coppers confiscated all of my things. If they still have 'em, she's there."

"Anything you can tell us about her companion?"

"No hair. Bald as an egg. But it was shaved. He looked to me like a copper. But people change their appearance for counterfeit passports. You probably wouldn't recognize him now."

"And that 'third party' you mentioned?"

"He's dead?"

Lee exchanged glances with Zoe. "Fact or a guess, Harry?"

"Only a guess," Harry continued. "He stopped bringing me business about a month after that transaction. When they disappear like that, they usually turn up face down in the Thames."

"Thanks, Harry," Lee said. "In your own way, you've been helpful. How much longer until they let you out?"

Harry waved a hand to the guard who stood by the door, as if summoning a personal assistant.

"I'm not in any hurry. The food here is pretty good. I'm old enough that the bad guys look up to me as a hero. And I'm taking some classes."

The news surprised Lee. Most criminals Harry's age

were content to live on their reputation. "What are you studying?"

"Politics. These days, being a convicted criminal is a plus if you're running for parliament. At least your constituency knows what they are voting for."

As the guard opened the door to let the women out, Harry remembered one thing more.

"Blair," he said. "Like Tony."

"Blair?"

"That was the last name on her passport. I thought it was unusual that she would pick that last name in England. It raises hackles, especially if you are a Tory. Blair with the Big Ones. That's how I filed her photo."

Lee shook Harry's hand.

"Thank you, Harry. If you run for MP, you have my vote."

————

"MEN AND BREASTS," ZOE SAID AS THE TWO DROVE away from Belmarsh. "They seem to go together like fish and chips."

Lee laughed. "It sounds like our suspect's attributes are hard to miss."

"And we have a name," Zoe added. "An armed robbery, and a couple of clues. A productive day."

"So, I've got you hooked on the Culpado mystery, eh, Zoe?"

Zoe sniffed. "Just a peripheral interest. I support my partner."

Lee pointed their vehicle toward the A2016. "Now to connect those clues with one of London's 8.7 million inhabitants… If she's even still in the country."

Lee focused on the line of cars coursing along the

motorway like corpuscles in a blood vessel. It was well past the end of their shift, and night was descending on London.

Zoe weighed in. "A single grain of sand in a beach a thousand miles long. It can wait until tomorrow. You've got a better chance playing The National Lottery."

PALOMA, ILLINOIS

"You're awfully quiet, Jessica."

Jessica Ramirez sat across from her partner, Officer Alexandra Clark, at The Paloma Bean coffee shop just off campus.

The days were getting longer, and most of the patrons came here in the afternoons for the free Wi-Fi and sips of overpriced liquid concoctions. The warmth of the afternoon sprouted several dozen students enjoying the sunshine on the green grass berm that spilled down toward the Mississippi River in front of the Paloma University Administration Building. Just two other patrons were in the place at this hour, and they seemed to look at one another across a two-top with the wary glares of lovers who were reassessing their relationship.

Whenever Jess returned from a trip, she spilled details. This afternoon she was silent.

"I haven't slept since I got back from Nashville, Ali. Nobody should have to witness an intentional murder."

"Is my right-wing sister swinging left against the death penalty?"

"Psychotics are different." Jess's attention was reflexively drawn to the rising heat brewing between the one other couple in the shop. "We can't rehab a nut job. I think this guy was innocent."

Ali's expression turned thoughtful. "He was definitely calm when you arrested him. But I've met some pretty calm psychos, too. That's how I know you're 'normal.'"

Jess twirled the single marshmallow that floated atop her Frappuccino with a stir stick. "I have half a mind to drop everything and take a trip over to England to see what this UK detective inspector can remember."

Ali rolled her eyes. "One observation in a sea of humanity and you want to chase it down? I don't get it."

Jess sipped the drink, hoping the caffeine would recharge her flagging spirit. "I saw Papa's face in that electric chair, Ali. I failed him as a daughter, and I failed a citizen as a police officer. He's dead because I couldn't protect him."

Ali tried plucking a mosquito from in front of her face. On days like today, the owners left the doors open and the damned things were a nuisance. "And you think that vindicating another dead man will make all that go away? We're all walking powder kegs of grief, regret, and cynicism, sister. Learn to let it go, or you'll make a bad decision and get yourself in a jam you can't get out of."

Jess fingered the buttons on her shirt, processing Ali's words. It was a rare day when they worked old cases and didn't have to be in uniform.

The sound of the guy's voice got her attention. The volume was up, and the tone was borderline menacing.

The barista heard it, too, and was heading in the couple's direction. Jess stood, holding up a hand to stop the employee. "I have this."

The guy's tenor was creepy, and the girl was clearly

uncomfortable. "This isn't working for me," the girl said, "I think I want to leave."

Her companion smiled. It was the smile you saw when the smiler had dark things on his mind. "That's okay, baby. I know where you live."

The color drained out of the girl's face. Her companion leaned in, resting his chin on a pair of beefy palms.

Jess grabbed a nearby chair, planted it backward at the table between the two, straddling it with her arms folded on the back. She opened her fist, displaying her shield and depositing it on the table in front of the guy so he could see what he was dealing with. He looked Jess up and down, as if trying to decide how he might prevail if things turned ugly.

Jess's gaze locked on his, her voice soft but with an authoritative tone. "I'm enjoying my frappuccino with my partner over there, and I heard you threatening this young woman. Got anything to say about that?"

The guy stumbled through a half dozen *ahs* and *ums* before Jess held up a finger to shut him up.

"I thought so. We cops don't have a lot of patience for that kind of behavior, so I'm deciding whether to call some of my colleagues to come to take you to jail."

The guy pulled back, putting some physical distance between himself and authority. "I was just joking around. I meant nothing by it."

Jess nodded. Another macho idiot. "Arresting you would be inconvenient for all of us. So, here's what I want you to do. Give me your ID because I've had misguided young people take off on me, and that option might just be on your mind right now. Then get up and pay your bill. And while you're at it, pay this young lady's bill, too. If that's not something you're comfortable with, my partner over there can have six cops on the scene in five minutes.

And I promise you, they won't be as patient as I've been. The choice is yours."

The guy didn't flinch. His ID was in Jess's hands in seconds. "No problem, ma'am. I'll go pay the check right now."

Jess turned to the girl as she wrote her companion's information on a card. "I apologize for intruding. You could have handled this, but I thought I could help. And if you would like to file a complaint, I'll have my friends pick him up on his way home. He crossed the line, and we can definitely do something about it if you want."

"Thank you," the young woman whispered, the color returning to her face. "I wanted out an hour ago, but I let him drive me here and didn't know what to do."

Jess softened. She thought she could hear her own mother's voice in her. "Well, my partner and I are still working on our caffeine over there. Would you like to finish your salad and iced tea with us? We can give you a ride home after unless you would prefer to call someone."

The girl returned Jessica's smile. "That would be great. Thank you very much."

The soon-to-be ex-boyfriend returned. "I took care of everything," he said, the tiniest hint of swagger returning to his voice. "Is it okay if I take my ID back now, ma'am?"

Jess handed the plastic card over, holding on to an edge to make sure he was listening. "So, I have your details right here. I suggest you stay away from this lady and never contact her again."

"Of course, ma'am. Thank you."

He bolted for the door.

It turned out her name was Amanda Sutherland. She lived alone with her mother. Jess's empathetic inquisitiveness drew out the details. Her father had died in a single-car accident. His blood alcohol count had been three times the legal limit.

"I put up with bad boyfriends because I feel like daddy's death is my fault," Amanda said, a tear appearing at the edge of an eye. "He wanted to take me to dinner, and I said, 'no,' because I was afraid he would drink, even though he never did when I was in the car. We got the call after midnight, and I've never forgiven myself."

Jess heard her own words spill out, wisdom she knew but couldn't assimilate. "In the end, we can only influence our own destiny. It was your dad's issues that took him from you, not something you didn't do. In time, I hope you can forgive yourself. We can't go back to what was. We can only build on what is."

Jess felt Amanda's eyes inspecting her. "What's it like being women in law enforcement?"

Law enforcement, Jess thought. Most kids called them cops.

Ali began the sermon. "You'll get more than your share of abuse. You'll reflexively take a different path home from the station every night, just in case some guy you arrested sometime might want to even the score. You'll see more than your share of death and dishonor. And you will develop a sixth sense for when someone is lying, which will be ninety percent of the time."

Jess smiled at the young woman. "But you will also save lives, prevent pain, occasionally get the bad guys off the street, and hopefully inspire someone who is on the edge of night to walk toward the sunlight. Few jobs are tougher, but if you have the right attitude, few are more rewarding."

Amanda slowly nodded, as if a new idea was forming. "And you learn how to deescalate trouble and deal with egos that are bigger than their brains?"

"We can fight with the best of the boys," Jess grinned, "but anytime we don't have to is a victory."

Amanda stared at the Smith and Wesson M&P handguns Jess and Ali carried on their belts. "How often do you have to use those?"

Ali patted her weapon as if it were a puppy. "Some of us can have a twenty-five year career and never fire our weapons beyond the practice range."

The girl tilted her head. "But that doesn't apply to you two."

"We never go into a fight intending to pull the trigger. But we train so that if we ever need to, it's reflexive."

"I think I'll take you up on the offer of a ride home, officers," Amanda said.

Ali flicked her knuckle with a finger. "She's Jess. I'm Ali."

"And could I ride with you sometime, Jess and Ali? My mom will go ballistic, but I'm wondering if a law enforcement career might be my life's purpose?"

––––––

"You know what your real problem is, partner?" Ali said as they pulled away from Amanda Sutherland's modest single-family home. "You understand exactly what you need to do. Like that dead drunk dad, you just won't do it."

"And what should I do, miss psychotherapist?"

"Forgive yourself. On the day he died, your father asked for your forgiveness, something you would have instantly given. He left this life proud of his daughter. I'd give my own life if my parents had even a grain of acceptance in their hearts. Time to start working on letting this obsession with Vega's Boss go. People with more resources and brains than we have are on his trail. Let them chase him."

Amanda's confessions steeled Jess's resolve. As long as The Captain remained free, others might die. "I do know what to do, Ali. When the time is right, I'll do it."

13

HEADQUARTERS—BRITISH SECRET INTELLIGENCE SERVICES / MI6— LONDON

Tom Anastos typed "Vladimir Prokofiev" into his office computer. The MI6 database was one of the world's largest repositories of international crime, terrorism, and political upheaval.

Bits and pieces of information from thousands of sources, aggregated and curated by a combination of artificial intelligence engines and a cadre of dedicated analysts who spent days and nights seeking connections.

If the name meant anything important, it would show up here.

The screen turned blue, a sign Anastos knew well. The topic was top secret and required a second level of authentication. He typed his special password into the machine and waited. A moment later, the data began scrolling.

Vladimir Prokofiev—Alias: The Captain or Капитан

Managing Director—The Maitland Corporation, Extensive UK real estate holdings (MORE), Exporter of arms and high technology (MORE), Close connections with allied and enemy governments USA / Russia

— (MORE), Suspected in an attempted bombing in the New York Financial District (MORE)…

The cursor blinked, encouraging Anastos to hit the return button for a more detailed scroll. As he was about to press it, the phone on his desk rang. He recognized the extension.

"Anastos."

"You're looking at Prokofiev. Why?"

His boss didn't waste words. Anastos tried to sound disinterested.

"A mild interest, sir. You know, the story about how the Russians are buying up all of our commercial real estate."

"I don't buy it, Tom. Come to my office right now."

Anastos could sense an additional level of intensity in Associate Director Gerhardt's voice. He had stumbled into something he shouldn't have.

"Yes, sir. On my way."

14

ROTHERHITHE—LONDON

"Let's at least grab some sustenance before calling it a night. How about The Mayflower?"

Lee knew food and beer were the way to her partner's heart, and Zoe's favorite pub was The Mayflower.

Cobbled streets and stunning views of the Thames surrounded the Rotherhithe icon. The Mayflower's beer-battered fish and chips were among the best in the city. Lee also knew that Zoe had a particular fondness for the pub's Sticky Toffee Pudding. The 400-year-old venue also allowed dogs on the ground floor, a plus for two animal-loving coppers with appetites that had been marinating since breakfast.

Zoe shot her partner a sideways glance. "You're up to something, Lee."

Lee feigned ignorance. It was not a stellar performance. "Not at all, Zoe. We foiled a robbery and got a lead. That deserves a little celebration."

THE MAYFLOWER WAS A PERFECT PLACE FOR A confidential conversation. The pub's noise level was high enough to make individual conversations unintelligible, but if you sat close, it was possible to be heard perfectly. The vibe was always upbeat, another plus. People came here to blow off steam. Nobody cared what two plain-clothes cops might talk about at a corner table under a flat-screen television near the back.

Lee and Zoe were on their second pints when the entrees arrived. The PC attacked her fish with the voracity of a wild animal.

"Best in London," she said, her mouth full of deep-fried cod. "So tell me all about this woman you saw one time, ten years ago. Why the sudden interest?"

Lee swallowed her panko-crusted chicken. "They still kill people for murder in the states, love. I got a call from a detective over there who had to witness someone fry in the electric chair for a murder without a body."

Zoe dipped a chip into a plastic cup of vinegar. "How can any court burn someone for that?"

"Apparently, they still do over there. The victim is supposedly a woman I thought I saw boarding the tube by the Strand. The thought of some poor bastard losing his life because I didn't chase down a lead is eating at me."

Zoe shook her head. "That was years ago, babe. You can't beat yourself up for it."

"That's why I dragged you to see Harry today, Zoe. I was hoping he couldn't remember Marie Culpado. But he could. And now I'm keen to find out if she's still in the city."

"And you don't have enough on your plate already? There's more than enough covert CID and priority crime to keep you happy. The old boy is dead. And some jury decided he did the deed. Let it be, as McCartney would say."

"I wish I could, partner. And maybe I will. Connecting a few threads won't take that much time, and I'll sleep better if I find out we're chasing a false lead."

"Well, keep me out of it. Maddox doesn't like free-styling, and I hope to follow in your footsteps as a DI someday."

Superintendent Maddox was a by-the-book chief. He was fair but had little patience for detective inspectors who bent the rules.

But this was a puzzle. And Lee loved puzzles.

Her eyes flicked toward the flat screen. "Bloody hell. Look."

There was a photograph they both recognized next to the anchor's face. Lee strained to hear the commentary.

"A well-known criminal figure died today at HM Belmarsh prison. Harry Duggan, the colorful Passport Forger, who became famous in the 1990s for helping several of the world's most notorious criminals enter this country illegally, was found dead in his cell. The prison governor said the sixty-seven-year-old folk hero died of a heart attack."

Lee could tell that Zoe's cop instincts were screaming at her. "Jesus, Liyanna. Do you think there's any connection?"

"Of course, there's a connection. We're no longer working on a cold case, my friend."

———

"I THINK I MIGHT JUST POP ON BY THE OFFICE WITH you after all, partner," Zoe Doyle said as the two officers turned left on Saint Marychurch Street, toward the Sands Film Studio and Tunnel Road where Lee had parked their vehicle.

Lee was checking her assumptions. "So, our working hypothesis is that Harry Duggan was murdered"

"Absolutely. He was the picture of health today. Something stinks, and it's not the Thames."

"Hello, girls."

There were two of them, burly-bouncer types, in black T-shirts and blue jeans, with biceps the size of rugby footballs that framed steroid-enhanced torsos. The shorter of the two still towered over the women as he spoke. "We hear you're friends of old Harry Duggan."

"Bad luck," said the second, producing a taser. "Afraid you'll both have to go for a swim."

He fired the darts at Zoe. Lee saw her anticipate and jump out of the way of the projectiles.

Lee whirled into a backspin kick, aimed at the taller man's head. The darkness affected her accuracy, and the kick went wide, giving her opponent a chance to grab the leg as it passed in front of his face.

"Nice stems, love," he said, twisting her ankle with his hand.

The DI rolled with the move into a handstand. Her second leg connected with the man's neck, and he went down.

Zoe's opponent threw his taser to the ground. He aimed a powerful punch at the PC's face right before darts from Zoe's taser pierced his shirt. She bent backward, dodging the blow, slamming her left foot into the intruder's groin. The combination was incapacitating. But the two attackers had apparently taken their share of shots in the past. Groaning in pain, they were quickly back onto their feet and advancing on the two women.

"You boys have to learn some respect," Lee said, landing a sidekick to the tall man's chest.

"We're police officers, and you are both under arrest," Zoe barked, pulling a shield from her pocket.

As Zoe's assailant reached for her neck, she slashed at his forearm with the sharp-pointed crown at the top of her badge, slicing the radial artery. When the man turned to put pressure on the wound, the PC jumped onto his back, wrapping an elbow around his windpipe in a sleeper hold.

Lee's attacker stumbled backward, reacting to the force of her kick. But he had skills, too. The man blocked each of her martial arts moves with the precision of a black belt. He found his opening and picked the DI up by her waist, throwing her body against Sands Film Studios' wall. Lee winced and ducked as a thick fist smashed against the brick-and-mortar facing, shattering the mason's work into tiny bits. The DI smashed an elbow down onto the extended arm, finding a joint and breaking it. Another 360-degree spin and the same elbow connected with the man's left jugular vein.

Lee felt the wall shudder as the second assailant backed Zoe against it, trying to break her grip around his neck. But the oxygen deprivation was doing its work, and that was the worst of it.

"Jesus, Mary, and Joseph. Pass out already," Zoe panted, trying to catch her breath. "My back's going to hurt tomorrow, and you'll damn well pay for the inconvenience tonight."

With a last effort, her attacker hurled Zoe into the wall a second time. Her arms splayed, and she let go.

The taller assailant waved his one good arm, and a black sedan pulled alongside. The two men fell into the back seat, and it sped off into the night.

Lee bent over, resting her palms on her thighs. "You okay, partner?"

Zoe sat on the pavement, legs spread in a *V*, her back against the bricks.

"Yeah. And I think we both learned something tonight."

"What's that, Z?"

"This Marie Culpado person is still alive."

15

HEADQUARTERS—BRITISH SECRET INTELLIGENCE SERVICES / MI6— LONDON

The offices of the Secret Intelligence Services at 85 Albert Embankment are nothing like Ian Fleming described. Vauxhall Cross—as the place was sometimes called—was a tremendous step up from the "irredeemably insecure" Century House in Lambeth and a far cry from Fleming's haunts at 54 Broadway. Commander Thomas Anastos knocked on a nondescript door, halfway down a tiled hallway below street level, where the more sensitive activities of MI6 took place.

"Come."

Anastos flipped through his mental Rolodex, reviewing his boss's history with the organization. Associate Director Gerhardt's career trajectory within MI6 as a field agent was legendary. He had the perfect combination of brains, fearlessness, and the most important trait that made a successful agent: he looked ordinary. He was the agency's rising star until late-onset muscular dystrophy put him in a wheelchair.

But that didn't stop Gerhardt. He found he had the skills to lead. The director gave him a secondary role in recognition of a man who had given his life to his country. Gerhard's tenacity and drive surprised everyone, and he grew into the second most powerful person at MI6.

Anastos thought his wardrobe was a better fit for a bureaucrat than a spy. The suit was low-end Marks and Spencer, not Saville Row. The white shirt could have used more starch, and the red-and-blue-striped tie hung loosely around his neck.

Gerhardt's voice was firm. His eyes exuded authority. Their movement guided Anastos to the leather chair opposite the associate director's desk.

"Talk," Gerhardt said.

Anastos complied. "Associate Director Taylor phoned me with the name Vladimir Prokofiev. Sounds like he created mischief on the other side of the Atlantic and is beyond the FBI's jurisdiction. The name was not familiar to me, so I looked it up."

Gerhardt nodded. "And the secondary security check before viewing the profile did not raise questions?"

Tom Anastos chose his words carefully. "I have the clearance. Is there a problem?"

"Yes, Commander. There is a problem. And it's about to become your problem."

16

PALOMA, ILLINOIS

"He said he'd only talk to me."

Jessica Ramirez pointed the Tahoe toward Maryland Street. The scene that was the catalyst for her adventures in Arizona conjured up a procession of memories she was still trying to forget.

"Why Antonio, and why now?" Ali wondered. "El Sindicato is at peace with the other street gangs. Our informers have said nothing about any trouble brewing. And why did he demand to talk with you?"

Jess wasn't sure. "The word on the street is that I saved his older brother's life, when in fact, it was Ricardo who probably saved mine in that meth house."

"You know how those stories get bent," Ali said. "Riki probably painted that picture to burnish his own image."

"That gunshot was definitely a battle ribbon. But it's also been Ricardo's exit from El Sindicato. He fell in love with a girl at the hospital and seems to be on the straight and narrow toward a career in the lab at Paloma General."

Ali pointed to the seedy bar where Maryland Street intersected with River Bend. The word Cócteles winked in orange neon above the door. "Maybe 'El Asaltante' found out the truth and wants you to know it. I guess we'll find out."

It was still too early for the influx of evening customers, but Jess could still smell the mixture of stale beer, sweat, and blood that were the three most popular products sold at the headquarters of Paloma's only Latino street gang. As her eyes adjusted to the dark, she saw a pair of teenage boys flanking a door with "Gerente" painted on the wall above it.

Ali stifled a smirk. "Manager. How appropriate."

Jess fingered her Smith & Wesson. "I'm not sure you were on the invitation list, partner. Best keep a low profile and let me lead the conversation."

———

ANTONIO ROJAS, THE ASSAILANT OR "EL ASALTANTE" in Spanish, sat behind an oak desk that was almost too big for the tiny room. Posters of Hispanic rock stars hung on the walls. An unbalanced ceiling fan swirled slowly, like a drunken customer at closing time. The only light was a single table lamp, a gift Jess assumed once lived in one of the city's finer homes, perhaps given to El Asaltante as an expression of respect for his position as El Sindicato's leader.

El Asaltante was short, barely five feet tall. He had the muscle tone of a convict for whom weight training was the one nonviolent lesson learned in prison. Tattoos covered both arms, with more in evidence beneath a Chicago Bears muscle shirt. A tuft of greased hair topped closely shaved temples. A joint burned in an ashtray within Antonio Rojas's reach.

The gang leader lifted a finger, and a guard closed the

office door. The second stood against it. Jess could see the print of a handgun beneath his shirt as he crossed his arms to draw attention to it.

Jess nodded toward the weed. "Put that thing out, Tony. If you want me to respect you, don't disrespect me."

Antonio Rojas smiled. He picked up the joint and took a long pull off it before crushing the tiny remains of the roach in the ashtray. "Jessi Ramirez. How's your sister?"

"Smart enough to know to steer clear of elementary school bullies who make poor decisions."

Antonio licked his lips. "The girl could kiss; I'll give her that." He pointed to Ali. "Why bring the bollo. Do you feel unsafe in your old neighborhood?"

Jess knew that Ali's command of Spanish included the common slang for lesbians. But her partner kept her mouth shut.

"What do you want, Tony?"

Antonio held his hands out in a gesture of innocence. "Just to return a favor. You saved my brother's life. Perhaps I can save yours."

"What do you mean?"

"The word on the street is that there is a sicario out there looking for you. And the assassin is not local. He may have offered the contract to one of the inferior Paloma pandillas."

Jess crossed her arms. "Are you going to tell me how you know this?"

Antonio slowly shook his head. "No, hermanita. What good would my networks be if I told the police how they work? You're one of the few mujer cops and the only Latina." Antonio rubbed his forearm. "We're easy to spot. Just watch your back."

Jess chuckled. "So, you're warning me that someone

out there is going to kill me, but you won't tell me who it might be or how you know?"

El Asaltante stood, leaning forward as his fingers pressed against the desktop. "Forewarned is forearmed. Abraham Tucker in *The Light of Nature Pursued*. 1768. See, hermanita? I paid some attention in class."

Jess turned toward the door while Ali monitored the gang leader. Antonio must have sent a sign because the guard slid aside and held it open for them.

"Jessi?" Antonio called after her. "This makes us even."

Jess turned to face the young man she had known since childhood. Despite the tats and his hands on his hips, he still looked like a kid. "No, we're not, pendejo. I'm betting there's enough weed on the premises right now to send you and your two mentees back to the joint for a nice long visit. I'm overlooking that. You still owe me."

———

"You were a badass in there, partner," Ali said as the two cops drove away from the bar.

"Do you think Tony is just trying to assert a little male dominance or is someone out there who means to do you harm?"

Jess could feel the fight coming back into her constitution. Perhaps the horrors of Nashville were going into the box where she kept all the other things she wanted to forget. "Who knows? These past few weeks have been full of surprises."

"Well, intel is intel. I think we should nose around and see if we can sniff out some facts."

Jess frowned and patted the pocket where she kept her cell phone. She noticed Ali feeling the soft tremor of the vibration alert in her pocket, too. A red light afforded the opportunity for the women to read the message.

Jess's eyes widened. Ali's mouth dropped open.

The two turned their screens so the other could read the single sentence, screaming at them both in capital letters.

MARIE CULPADO IS ALIVE.

METROPOLITAN POLICE
HEADQUARTERS—LONDON

While the city itself is under the City of London Police jurisdiction, the Metropolitan Police Services, informally known as The Met serves 32 London boroughs, co-coordinates counterterrorism activities, and protects the royal family and certain members of the government.

Chasing down an American who was supposedly dead for over a decade was arguably not part of the job for the 40,000 plus men and women who took home a Met paycheck.

For Liyanna Evans's boss, it was now more than a minor annoyance. Desmond Maddox glared at Lee and Zoe from behind his desk in a small office that didn't come close to reflecting his responsibilities. The man was north of six feet tall with a boxer's build and a bearing that betrayed his service as a Royal Marine.

"Tell me everything," he commanded in the terse style that could terrify his officers.

Lee produced a scan of the newspaper story that had

triggered her recognition of the woman she thought might be Marie Culpado, handing it over to her boss.

"Ten years ago, I thought I saw the woman pictured in this press story. I noted the reporter's name who covered the trial in the States and called him to see if there were a possibility she might still be alive. That was how my contact information got to an American detective who arrested the woman's alleged killer. She contacted me four days ago and told me that the suspect in her murder was convicted and executed. Something didn't sit right with her about the whole thing, and I admit it bothered my conscience that an innocent man might have been killed because I didn't press hard enough on a lead."

Maddox closed his eyes, pressing his fingers against his temples. "So you visited Harry Duggan. What did he tell you?"

"Duggan thinks…" Lee took a breath. It was still hard to imagine Harry in the past tense. "Duggan thought that this Marie Culpado came to London with a companion. He claimed to have provided them with false documents."

Maddox finished the story for her. "And now Duggan is dead. Two men assaulted you and PC Doyle outside of a pub, and you think there's a connection."

"Yes, sir. It doesn't feel like the two events are coincidental."

Maddox pulled a well-worn folder with "Harold Duggan" written on the front from his center drawer, tossing it onto his desk. "Harry Duggan had many enemies. So do you, DI Evans. Perhaps the timing is coincidental."

Zoe tried to come to her partner's aid. "Our attackers specifically mentioned Harry's name when they jumped us."

Maddox shot icicles at her. "There are a dozen explanations for that, PC Doyle. We live in a two-thousand-year-old city. Hatred that crosses a dozen generations simmers everywhere. The more important issue is this: You both have very full plates without chasing an ice-cold lead from ten years ago that has nothing to do with our mission." Maddox turned his glare to Lee. "I want you to drop this."

Lee wasn't sure she could.

"And no investigations on your own time. Is that clear?"

Lee tried to make her response sound more acquiescent than it felt. "Yes, sir."

Maddox turned his attention to Zoe. "Doyle, I'm reassigning you to the Royal Detail. The palace has asked for extra security for Prince William's kids. Report to Buckingham division in the morning."

Focusing on Lee, Maddox continued, "Evans, you're off the street. Sixty day's temporary assignment to research."

Lee and Zoe fell silent, too stunned to respond.

Lee saw the boss react to the discolored bruises that pockmarked the two cops' faces. "You both look like hell."

Zoe finally found her voice. "You should see our assailants."

Maddox waved a hand, a signal dismissing his charges. "I have. They were found an hour ago, floating face down in the Thames."

COMPUTER SCIENCE LAB—PALOMA UNIVERSITY

"Okay, Andy. What the hell is going on?"

Alexandra Clark and her partner stood amid the technological chaos of the computer science lab at Paloma University. A dozen desktop CPUs were in various states of disassembly on the lab's benches. Monitors flickered with the output of a hundred different programs scrolling and blinking. Six large flat screens hung in two rows on one wall displaying Internet traffic in real-time. Five disheveled students surrounded Andy Milluzzi, the lab's student supervisor.

Andy held Ali's and Jessica's cellphones in his hands, studying the identical messages on the two screens.

"The SMS system is pretty much untraceable if the caller ID data is blocked. Someone would have to know both your phone numbers. Got any friends at work who might be pranking you?"

"Jessica has her share of enemies." Ali turned to Jess. "Who knows about the Culpado stuff besides the chief?"

"Not even the chief is aware of my encounter with Jack

Crawford. He would know Marie's name from the case records. Anybody could look up the details of the trial on the web. But why would a person target both Ali and me at the same time?"

Andy shrugged. "Can't help you figure out that one. My guess is this is somebody you know. The carriers keep info about cell accounts close to the vest. They keep their customer databases behind some mongo firewalls with world-class encryption. It's not something your average cop with a weird sense of humor could access without a warrant."

Ali gave Andy a dirty look. "Come on, Andy, you can do better than that. What if this were the tip of a deeper iceberg? Just for grins. What if somebody cracked those databases? How would those text messages get from there to here?"

"It would probably happen under the auspices of the Chinese, the North Koreans, or the Russians. It could also be our own National Security Agency or the CIA. They have the tech and the brains to do something like this. You guys would have to figure out the 'why.' What would an entity like that do if they had that kind of access?"

"You tell me, kiddo," Ali prodded. "What's the dystopian scenario. These days, anything is possible. Give me the worst case."

Andy looked to a fellow student. "Gina is our dystopian genius. Share your favorite conspiracy theory."

Gina ran her fingers through the dreadlocks that framed her mahogany facial features. "Not theories, Andrew. I base my analysis on what we know to be percolating out there. Our adversaries would love to break into the power grid. That system is notoriously unsafe. The holy grail is a multi-level hack, where they can control our devices. That's harder because there are so many operating system flavors. But it's public knowledge that the Chinese have a bunch of people working on just that scenario."

Ali touched Jessica's arm as Gina pulled a marker out of her pocket and rubbed a section of the lab's whiteboard clear with the arm of her sweatshirt. "I am woman, hear me roar," she whispered.

Gina drew a group of different devices on the white background. "Cell phones, computers, even your light-bulbs are smart devices these days." She drew lines from the icons to a drawing of a cloud. "If they are connected to the web, a hacker who knows how the operating system worked could control them. They could read the GPS data on your phone, Officer Clark, and know exactly where you are. They could listen in on your phone calls and read your texts. With the right psychology, they could do what social media does, direct your thoughts and actions toward what they want you to believe and do. It's pretty dark stuff, but we learned just how gullible people could be during the last election cycle. Plant the right ideas in someone's brain and they march toward the cliff like a lemming."

The information was enough for Ali to come up with an assignment. "Okay, guys. Here's what I need. Let's solve for Gina's scenario. How would we figure out if someone had done exactly what she is implying? How would it show up in operating system code? Could we see it in the way the packets flow across the web? I'm talking about the most elegant and frightening hack you can imagine, something nobody can see unless they are looking for it. Draw me a picture of how that would work. And then I want you to tell me how to stop it. Sound like fun?"

Andy Milluzzi grinned. "Absolutely, Officer Clark. I know a guy at Apple. We can start there since that's the OS you both use. Do you mind if I download your operating system and the contents of your phones to a desktop? We can compare it to what should come from the manufacturer and see if anything is different."

Jess shot her partner a concerned glance. "These are department phones, Ali. I'm not sure O'Brien would approve."

"O'Brien wouldn't understand half of the picture Gina just painted, Jess. If there's even a modicum of a chance that what she describes is true, this will be a lot bigger issue than whether two college town cops gave some computer geeks the contents of their smart phones."

"That makes it worse, Alexandra. We'd have the FBI, CIA, NSA, an alphabet soup of shit on our shoulders pretty quickly."

Ali held out her hand. "So you're in?"

Jess acquiesced. "Of course, I am. Just know that if the chief comes after me for this, I'll tell him you took my phone without my permission."

She handed her device to Andy. Their favorite nerd dropped the two phones into charging USB holsters and tapped a command into a keyboard.

Gina chimed in. "If it's a big enough hack, you won't see it that way. The bad peeps would have inserted their code at the source."

"The Phoenix Code," Jess murmured.

Ali nodded. "Y'all helped us last year with that little adventure in Arizona and New York, and you saved a lot of lives. It may well be that we're overreacting. But let's pretend that Gina's vision is on the money. If you find anything weird, ping me right away. Jessica has contacts at the FBI who will be very interested if someone has broken into our communications systems."

Andy Milluzzi regarded his team. "Some stuff we might have to do to help you will be illegal, Officer Clark."

Ali chuckled. "As in, Jess and me giving you access to every bit of data on our company cell phones? When has anything outside of the envelope stopped you before. You've still got the SHTF code?" Jessica's face expressed confusion. "SHTF… Shit hits the fan. It's a cell code that pings an attorney I know and me."

Andy flipped open his Android device. "Got it. One punch or a voice command." He turned to his team. "We all sleep better at night knowing that we don't have to call 9-1-1 for help."

The computer that was downloading the contents of Jessica's and Ali's phones spoke. "Over here."

"Geordi La Forge," Ali said, recognizing the sound byte voiced by actor LeVar Burton. "Why are all digit heads also Star Trek nerds?"

"You guys be careful," Jess said. "We've just asked you to go 'where angels fear to tread.'"

"And yay, though I may walk through the valley of the shadow of death," Andy recited, "I shall fear no evil. For my friends are more dangerous than my enemies."

Jessica shook Gina's hand. "Glad you're keeping these boys in line, Gina."

Gina grinned. "You sometimes have to be patient with men. Boys take a while to comprehend stuff."

"Seriously, team," Ali added, "Thanks so much for doing this for us. If you feel at all uncomfortable, unplug and call us. Safety first."

Andy handed Jessica and Ali their phones. "What's life without a little excitement now and then. You two be careful. You're taking bigger risks than we ever will."

———

THE AFTERNOON SUN WAS DANCING OVER THE Mississippi as the two cops left the Paloma University Physics Building. "You know what's depressing?" Jess asked. "Those kids will make a thousand times what we'll earn during their lifetimes. I should have paid more attention in calculus class."

"If you love what you do, the money is secondary," Ali answered.

"Tell that to my financial analyst," Jess quipped. "At this rate, I'll retire owing money."

The cop radar that was hard-wired into her brain pinged. "Check it out. A regular customer."

Jess saw Ali make the ID, too. "Jimmy. What's a three-time loser doing hanging around campus?"

"Let's find out." Jess yelled at the retreating figure, "Hey, Jimmy. Turning over a new leaf?"

She saw Jimmy's recognition. He broke into a run. "Catch me if you can, motherfuckers."

"No respect," Jess said. "He's overtly challenging us to chase him."

"This isn't Jimmy's neighborhood, partner," Ali said, jogging toward the Tahoe. "Out of place means something is going down."

As Jess was about to buckle her seatbelt, she froze. "Ali, look."

Jess pointed to the bottom of the dashboard. A wire slipped away from its concealment and swung free above the gas pedal. "Speaking of 'out of place.'"

The two exchanged a wordless glance and bolted from the vehicle, seconds before it exploded into a mushroom cloud of smoke and fire. Jess felt the blast concussion as the force threw the two cops onto the lawn next to the parking lot.

She watched the conflagration that had once been their

service vehicle. The heat ignited the gas tanks of a pair of illegally parked student vehicles on either side.

"You okay, partner?" Ali asked.

Jess nodded, mesmerized by the flames and the curling black tendrils that rose into the afternoon sky.

"I guess we owe El Asaltante a favor, after all."

19

THE MET—LONDON

Zoe Doyle found the breaking news story on the Guardian website.

Two Bodies Pulled from the Thames. Cops Hint at an Organized Crime Hit.

"Here they are. No names, but there's cell phone video of a couple of floaters who share bodies that look an awful lot like the two sods we danced with last night… What are you doing, Lee?"

Zoe watched her partner typing a message into her cell phone as the two left Scotland Yard at the end of their shifts.

Lee kept her eyes focused on the smartphone's screen. "Maddox told us we couldn't investigate. He didn't say, I couldn't report."

"To whom?"

"To Detective Ramirez."

"What are you telling her?"

"Everything. If the roles were reversed, I would want to know."

Zoe thought about their boss's parting shot. "I bet you

wanted to ask Maddox if the fact that the goons who jumped us ended up dead was a coincidence."

Lee kept typing. "It's not. And he knows it."

"So, you're just going to follow orders and let it be?"

Lee pressed the send button. "Yes."

Zoe smirked. "You're not a very good liar, Liyanna. Be careful with this. Something tells me that Maddox is getting his instructions from pretty far up the chain."

"Maddox can't tell us what to do with our own time."

"Yes, he can, Lee. We're cops twenty-four-seven."

"And good cops follow their instincts. Mine are telling me there's more to this than anybody knows. It smells like it's within the Met's jurisdiction at the very least, perhaps even MI6."

Zoe put a hand on Lee's arm. "Then let people who are smarter than us handle it."

Lee pressed the send button on her phone, opened the door to her vehicle and gave Zoe a hard look. "All we did was scratch the surface of this thing, Z, and looked what happened. Harry Duggan dies. We get accosted. The two sods who jumped us end up sipping. And Maddox sends you to the palace and me to purgatory. If this Marie woman is still alive, she's in grave danger. I'm not sure I can let this one go. Nobody seems to care about her but you, me, and a cop in Illinois."

Zoe held up a finger. "That's where you're wrong, partner. I think many people care about this. We just don't know why."

Lee's face broke into a grin. "We don't know why… *yet.*"

20

RESEARCH LAB—BRITISH SECRET INTELLIGENCE SERVICES / MI6— LONDON

The MI6 research laboratory doesn't have modified Aston Martins or exploding cigarettes in its inventory.

Director Gerhardt swung his electric wheelchair around so that he and Commander Anastos could see what the young lab technician, CJ Riemer, was working on. The wiry kid pointed to a pair of familiar smart devices becoming a common fixture in more and more British homes.

"You have both probably met 'Frieda' before," CJ said, patting the hockey puck-shaped item with a hand. "She's the most ubiquitous piece of electronics in the world, telling more people the temperature and turning more appliances on and off than all her competitors combined."

CJ pointed to two flat screens on the wall that quietly scrolled lines of digital code in white characters on a dark blue background.

"This is a visual output of Frieda's data stream. When you say her name, they call it the 'wake word,' she comes alive and tries to do what you ask."

"I don't like the idea of any device with a microphone on the premises," Gerhardt grunted. "No matter what the manufacturers say, we have no confidence that they ever stop listening."

CJ concurred, "Frieda is programmed to sleep unless she's awakened. That means her microphone should only come on when someone speaks her wake word."

He tapped the device on the left. "I bought this one today. She's fresh out of the box. We'll talk about where we found her sister in a moment. Watch."

CJ spoke to the devices. "Frieda? What time does Manchester United play Arsenal tonight?"

The two devices spoke in unison. The friendly female voice everyone knew from dozens of television commercials touting the product brightly answered CJ's question.

"Manchester United and Arsenal meet tonight at nineteen hundred thirty hours at Old Trafford. Would you like to order tickets?"

"No, thank you," CJ said.

He turned to the two flat screens. "Look at the two data streams, gentlemen. They begin with the unique device ID number. The code that follows is almost identical. The connect command wakes up the servers that process the request, followed by the binary representation of the question. Note the brief delay, and then the answers appear."

"The device on the right is still spitting out characters," Commander Anastos said.

CJ nodded. "Indeed, Commander. Frieda number two is still listening. And look at this." The technician issued another command, "Frieda, power down."

"Shutting down now," the two voices cooed. "Press the red power button to turn me back on."

CJ pointed to the LED power indicators on both units.

It was dark. "The lights say the devices are off. But notice…" The tech pointed to the right screen. The data flow continued to output, spitting packets every time it heard a sound. "This girl is still listening and reporting. We've done some cursory packet tracing, and the information is not going to the company servers."

"Where is it going?" Gerhardt asked.

"To a spoofed IP address somewhere outside of England," CJ answered. "She's all ears and reporting everything she hears."

Commander Anastos scratched the stubble on his chin. "What does it mean?"

"It means," CJ said, "that someone has hacked the operating system to turn Frieda into his personal spy."

"How did you acquire this little gem?" Anastos wondered.

"Purely by chance. I have a mate who works for sanitation, and he grabs stuff out of trash cans he thinks he can salvage. He gave me a ring when Frieda misbehaved."

"Misbehaved?" Gerhardt repeated the word as a question.

CJ patted a black square box with a CAT5 connector on the back. "This is my friend's smart hub. It controls his television, lights, and… this one got my attention… the door to his flat. Frieda decided last night that she wanted to play with his toys. He heard the lock click open, figured out what was happening, and pulled Frieda's plug."

Gerhard frowned at Anastos. His own knowledge of technology surpassed the Commander by a mile. The Director wondered if his subordinate could keep up.

"There's more, gentlemen," CJ continued. "When he told me about it, I asked my mate if I could borrow this little square baby. The data stream from the hub is flowing across this third screen. Notice anything interesting?"

The two men studied the flow of numbers and letters. Anastos saw it first. "That sequence is almost identical to what Frieda Number Two is spitting out."

Gerhard could tell that CJ was pleased.

"Well done, Commander. You have a future in computer forensics. Frieda Number Two here has infected my mate's control hub. It's now talking to the same unknown server and listening for commands."

As CJ finished, Frieda Number One started spitting out data. The color drained from the technician's face.

Gerhardt's expression morphed into concern. "What is happening CJ?"

The tech pulled the power plugs from all three devices with lightning speed.

"The device I bought this morning just got infected with Frieda Number Two's troublesome code. She's now on someone else's team."

Gerhardt watched the wheels turning in the young computer whiz's brain. CJ pulled a cell phone out of his pocket.

The Director darkened. "You're not supposed to have those things in this building, CJ."

"I know, sir. I suggested the regulation. But I wondered about something and wanted to test my hypothesis."

CJ dropped his phone into a power holster on the lab bench, firing up a fourth flat screen. The white characters began to race across the display.

"Shit." He turned to the two men. "Turn off your cell phones right now, gentlemen."

Gerhardt frowned. "We locked our devices in our vehicles, CJ. We follow the rules."

CJ began typing commands furiously into his terminal. "I don't know if it happened here, there, or anywhere, but that code has infected my cell. I'd get everyone in the building down here at once to see how many others have phones on the premises that are compromised."

"Who would do this?" Anastos asked.

Gerhardt tapped the controls of his wheelchair with a pair of fingers. The device spun toward the exit. "Drop everything else you're doing to find that out, Commander." Just before he pressed the accessible exit button, Gerhardt stopped cold. "CJ, where did your friend get that device?"

CJ remained focused on his terminal. "Out of the rubbish bin in 91 Waterloo."

Gerhardt turned his wheelchair to make eye contact with Anastos. "91 Waterloo. The Maitland Corporation."

POLICE HEADQUARTERS—PALOMA, ILLINOIS

J essica Ramirez sat, alone, across the large oak desk that was the centerpiece of the Paloma Chief of Police's office. She felt like O'Brien didn't even know she was there. The only connection was his concentration on the thick personnel file with her name on it.

After what felt like an age, the Chief finally regarded her. "You have a knack for attracting trouble, JRam."

The nickname she had received on day one at the academy had followed her for a decade. Once upon a time, the moniker bothered her. Now it was part of who she was.

"We found Jimmy." O'Brien tossed that one out as if it were an afterthought.

Jess perked up. "Did he tell you anything?"

O'Brien turned his attention back to her file. "The dead have little to say. Single bullet in the head. A professional job... As usual, you've drawn the attention of some pretty bad people."

Jess scanned the hundreds of criminal encounters that

were part and parcel of a career where she'd purposely put herself in harm's way. "Crouch?"

The chief rolled his eyes. "Yes. Crouch. He's been running his operation from Statesville, and a scum-bag lawyer got him released pending a retrial. It sounds like he's out for retribution."

Jess felt her temper flare. "I was a minor player in that ballet. Why isn't Crouch going after the district attorney and the sting team who set him up? Abernathy and Harrison should be on the top of his list."

O'Brien slid a briefing paper across the desk. "They are. Apparently, there was a coordinated attack on all three of you yesterday. Some valet kid turned the keys on Abernathy's Caddy after lunch at some restaurant. Same C4 explosives that vaporized your vehicle. The poor boy is playing a harp."

No cop likes it when a kid dies. Jess could see O'Brien's legendary composure crack. "They think they killed Harrison. He has a doppelgänger out there who got popped by mistake. They came closest to success with you and Clark yesterday afternoon."

Jess tried to wrap her head around the news. "Crouch's deal was federal. Why isn't the FBI involved?"

O'Brien gave her one of his looks. The one that told her he knew way more about her personal life than was appropriate. "They are. Your boyfriend in DC pulled some strings. I'm supposed to encourage you to take thirty days off with pay and leave the country until they can catch the people responsible."

Jess's thoughts instantly vectored to la familia. "I'm not going. If they can't target me, they know the way to extract retribution is to target my family."

The chief took a long breath. "I've already spoken with your mother. She's as stubborn as you are. But I've convinced her that she, Maria, and your grandmother deserve a department-funded vacation in Mexico for a few weeks. I have officers at the house right now helping them pack. They leave from O'Hare tonight at seven."

Jess tried to process this extraordinary news. It had FBI Special Agent Michael Wright's name all over it. Her lover was looking out for her and her family. The usual mixture of anger and desire pounded in her head like a migraine. "Then," she stuttered, "I-I think I should go with them. They might need my protection."

O'Brien shook his head. "The Feds think it's best to keep you away from them. Crouch wants you. But he's a small-time gangster. His reach is still only regional. If you're on the other side of the world, Agent Wright thinks you'll be safer."

"Safer." That didn't mean *safe*.

Jess gave it one last try. "I was involved in Crouch's capture, Chief. That's why he's after me. Doesn't it make sense that I should be part of the team to lure him out into the open?"

"No, JRam. My orders are coming from far above Agent Wright's pay grade. He's just the messenger boy."

O'Brien's tone softened. It made Jessica wary. "You've lived your entire life right here in Paloma."

Jess instantly vectored to the horrors of Nashville.

O'Brien had conveniently forgotten about that minor detour. "Think about someplace in the world you've always wanted to see. And make that decision quickly, or DC will make it for you."

———

JESSICA RAMIREZ SAT ACROSS FROM ALEXANDRA CLARK at The Vine and Barrel, Paloma's most popular watering hole. The owner gave Jess and Ali carte blanch there, after they arrested an unruly patron at Christmas.

Ali raised her bottle of Pilsner Urquell, clinking its base against the tall glass filled with Jess's third Margarita. "So where are you going to go, partner? The world is your oyster, and the company is paying."

"I want to go catch that bastard, Crouch," Jess slurred. "Yeah, Jimmy was a loser, but he wasn't a bad guy at heart. I'd love to put a hollow point between Crouch's baby blues."

Ali rolled her eyes. "When you get angry and drunk, what little good judgment you may have evaporates, Jess. This is your golden ticket. How are you going to spend it?"

Jess took a bigger slurp of her Margarita than she should have. A rivulet rolled down her chin. "I can't believe they just up and shooed la familia to Mexico. By rights, I should be there with them. If something happens down there…"

Ali interrupted, "You'll never forgive yourself. Listen, Jessica. You are not responsible for what happened to your father. And Michael Wright wants into your pants so badly that he'll do anything to impress you. Mama and crew will get Secret Service-level protection down there. Let it go, partner. Focus! If you could go anywhere, where would it be?"

Jess pulled her cell phone from her pocket and flipped the display in Ali's direction. "You know exactly where I'm going to go, Alexandra."

Diamond-like white reflections of the dim spotlights accented the words MARIE CULPADO IS ALIVE.

Ali took another long drink from her beer bottle. "I was afraid of that. Don't you think O'Brien has already figured out that you would come to that conclusion?"

"I think this mob hit stuff finally cracked that knucklehead's skull. He feels sorry for me. Protective is a man's vibe. Maybe he's, at last, got some remorse for forcing me to watch that fucking execution. He knows that lit a fire under my ass, and I won't rest until I figure out what really happened. Letting me jump from one frying pan into another is his way of expressing affection."

Ali shook her head. "You're as crazy as he is, Jessica. Is there anything I can say to talk you out of this horrible idea?"

"You know there isn't, partner. And deep down, you want me to go for it."

Ali drained the last of the Pilsner Urquell from the bottle. She motioned to the server to bring the cops two more drinks.

"I totally do. Go get him."

"But on my way," Jess slurred, "I need to see a guy in Washington."

WASHINGTON, DC

Michael Wright considered the beauty sitting across from him. "You attract some pretty interesting men."

The love of his life mesmerized the FBI Special Agent. He wanted to thank this Crouch dirt bag for helping to bring Jessica Ramirez to Washington, DC, even if it was just for a one-night stand.

Nothing had changed since Michael had impulsively asked Jess to marry him from a hospital bed in Phoenix last year.

"And the mood lighting here at The Dabney makes you look more attractive than ever."

Michael studied Jessica's beauty in the converted row-house at 122 Blagden Alley NW, satiated with the five-star cuisine and enjoying after-dinner cocktails on the taxpay-er's dime. Once again, Michael thought, Jessica would judge his lavish expenditures as a total waste of her tax dollars.

To his surprise, her mood wasn't combative. Her voice

was soft, almost sexy, and she was actually wearing make-up.

"You always flatter me, Michael. Be honest. What can you possibly see in a Latina from an Illinois river town who has done nothing but treat you like crap since the day we met?"

Michael felt a shiver of delight. Their arguments had passionate bookends that still were the stuff of his most prurient dreams.

He chuckled and took another sip of his single malt scotch. "I wouldn't say 'totally.' You have to admit that in many ways, we fit well together."

"I'll ignore the sexual reference. I owe you a debt, Michael. Thank you for doing what you did to keep my family safe until your guys put Crouch back into the slammer. Is O'Brien really paying for all of this with city money, or is our vacation funded by the national treasury."

Michael winked. "Let's just say that the safety of the Ramirez family is in the best interest of the country at the moment. You saved a lot of lives last year. It's the least we can do."

Jess leaned forward. Michael noticed her V-neck plunged deep enough to provide a delectable view of what was beneath it.

"That thing you said at the hospital. Now that the drugs are out of your system, I hope you realize what a mess that could be."

Michael took a deep breath. Nothing had changed. He wanted Jessica more now than ever. But how to tell her... that was delicate.

"I've been married before, Jessica. It was early in my career, and I don't think either of us knew what being a cop meant. You do. I don't want to tell you where to live or what to do with your life. We're very much the same. Passionate about our work. Bullheaded. Our values sometimes drive us past the edge of the envelope to get the job done. We take risks for the small guy and don't take shit from the big guys."

Michael regarded the woman looking back at him from across the table. The restaurant lighting accented the flecks of gold in her beautiful brown eyes. The geography of her face reflected a proud family tree with a history dating back to the days when Spain was a world power and could afford to send Columbus into the unknown. The sleeveless top she wore flattered a pair of arms perfected by every weight machine at the gym.

He memorized every line of her personnel file, noting with disgust how the system had tried to break her. But Michael had also seen Jess in action. She was a stellar cop who could compartmentalize and focus with the best of them. But the rare moments when she let down her shields revealed a passionate heart, a shared dedication to family values, and a sexual attraction that drew him to her like a magnet. Michael wished she wasn't so damn practical.

"I don't know, Michael. There's something about this idea of 'completion.' Two people who are too much the same are like two Capricorns hooking up. It's a recipe for disaster."

Michael felt reflective. "Have you ever been in love, Jessica?"

Jessica put her hand on top of his. "I am, Michael. That's what is making this so hard. Every intellectual fiber of my being is telling me we can't possibly work. But my heart wants you so badly that it hurts. Ali tells me I get in trouble when I let my heart rule my head." Jess rubbed a finger on top of Michael's knuckle. It felt like she had her hand inside of his pants, and it was driving him crazy. "And right now," Jess added, "we both have unfinished business."

"What's to finish?" Michael asked, "We'll get Crouch in a week and then it's back to the normal drill. 'Protect and Serve.'"

Jess blinked. It was one of those slow eyelid movements that have invited intimacy since the beginning of time.

"Tell you what, Michael Wright. For tonight, let's play the roles. You pick up the check and get the car. I'll make sure my lipstick looks good. We'll go back to your place and do what married people do."

Michael felt his heart rate surge, pressing the blood flow southward toward his passion. "Married people would lie in bed, looking at their cell phones with *Saturday Night Live* on in the background, until they fell asleep, drooling on their pillowcases." He put a finger on his pulse. "I prefer some extended cardiovascular activity."

The look on Jessica's face told Michael he had just scored some points. "Okay, Michael. Take me home and make love to me. Just get me to Dulles in time for my flight tomorrow evening."

"I can't believe it," Michael said in feigned surprise. "Detective Jessica Ramirez follows orders?"

"They are your orders, idiot. You're the one who told O'Brien to get me out of the country. I suppose I'm here to thank you for that."

"And where will you be sightseeing?"

"If you want me to fuck you, stop pretending you don't know, Michael. London, of course. I may even jump over to Spain and see if I have any rich ancestors."

"First things first." Michael produced a small, square blue box, placing it front and center on Jessica's placemat. He enjoyed watching her face contort in horror.

He could imagine her thoughts. "Not here. Not now."

"No, Jess. This isn't that magic moment. Just a memento to remind you of our adventures."

Jessica approached the item as if it were a hand grenade. Her fingers delicately opened the box. Her expression transformed from fear into delight. "It's beautiful, Michael," was all she could get out.

"I have a sister who was born with Down syndrome," Michael whispered. "It's a necklace, made by another Down syndrome mom in honor of her daughter. Juliette is my only sibling and the only other woman in my life."

Jessica examined the five-point star that hung from a tiny chain. It looked as if it were woven from strands of gold. Inside she could see a cluster of precious blue stones.

"You never told me about a sister."

"There's a lot I would tell my fiancée that I would never tell a co-worker."

"What does the design signify?" Jessica asked.

Michael took the necklace into his fingers, letting the golden star and the blue stones shimmer in the restaurant's mood lighting. "The three stones represent the three copies of chromosome 21. Most people are born with two. Those with Down syndrome have three. We can see them within the strands of gold that make up a star, that star each of us hopes we can grow up to become."

He slid his chair around the table, unhooking the tiny clasp and placing the chain around Jessica's neck. The star hung perfectly, just above her collarbone.

"Whatever happens with us, I hope you'll wear this in recognition of all that we can be and not what we are."

Jessica fingered the necklace. "Quoting John Denver now?"

Michael held out an arm. Jess took it, pinching his butt

with her thumb and index finger. "You're getting a little soft, Agent Wright."

Michael's devilish smile gave meaning to his answer. "Exactly the opposite, Detective Ramirez."

23

GATWICK AIRPORT—LONDON

Detective Inspector Liyanna Evans had mixed feelings about being banished to research. On the one hand, she missed the excitement of being on the street. But on the other, it gave her unimpeded access to every resource to continue her investigation into the Culpado matter. That Maddox would know this and didn't wave her off was proof that her boss wanted to learn more about it, too.

The text that Detective Jessica Ramirez was on her way to London re-energized Lee. Maddox may have taken away her partner, but providence was providing her with exactly the co-conspirator she needed.

Lee liked Jess instantly. Five feet, seven inches tall, about sixty-one kilograms, fit but feminine with brown eyes and skin that had Latin roots.

There was something about her attitude that resonated with Lee. It was hard being a woman in a man's profession. The edge in her voice and the intensity of her focus told the London DI that, like Lee, Jessica always had something to prove.

She was also a hugger, with an amiable smile that Lee could imagine turned ice cold when she smelled a potential perpetrator.

"How did a South African end up a DI with the Met?"

"I thought my accent was Scottish."

"I'm not that good. I checked you out on the Internet."

"I try to keep things off the Internet. What did it tell you?"

"You are my age. Thirty-four. Emigrated from Joburg at eighteen. Joined police services as PC. A self-made girl, firsts in criminology, law and criminal justice. You pulled that off while you were walking a beat. Pretty impressive. A fast mover. Not many women make DI in a decade. Never married, but you peel the boys off you like a supermodel."

"Where did you get that last part?"

Jessica laughed. "Speculation. That was a given in my department when I started. 'Screw or be screwed.' Or is it 'shag or be shagged'?"

"What makes you think I'm not married?"

"No indentation on the ring finger. I get paid to be observant."

Lee wanted to know more about this detective who dropped everything to chase a dead end.

"Right on almost all accounts. You missed one, though. I was born here. Parents on vacation when the time came. My dad is a Scot, and my mother is South African, a Zulu, so I'm a dual citizen. Growing up in Johannesburg was the perfect training for a copper. It's a hellhole of violence and death. London is almost boring in comparison."

Lee took a step back, framing Detective Ramirez in her mind.

"Your turn."

Jessica shared her own backstory, how she became a

cop, and the adventures in Arizona that led to this meeting.

Lee felt her cop skepticism kicking in.

"Why are you doing this? Nobody just drops everything and flies halfway around the world on a hunch."

"I saw the man I arrested die. Parts of the investigation didn't feel right. He had no family and only one advocate who couldn't get anyone to listen. Nobody cared about Vincent Culpado. I need to know what happened, to put my own conscience at rest."

"But you're spending your own money and burning vacation time on a single observation from ten years ago by one CID cop who isn't even sure the person she saw is the one you are looking for."

Detective Ramirez smiled. "That's enough for me. Are you game to find a needle in a haystack, Detective Inspector?"

Lee was. The force of Jessica's personality and the sheer hopelessness that she would ever find this woman had the DI hooked. "I'm on board. And call me Lee."

——————

"So, what do we do next?"

That was Lee's question after she briefed Jessica on everything that had happened on her side of the ocean.

"First, we look at Harry Duggan's stash and see if we can get a glimpse at what Marie Culpado looks like. And we talk with the district attorney who sent Vincent Culpado to The Chair."

This bewildered Lee. "You just got here, Jessica. And you are under orders to stay out of the country. How are you going to make that happen?"

Jessica smiled, punching a set of numbers into her cell phone. "I know just the person who can help us."

24

PALOMA, ILLINOIS

If you've been a cop for any length of time, you develop a sixth sense for an impending shit storm. Alexandra Clark's sixth sense was vibrating like a 7.5 earthquake when she saw the caller ID on her phone.

"You're calling me already, partner. Have you found Crouch and bagged Marie Culpado?"

"No on both accounts, Ali. I need your help."

"Whenever you say that, I know I'm about to do something I'll regret."

"Thank you for the supportive feedback, Alexandra. So, are you going to help me or not?"

"Of course, I am. What do you need?"

"I'm emailing your private account with the details. I think someone put pressure on the Nashville District Attorney to convict and kill this Culpado guy. I need you to work your magic and see if he'll tell us the truth."

Ali could smell trouble brewing. "You want me to go to Nashville and sweat a government employee who has no reason to cooperate?"

"Exactly."

"You know how well that's going to work. I'll probably get arrested."

"So, are you in?"

There wasn't a moment's hesitation in Ali's answer. "Absolutely. I can be there tomorrow."

J ess thought the place resembled the huge warehouse scene at the end of *Raiders of the Lost Ark.* Two rows of incandescent lights barely illuminated fifty-thousand square feet of stuff that Jess thought might be more proper as items in someone's garage sale.

"I'll give my research pals one thing," Lee said, running a finger down a blurry photocopy of the place's architectural layout. "They know how to organize rubbish."

"How long do you keep stuff before disposing of it?" Jess wondered as she followed her British counterpart through the maze of thin aisles bordered by ceiling-high steel shelving.

"We're English," Lee said without looking up from her map. "There's stuff here from before World War I."

Jess squinted. "Those perpetrators are long dead. Why hang onto everything?"

"History, my dear Jessica. Eventually, everything finds a place in some museum. Ahh, here we are!"

The personal effects of the late Harry Duggan, master

forger, took up about three square feet of space in the sprawling warehouse. All that betrayed its history was a seven-digit number, scribbled onto a card taped to the bottom of a shelf.

Lee pointed to a singular box in the middle of the cache. "That's the one. And there's not too much stuff to go through. If what we are looking for is here, we'll find it."

Jess held the shoebox-sized file container while Lee put on plastic gloves and thumbed through the records. "Old Harry had some pretty famous clients."

Jess recognized some faces that flipped by, including a few that had once adorned Wanted posters in the Paloma Police squad room.

Lee continued her inspection. "If he organized alphabetically, she should be near the front... Yes! We've got it!"

Lee pulled two cards from the box. "Blair" was written in Harry's distinctive scrawl. "This," the DI said, showing Jess a woman's photograph, "is the person I saw get on the tube at The Strand. Cops don't forget a face."

There was a second card with "Jonathan Blair" written on it. He was bald. No facial hair. Nondescript. Perfect for someone who wanted to blend in and disappear.

"We'll run this boy through the AI scanner at the office," Lee said, sliding both pictures into a fleece pocket. "You said your partner is heading to Nashville. If I send her a copy, do you think she could get them to confirm the ID?"

Jess grinned. "Oh, yeah."

26

NASHVILLE, TENNESSEE

T he Nashville District Attorney's office is at 222 N. 2nd Avenue, a block west of Bicentennial Park. To the east of the park is the Cumberland River, where Marie Culpado was last seen alive.

You don't just walk in and get to see DA Bob Goulding. So, Ali had to spill enough of the story to get his attention. She told Goulding's admin that she was a private citizen with information about the Vincent Culpado case and wanted fifteen minutes of his time. Apparently, those were the magic words because it took only a moment for the woman to come back on the line and confirm an 11 am appointment.

The admin ushered Ali into a conservatively furnished office. The DA was a big man, six feet three inches tall and heavy, about 280 pounds. His suit was beyond the budget of a government employee. It flattered his physical excess.

Goulding was young enough to still have his hair but old enough to want to color it. He flashed a careful, porcelain smile as he stuck out his paw. "How can I help you, Miss Clark?"

Ali had rehearsed her act with Jess the night before. She would have to fire all her weapons out of the gate, with no idea if they would work. "Thank you for seeing me, Mr. Goulding. I have firsthand information that Marie Culpado is alive and living in London. Is this something that you were aware of when you pressed the jury for the death penalty for her husband?"

Goulding's right cheek twitched, but he held the smile. "What's your interest in this case, Miss Clark?"

"Peripheral. I'm just a private citizen in search of the truth. If I know Marie is alive, then others know it. My next stop is to visit Tony Eldridge at *The Tennessean*. Before I talk with him, I wanted to give you the opportunity to help me understand why the State would purposely murder an innocent man."

There was the twitch again. The smile was fading.

"This is all very interesting, *Officer* Clark. Yes, I do my homework, too. What would your chief think about a policewoman operating outside of her sworn jurisdiction, interfering in something that's none of her business?"

Ali expected this. "Let's not fuck around, Bob. I'm immune to threats. You're welcome to call my chief. He'll tell you what a pain in the ass I can be. Are you going to enlighten me on the Culpado thing, or do I let Mr. Eldridge draw his own conclusions on the front page?"

His eyes were menacing slits. His voice was ominous. "You're in way over your head, Officer Clark. And you can tell your friend, Detective Ramirez, that I said so. This is far above all of our pay grades. You may be a big fish in your small Illinois pond, but if you pursue this, they will crush you underfoot like a couple of Tennessee cockroaches."

His attitude pissed Ali off.

"You're sweating, Bob. What kind of pressure are you under?"

"Your bravado is admirable. But you're out of your league. We both are on this one. Leave it and go back to chasing shoplifters."

She hated it when DA's patronized her. "Here's how I see it, Bob. The only people who could make a guy like you risk his career and his character are the feds. They promised you that you would have a backup if anyone started asking questions. For all I know, they may already have shut down Tony Eldridge, too. Just tell me the truth. If I buy your story, I can talk with Detective Ramirez about cooling her jets."

Goulding twitched again. But this time, he didn't have a snappy response. When you got a DA to deliberate, that was something. The federal thing was a shot in the dark. It was the only reason Ali and Jess could think of that might force a good man to do something bad. Like Sherlock says, "Eliminate all other possibilities and what remains is the truth."

The DA looked at his watch. Was he stalling or still thinking?

"Okay, Officer Clark, I'll level with you. But I must ask, on your honor as a peace officer, that you immediately stop all inquiries into this case. Do we have a deal?"

Ali stood and turned toward the door. "It's nice to have met you, Bob. See you in the papers." She was about to turn the handle when he answered.

"I got direct instructions from the FBI. I didn't want to do it, but they can make threats that stick. There it is. That's all I can tell you. I implore you, drop this. If you don't, many lives will be in danger, including your own."

Ali turned back to face him. A cop can almost always sense when someone's lying. It happens so often that when you hear the truth, it's uncomfortably refreshing. Bob Goulding was telling her the truth.

"Okay, Bob. I believe you. It had to be something horrific, or you wouldn't put your reputation at risk. Thank you for the honesty."

Goulding was standing now, leaning forward with his palms on the top of his desk. "What will you do now, Officer Clark?"

"I'll talk it over with Detective Ramirez."

Everything about Goulding's narrative felt like slime. But somewhere inside that suit, there had to be a shred of character.

"We all get into the game with high ideals," Ali said. "They crumble when we see the world as it really is."

"Here's the thing, Bob. We took these jobs because we believe in justice and the search for truth. We are sworn to protect the innocent and pursue the guilty. For whatever reason, someone forced you to do the antithesis of everything you stand for. That's troubling. I appreciate the slice of candor. But, like you, I need more evidence before rendering judgment."

The sweat was running down the DA's sideburns. Whatever this was, had him shook. "If you don't stop this, what you're looking for will come to you. And it won't be pretty."

Ali felt genuine empathy for the guy and tried to communicate it. "Thanks, Bob. I'll watch my back. You had to know that this would all come out at some point. I hope you have a plan-B."

The DA nodded. There was resignation in his expression. "Be careful, Officer Clark. You have no idea what's inside of this powder keg you are opening."

———

Ali was asking Goulding's admin where she could find a coffee shop with some Wi-Fi when they heard the gunshot. The woman beat Ali to the door.

District Attorney Robert Goulding's torso was bent over his desk. His head rested on its chin like a bearskin rug. A Taurus Judge revolver smoked in his right hand. The .410 slug cleaved his skull from side to side, painting the far wall with a crimson and gray mixture of a troubled existence.

Whatever Jess was into was enough to force the man to take his own life.

The admin froze, clearly in shock. Ali put her hands on the woman's shoulders and focused on her stunned expression.

"Call 9-1-1. Let's get some help."

The admin nodded and left the room.

Ali had only seconds to scan the place before she would have to bail. She saw it on the edge of the desk, about a foot from the hand that pulled the trigger.

It was a sheet from the DA's personal notepad with two names and an address. Above the scrawl was Ali's name, underlined.

She slipped the paper into her pocket. "Now you're tampering with evidence in a murder case, Alexandra," she said to herself, deciding that it was time to get the hell out.

———

She saw the suits in the lobby. Identical down to the sunglasses. They were kind enough to wait until she was on the street before accosting her. At least there were more options out in the open.

"Alexandra Clark?"

"What do you want?"

"You must take a ride with us, ma'am."

"I prefer my own company, thank you."

A hand grabbed her arm. Ali could see the other man reaching under his suit coat, where she knew guys like him carried their heat.

The voice was cold, insistent, official. "This isn't optional."

He pointed to a blue Ford sedan with an open door. There was a small crack in the windshield on the passenger side.

The grip was firm but not firm enough. Ali broke it with ease and sprinted south toward Bank Street. The lunch hour congestion on the sidewalk was thick. It was an advantage, and Ali needed any advantage she could get.

The suits had as much trouble threading through the maze of humanity as she did. But Ali had about ten steps on them. That was enough.

She made the left turn on Bank and ran in the street against traffic. Ali was fifty yards ahead of them when she took another left on First Avenue and melted into the thicket of people and trees in Bicentennial Park.

27

FBI HEADQUARTERS—
WASHINGTON, DC

Terry Taylor recognized the number. The boss almost never called his cell. The director of the Federal Bureau of Investigation preferred the privacy of his office, where confidences had a better chance of preservation and verbal promises could easily be broken.

"There's a problem with the Nashville matter."

Terry frowned. Directors came and went. He had served a dozen of them. This one was particularly wedded to the inhabitant of 1600 Pennsylvania Avenue. The director was smart enough to give Terry his freedom. Sometimes that freedom came with a political price tag.

Taylor could hear his boss inhaling a Marlboro on the other end of the line before continuing.

"Two Illinois yokels are asking questions."

Taylor rubbed the Marine crew cut that had been part of his brand since Parris Island. Friends said it stimulated his thinking.

"Civilians?"

"Law. Handle it."

The gravel voice disconnected the call before Taylor could affirm the order.

MET HEADQUARTERS—LONDON

J ess twirled the two 4x6-inch passport photo cards through her fingers like a magician knuckling a silver dollar. She sat next to Lee in the small cubical Research kept for temporary visitors. The detective felt her phone vibrate and saw Ali's icon pop up as an incoming call.

The connection was excellent. Ali sounded as if she were sitting at the next desk.

Her partner's voice dripped with its usual combination of sarcasm and excitement. "This is getting interesting."

"Talk to me, partner."

"The DA shot himself in the head after my visit. Two goons in suits tried to abduct me when I left the building. And there are guys with guns and sunglasses watching my rental car. I'm guessing a few more people know about your little trip to London."

This stunning development came close to cracking Jess' legendary game face. Close, but not close enough for Lee to realize that there was trouble. "I'm pretty sure that Marie Culpado is alive, Ali. Or at least she was when she and her boyfriend snuck into the UK with fake passports ten years ago."

"Are you listening to me, Jessica? You've got a tiger by the tail. I think it's time to talk to Michael Wright about this. I smell FBI all around me."

The name triggered a flood of conflicting emotions that Jess didn't want to process. The dinner. The exquisite night of passion. And the new, uncomfortable feeling of missing Michael when he dropped her off at Dulles.

She wore his necklace, but she was still unsure if she could ever wear his ring.

"Where are you now?"

"I'm at a Wi-Fi coffee shop. Got the countermeasures turned on. If these guys are, in fact, federal, they already have talked to Chief O'Brien and can track my cell, so I'll keep this short. DA Goulding left me a love note before he pulled the trigger. Names and an address. Do Rufus and Charlene Yates mean anything to you?"

They did. Just unusual enough to make an impression on a cop with PTSD, forced to witness an execution.

"Yes. They are supposedly Marie Culpado's parents."

"Well, that's my next port of call. The late Mr. Goulding left me that morsel."

"Be careful, Ali. I'm regretting getting you into this mess."

Jess's partner laughed. "Are you kidding? This is the most fun I've had since you almost got me killed in Flagstaff. *You* be careful, partner. Do you want to call Michael, or should I?"

She could feel Ali sensing the hesitation. Partners in the police profession got good at that sort of thing.

"I'll do it. I'll call him after I visit Rufus and Charlene. Geez, you'd think they could come up with more innocuous aliases."

"You're the best, partner. Watch your back."

"You watch yours. I'm not over there to watch it for you."

Jess had Ali on speaker so Lee could hear the conversation.

"I'm wishing I had not dragged you into this, Lee. Things might get dicey for you."

Lee focused on typing a query into her terminal. "I grew up in Johannesburg, Jessica. It was open warfare down there, especially for 'colored people' who look like me. I've seen friends shot dead and have had guns pointed at my face. This feels like a vacation."

Jess knew she was underplaying it. Ali was rarely serious. Her words of warning were sinking in. Jess slid a finger along the indentation that ran from the wrist to the elbow of her right arm, a past battle scar she treasured to remind her of that place where courage and stupidity intersect.

It felt like she was at that very intersection now.

Lee finished typing and hit the return key. "Now, let's see what one of the world's most sophisticated databases can tell us about our friends, Marie and Jonathan Blair."

It didn't take long. In what seemed like an instant, the screen beeped, and a red box appeared with the words "Information Restricted—IT Security Notified" inside.

Lee grimaced. "Oops. That's not good."

"What just happened?"

"Well, whatever covert research we may have been doing off the clock just got everyone's attention."

Her cell lit up. The word "Maddox" appeared on the screen.

"Bollocks. That's the boss. I'm feeling a chunder coming on."

She opened the connection. "DI Evans speaking. Yes, sir. I'm in the building. Yes… I will report to your office now."

Lee shot the detective a glance. It was an expression Jess knew well. The heat was coming, and she was preparing for it.

"Wait here."

29

NASHVILLE

R*ufus and Charlene Yates. You have to be kidding me. Someone probably picked those monikers out of an old phone book.*

But they must still exist, or Goulding wouldn't have given Ali an address with the names.

She abandoned any idea of retrieving the rental car and flagged a passing Uber. No telling if spies were watching her Internet traffic. The driver was at the end of his shift and willing to take another fare without sharing a cut with his contract employer.

Ali handed him an address and a twenty while she tried to add up the equation.

They sacrificed Culpado to protect his wife, who was now allegedly living underground in London with another husband. It took some major pressure to get a district attorney to be complicit in what was essentially murder one.

Why?

What was it about Marie Culpado that made her that valuable to the United States Government?

It didn't take a genius to connect the dots. She had to be under protection.

It was still too early for Ali to put that theory into stone. Perhaps Mr. and Mrs. Yates could enlighten her.

She had the Uber guy drop her off a block away from the address. Ali flipped him two more twenties and asked him to hang around for a few minutes.

As the home came into view, she could see a phalanx of police cars and EMS on the street. A uniformed cop kept a knot of neighbors at bay.

She joined the gawkers, asking nobody in particular, "What's going on?"

A woman Ali assumed to be one of the local gossips put a hand next to her mouth, the universal symbol for sharing a secret she wanted everyone else to know.

"Someone killed Rufus and Charlene. I heard the shots and called 9-1-1." She pointed to a gurney with a black body bag on it, flanked by two men with coroner jackets.

"That has to be her. She was the short one."

Ali made a mental inventory of the scene. Four black and whites, an ambulance, the coroner's van, and three unmarked units. One jogged a memory. She recognized the blue Ford with the cracked windshield.

On the front porch, Ali's two boyfriends were in a heated exchange with what looked like the cop in charge. She couldn't make out the words, but she knew the look. The locals don't like it when federals flex their muscles.

The guy who tried to grab her arm seemed to be the senior player. He made a cutting motion with his hand as if to signal that the conversation was over.

Ali could hear the head cop's voice calling after the two in blue as they walked toward their vehicle. "We'll see about that."

Badges were hanging around their necks. Even from a distance, she recognized them.

FBI.

30

THE G8 SUMMIT—BRUSSELS

Governor Darell Sisson and his party compatriots sat across from the Group of Three. The memory of watching the aircraft he was originally scheduled to fly drill into the depths of the Atlantic Ocean was still intruding on his concentration. He tried to shake it off and focus.

Each man in the trio had a cadre of bodyguards in tow. It felt to Sisson as if there were more soldiers at the meeting than there were participants.

In the hotel's main conference room, the world press listened to leaders mouth the same, tired political sound bytes.

Things only change, Sisson thought, *when you talk with the people in charge.*

It occurred to the governor that these were the new "knights of the round table" as he studied the configuration of the gathering. The adversaries sat in two semi-circles. Sisson and his fellow governors were almost shoulder to shoulder on one side, binders with economic data before them. The three oligarchs with ties to Russia, China, and India, sat on the other. Although each was clearly fluent in English, earbuds connected them to translators who sat at a separate table off to the side. Identical digital note pads were the only accouterments in front of them.

Sisson stood, walked around to a break between the two semi-circular tables and entered the space between them, facing his foreign audience.

"Let me begin by thanking each of you for taking the time out of your busy schedules for this extraordinary conversation. I won't spend any more of it with platitudes or a long introduction. We are here to discuss the efficacy of the American consumer market, a juggernaut that is still the largest in the world and a powerful force for commerce and profit."

The governor waved a hand, and a bar chart flashed on the wall behind him, denoting the world's markets. The United States was, by far, the longest bar, dwarfing even the countries these three powerful men represented.

"Unfortunate messaging about the United States becoming a 'dying nation' being spread by misinformed individuals on social media has bled into the mainstream. It is a subject of discussion by the politicians in the auditorium next to our little gathering."

Another sign and the image behind Sisson dissolved into a series of headlines: "America is Impotent on the World Stage. US Consumers are overextended. High debt. Can't afford what they buy."

Sisson continued, "We know that each of you controls vast media empires that may contribute to this misinformation. And we felt it was important for you to know that it is not representative of the hard-working men and women each of us represents."

Sisson took a step closer to the three men. He could see the row of bodyguards tense.

"America is a confederation of individual states. Our presidents come and go. The shifting sands of federal policy ultimately have little impact on history. The states are the engines of commerce that continue to make America great."

The Chinese billionaire who sat, hands flat on the table, to the right of his Russian and Indian counterparts, bent a palm upward.

The governor halted his presentation, bowing in the man's direction.

The voice was quiet but powerful and foreboding. Sisson could feel the room temperature drop.

"These are the facts, Governor Sisson," the oligarch said. "Consumer debt in your country tops fourteen trillion dollars. That's forty-two thousand two hundred and ninety-six dollars in debt for every man, woman, and child in the United States. The median household income in your country is slightly over sixty thousand dollars a year. Your constituents spend nearly every cent they earn. You save just four point nine percent of your income. Your economy is growing at just two point three five percent per year. You rank one hundred fifteenth out of one hundred ninety-three nations."

The man paused for effect.

"The world knows that America is in trouble and can't pay her debts. Despite this admirable overture, we have little confidence that this will improve. We fear it will soon do quite the opposite."

Sisson could see his grand meeting disintegrating. "But the stock market," he began.

Another raised palm shut him up.

"The American stock market is the realm of gamblers.

When a small group of people on a social network can band together to raise the stock price of a failing company, that is proof that your markets reflect unreasonable exuberance, rather than the true value of your economy."

The Chinese oligarch pressed his chair backward. His two counterparts followed suit.

"We must prepare for a global community, where the United States is no longer an economic powerhouse, nor a reliable partner. That, gentlemen, is our conclusion."

Darrell Sisson was never at a loss for words. He worried his fellow governors would note the change. Before he could gather himself to respond, the three men and their security entourages disappeared through a side entrance.

Governor Chris Buchanan stood. Sisson's chief rival in the early polls of possible presidential contenders spoke to the stunned group of leaders. "Well, gents, we've just seen Darell's oval office prospects vaporize before our eyes. We may wish we were all on that plane that took a dump in the Atlantic before this debacle is over."

———

OUTSIDE OF THE CONFERENCE ROOM, THE GROUP OF Three exchanged wordless glances. "Are we still in agreement?" the Indian said.

All nodded in affirmation.

MET HEADQUARTERS—LONDON

"Let's have it, Inspector Evans. You're investigating the Culpado matter after I told you not to. Why?"

Lee was always straight with her boss and gave him everything, the text she had sent to Jessica, her arrival in London, and the trip to the archives. He was a good listener. Nodding without comment. Lee had an uncomfortable feeling that he knew more about this than she did. The expected dress-down didn't come after Lee finished her tale. Just instructions.

"You are to drop the investigation immediately, Detective Inspector. Put Detective Ramirez on a flight to the States within twenty-four hours. You will personally make sure she boards the aircraft. Until then, she is in your..." he hesitated, "in your custody. Don't let her out of your sight. Is that clear?"

"Yes, sir."

NASHVILLE

"**M**ichael Wright. It's Alexandra Clark. It sounds like you have no lasting side effects from your adventures in Arizona."

Jessica's FBI boyfriend seemed happy to hear from her.

"Gates! How is my favorite computer nerd? Are you ready to come work in DC?"

He didn't know.

"I'm not sure you'll want to be associated with my smiling face after this conversation, my friend."

"What's happened?"

"I think your partner stumbled into FBI territory, something in Associate Director Taylor's orbit that the Bureau is trying to keep under wraps. I need to know how much trouble we may be in."

"Hmm…"

Ali could hear the wheels turning in Michael Wright's head. He was flipping through the database in his brain to get ahead of her.

"OK. What snake pit did Jess drag you into now?"

Ali feigned annoyance. "You always assume it's her. Give me some credit for causing my own trouble."

"I know you, Gates. You're the smart-aleck friend who enables a good girl's poor judgment."

"As in her poor judgment about men?"

"If she had good judgment, we'd be living together. Spill the details."

"Know anything about a missing wife and an alleged murderous husband in Nashville?"

"You'll have to give me more than that, Ali."

"Does Vincent Culpado ring any bells?"

There was silence on Michael's end of the line. The name obviously did.

His answer was cryptic. "Tell me more."

"Ahh, you know the name. Chief O'Brien ordered Jess to witness Culpado's execution. His usual sick attempt to break her spirit. You probably already know that Jess caught the perp a decade ago when he was on the run. Nothing about the experience felt right, and she asked some questions. She thinks the dead wife is alive and possibly living in London. She sent me to Nashville to have a talk with the District Attorney. He blew his brains out after our interview. Two people who Jess says were the wife's parents were shot and killed about two hours later. In between, a couple of boys who look an awful lot like you tried to grab me. You know how I don't like unwanted physical contact. I saw them at the home of the dead parents, pulling rank on the local law. Their shields told me they are your brothers in arms. Have we stumbled onto somebody important who you guys are trying to hide?"

"Give me a moment, Ali. The boss is on the other line."

If that was the case, the conversation didn't take long. The voice that came back was Michael's command voice.

But there was something else Ali could hear in the mix. Michael Wright was afraid.

"OK, Ali. Here's what I need you to do. Call Jessica right now and tell her to leave London immediately. If I know her, she's undoubtedly found a friend at the Met. Tell that person to forget that she ever heard the name Culpado. Her career and maybe her life will depend upon it. By now, our boys know who you are and where you are staying in Nashville. Go to your hotel and wait for them there. I'll make sure they keep you safe. Do not talk to anyone else about this. Do you hear me, Ali? Say nothing. I need to make some phone calls now to protect the two of you."

Ali frowned. "It's that bad?"

"It's that bad, Alexandra. You girls have to play ball with me on this, or nothing I can do will shield you. This goes way beyond things like careers and jail time for interfering. You have stumbled into something with international implications. I'll do what I can to back you out of it. But for once, please listen to me and do exactly as I say."

He was pleading. Ali had never heard that from him before.

"OK, Michael. I'll call her right now. I'm sorry if any of this ends up dumping shit on your doorstep."

"I'll deal with that. Make the call and get to your hotel as soon as you can. Do it without drawing attention to yourself. You're already in danger and it may take some time for me to reorient some attitudes."

What the fuck? Reorienting attitudes? International implications? Beyond careers and jail time?

Ali knew that there was no way she was going back to her hotel.

She needed time to think.

33

THE STRAND—LONDON

L ee and Jess sat across from one another at The Wellington, a pub favorite in the Strand. Jess was on her second Lagavulin single malt scotch. Lee was nursing a Guinness Stout.

Jess winced as the alcohol stung her throat. "So, he didn't chew you out?"

Lee studied the tiny ropes of carbonation bubbling upward in her glass. "Not a word. I think his orders were coming from the top of the chain. He was calm and direct. That's what troubled me. It was as if his own career was on the line."

"And I'm persona non grata after tomorrow."

"I have 24 hours to get you out of the country."

"And you'll follow orders?"

"You know I will."

"So that gives us another day to make sense of all of this."

"I don't know, Jessica. The boss gave me the impression that we've opened some doors he would rather have closed."

Jess had to agree. They were locked out of the database, so what they knew about the Blairs was what they were going to get. Every avenue Jess had taken had been a dead end. Perhaps it was time to throw in the towel.

That's when she heard the first shots.

They were a trio of professionals, complete with ski masks and smoking AK47s. The opening volley was designed to get everyone's attention. They were looking for specific targets. Jess had a bad feeling about that.

She pulled Lee from the stool and toward cover behind the bar. A voice in an accent Jess couldn't place shouted above the screams of the patrons.

"Everything will be all right, people. Just do as we say, and nobody will be hurt. We are looking for two women: a Spaniard and a Black. Point them out to us and the rest of you get to keep on living."

Lee and Jess locked eyes. She tilted her head as she spoke.

"A Spaniard and a Black?"

Jess was instantly incensed. All the frustrations of the case conspired to light up her Hispanic temper like a flame-thrower. "I'm a Latina, dammit. No guns and no backup. What a cluster."

They both heard the shot. Jess knew from the sound signature that it was a 9-millimeter.

A hail of bullets rained against an overturned table

"That's a mate," Lee said. "Looks like the boss didn't trust me to keep you on a leash by myself."

"He's got a weapon and we don't," Jess hissed back, getting hotter by the second.

She crawled behind the bar, trying to keep her anger under control and looking for the biggest bottle of booze she could find. Jess saw an unopened Macallan and grabbed it.

Another shot rang out from the 9 mil. Time to help a fellow officer.

Jess popped above the bar. The three men were all focused on emptying their magazines into the table. One was close enough to touch.

She smashed the whisky bottle across his forehead. The son of a bitch didn't break. But it dazed him enough that he lost his grip on the AK. Despite her blood alcohol level, Jess snagged it and sprayed about 20 rounds into his chest.

He had on a Kevlar vest!

Jess spat an obscenity and popped him with a single shot to the head before dropping behind the bar.

Jess saw the two survivors recognize their target and turn the fury of their machine guns in her direction as she scampered back to Lee's position.

Lee wasn't there.

Jess knew where she would be and poked a head around the edge of the bar to get a look at the table where the backup was hiding.

He was dead.

Lee wasn't there to revive him. She was there for his gun.

Jess rose above the bar and drew a bead on the two remaining bad guys, high enough to be above the protection of their Kevlar vests. Jess didn't know how many rounds were left in her magazine, so she configured the AK for single-action.

A shot tagged number two in the shoulder. He reflexively grabbed the arm to stem the bleeding. Jess took him out with a round to the head.

That left perp number three. If the size of his weapon's drum magazine was any indicator, he was the leader.

Lee dove back toward Jessica's position as he started firing.

The sound of the AK was coming closer. The drum mag must have been gargantuan because there was no letup in the hail of lead as he walked closer to his targets.

"Do we want this guy alive for questioning, Lee?"

"Maybe not. I don't like his cavalier attitude toward the sanctity of human life."

"I'll get his attention. You take him out."

There was a stool within Jess's reach. She heaved it over the top of the bar, vaulting behind the long line of beer taps.

The perp swung the AK in her direction, it's red-hot barrel still firing.

Lee rose above the bar as the stream of bullets followed Jess's movements. Her handgun coughed three times, each bullet finding its target.

The last of the trio crumpled to the ground, his finger still on the trigger of his weapon as the last rounds embedded themselves in the thick oak at the base of the bar.

"Good shooting, partner," Jess said, "How is our colleague?"

Lee's voice cracked. "Bled out. I knew him. Two young kids and a wife."

Her hands were shaking. Jess gently took the semi-auto from her fist and hid both of the weapons under the bar.

"We probably don't want to have this on us when your friends get here."

"I don't want to be seen by my friends, Jessica. Let's disappear before any of them make an appearance."

"I thought cops everywhere looked out for one another."

"So did I," Lee answered. "Only Maddox should be able to track the GPS on my cell. Only my brothers and sisters in arms should have known where we were. I'm beginning to wonder who is friend and who is foe. I need some time to get some clarification… from a distance."

The two hurried to the door hearing raised voices as the patrons began to comprehend that the evening's entertainment was at an end.

The text ringtone on Jess's cell buzzed when they were out on the street. She recognized the number but couldn't place it.

The message was an address.

34

NASHVILLE

The Village Inn restaurant was close enough to the hotel so Ali could bolt there if she got the sense that Michael's orders had been communicated. But it was far enough away to keep Ali somewhat anonymous as she pondered her options. It had Wi-Fi and caffeine; all her adrenaline-charged body needed to sustain life.

The Yates murders were already on CNN, as was a suspected terrorist incident in the heart of London. Three shooters were dead. Miraculously, there was only one patron killed among the many that jammed the Wellington Pub. An armed undercover officer was apparently on the scene. Beyond that sparse intelligence, the cops weren't talking.

Ali wanted to know more about what she was up against. Michael's admonition to stay under cover until she got to her hotel was a warning. His compatriots might have different instructions regarding her safety, and he wanted to amend them.

She fired up her laptop and had little luck finding

anything out about Rufus and Charlene Yates. They were two people without a past.

Ali was about to give it up and follow instructions when the two FBI suits appeared.

The countermeasures she was using with her technology were apparently more vulnerable than she thought..

They sat on either side of her, suit coats open, weapons clearly visible in shoulder holsters.

"Gentlemen. Can I assume you are here to pick up my tab?"

One twin scooped Ali's computer and cell phone into a briefcase he carried.

The other spoke. "You must come with us, Officer Clark. Your shield and weapon, please."

"No phone calls from your bosses in DC?"

"Follow instructions. Your weapon and your badge."

There didn't seem to be any way out. Ali held out both hands where the boys could see them.

"The holster is behind me. My badge and my handcuffs are next to the weapon. Would you like to relieve me, or should I do it?"

They both put paws inside their suit coats at the same time. Ail wondered if they taught synchronized swimming at the FBI Academy, too.

"You do it. Slowly. Everything on the table."

There was an explosion by the cash register. A bullet ripped through the forehead of the agent on Ali's right, painting the wall behind it with a similar parabola of bodily fluids she recognized from her experience in the DA's office.

The second agent launched himself away from the booth and toward a lead planter that split the dining area in half. Gunshots followed him.

Ali slid under the table, trying to get a make on her assailants.

There were two of them, equally well dressed but clearly not allies. And why weren't they shooting at her?

Ali heard shouts in what sounded like Russian. They both stood, legs apart in a firing stance, handguns blazing at the planter.

She realized they couldn't see her movements from their position. Ali took advantage of the situation and crawled in the gunfire's direction.

When they ran out of rounds, she heard the sounds of clips dropping on the tiles. They would have to look down to reload. There was a nanosecond of surprise.

When the two bad guys refocused, they were in her sights.

"Bye, boys."

Ali double-tapped both twice, just to make sure. She was too close to miss.

The restaurant was nearly empty, but that didn't stop the wait staff from screaming. Ali showed her shield and told the hostess to call 9-1-1.

Then she went over to see how agent number two was holding up.

He was alive, barely. Blood was draining from a half dozen holes in his body.

She couldn't stop it.

"Who can I call for you, my friend?"

His voice gurgled when he answered. Blood came out of his mouth with the words, "More are coming. Get away while you can."

Alexandra Clark ran for the door, remembering too late that her laptop and cell phone were still in Agent Number One's briefcase.

35

THE STRAND—LONDON

"I left my bloody cell phone at the pub."

Liyanna Evans knew it wouldn't take long for any copper who found it to make the connection.

But there was a bright side. Maddox couldn't contact her with any further instructions. That bought some time to strategize.

It was already dark as the two women hustled toward Covent Garden. Lee could tell that Jessica Ramirez was on an adrenaline high. Her words came fast, almost a stream of consciousness.

"The text message said 75 Charlton Street—Flat 404. Does that ring a bell? I know that damn phone number. Why do I know that damn number? And why would someone be texting us an address out of the blue?"

It felt like she was spinning up her brain to squeeze the answers she was looking for out of some corner of her memory. Whatever her process, it bore fruit.

"Crawford! That's Jack Crawford's number."

Lee made the connection. "Culpado's friend who tried to hire you?"

She pulled a business card out of her pocket. "That's the one. He doesn't even know I'm over here. At least he shouldn't. Is Charlton Street a London address, or is he trying to send me somewhere in Nashville?"

Lee knew the area. There was a Charlton Street in Somers Town. Number 75 would be right next to the medical center. The nearest tube stop was Brixton.

She flagged a taxi.

"75 Charlton Street is nearby. Let's go have a look. What do you know about this Jack Crawford?"

"Very little. He said he was Culpado's friend. But I have no evidence to confirm it." Jessica seemed to switch gears. "Do you have friends at British Telecom who could talk with the American cell carriers about triangulating the location of Crawford's phone?"

"Perhaps. It will take time. What are you thinking?"

"Just trying to cover the bases. Why the hell hasn't Ali checked in? It's been over an hour."

"Let me borrow your cell, and I'll call a mate at BT to see how he can help. He's a straight arrow, so I'm sure word will get back to Maddox about my request."

"I think after our adventures at the Wellington, your boss may have a different point of view about things. When people target cops, the brass gets protective."

Lee rang up her contact at British Telecom and gave him Crawford's number. The kid said he would work his magic and get back to her.

Ali wasn't answering.

That burned up the travel time to Charlton Street. The two stood in front of number 75. It was a four-story building that abutted up against the medical center complex. By rights, Lee should have taken Jessica's cell phone and called her boss. She floated the idea, and Jessica didn't like it.

"The clock is ticking, Lee. The bad guys took their shot at us when they did for a reason. Someone thinks we have enough of the puzzle to solve this thing. If we wait for your official channels to spin the gears, we may miss something important."

"You are not suggesting that we freestyle an engagement with the people in flat 404."

"That's exactly what I'm suggesting." Jessica said it over her shoulder as she pressed the entire line of doorbells for every flat in the building. "Here's hoping somebody buzzes us in. There's a security camera. Show your shield. That usually does the trick."

Lee did. A moment later, there was a soft magnetic click, and the door to 75 Charlton Street swung open.

———

THERE WAS NO RESPONSE WHEN THEY KNOCKED ON the door at flat 404.

"I guess we wait," Lee said.

Jess was already jogging down the hall toward the fire escape. "The hell we do. Follow me."

A moment later, she was on the external iron staircase that gave residents safe passage in case the danger blocked the elevators or the main stairway. Jess was counting the number of balconies between the fire escape and flat 404.

"One, two… three. That's the one. Come on, I think this ledge is wide enough to give us a foothold."

"Is this how they do things at your department in the States?"

Jess was already pressing her fingers between the bricks. "Sometimes you have to improvise, Lee. It feels like there isn't much time, and we need to see what's inside that flat. Forcing the cheap locks on the balcony slider will be easier than busting down the front door. And it will draw a lot less attention."

Jess slid along the thin concrete facing that stuck out about six inches from the red brick wall, her fingers jammed in between the bricks and the thin layer of cement that held everything together.

Lee hesitated. "I have a thing about heights, Jessica."

"So did I. Just imagine your life depends upon getting to that balcony. And don't look down."

Lee followed Jess, sticking like glue to the side of the building until they clawed their way onto the balcony of flat 404.

Opening the slider was easy for Jess. She flipped the lock open with a credit card. Ten minutes after debarking from their taxi, Lee and Jess stood in the darkness inside 75 Charlton Street—flat 404.

———

NOBODY WAS HOME. BUT WHOEVER LIVED THERE HAD recently left. A half-smoked cigarette still glowed in an ashtray, and the indentations on the couch felt warm to the touch.

"We just missed 'em," Jess said, crushing the butt. "Cigarettes are a dirty habit. And the damn things start fires."

"I think you just fouled up a crime scene with your fingerprints, Jessica. Unless you plan to take the butt with you."

"The only butts I care about are ours. What's out of place?"

The flat seemed to be normal until Jess inspected the wastebaskets.

"Ahh! Pay dirt!" Jess held up a crumpled scrap of paper.

They had to take it to the edge of the balcony to make out what had been written on it in the dim illumination from the streetlights below.

London St-Pancras to Paris Gare du Nord—2200

Lee checked her watch. "That's the Chunnel Train. It departs in thirty-four minutes."

Jess moved toward the front door to the flat. Something stopped her. "Best to go back the way we came. There may be security cameras in the hallway. I've already dirtied up your crime scene enough."

"I don't know where you get your brass monkeys, Jessica. The prospect of falling four stories to the pavement has me cocked up."

Jess scampered back onto the fire escape. "Oh, I can't stand heights, either. But I learned that if you concentrate, you can keep fear in the box for just enough time to do what you need to do."

"Is that something they teach you at the police academy?"

Jess shook her head. "I learned it in the real world, chasing after someone who tried to kill me. Nothing focuses you like imminent death."

There were sirens in the distance, and they were getting louder with each passing moment. By the time the two were back on the fire escape, there were four street units and a van full of special weapons personnel on the street below.

It was too dark for them to see anyone on the fire escape.

"Ahh," Jess said. "So, there are others interested in 75 Charlton Street, too."

The vehicles discharged their human contents. Police officers with weapons at the ready entered the building.

Lee could hear them mounting the stairs. Incredibly, nobody remained with their vehicles.

The two stepped down from their own stairway to heaven as quietly as the iron would allow. "We should tell them that we're here," Lee said.

Jess waved her away.

"We just finished breaking and entering," she whispered. "I don't think you want to have to explain that."

It was a warm enough night that windows were open. Jess could hear the army of boots reach the 4th floor and a single voice shouting, "Police! Open the door now!"

Jess pulled Lee away from the excitement and toward St. Pancras Station. There were less than twenty minutes to catch the train.

Even from a distance, they could both hear the battering ram.

And then, the entire east-facing of 75 Charlton Street disintegrated in a concussive, blinding flash.

36

GREENHILL'S APPLE STORE—
NASHVILLE

lexandra Clark was grateful to have some money left on one of her credit cards. It was enough to put a smile on the face of the young nerd at the Greenhill's Apple Store. If they were handing out commissions, a top-of-the-line MacBook Pro and the latest iPhone would augment hers.

It would take a while to reload everything from the cloud. The first thing Ali did was have the girl send the destruct code to the gear she assumed was now in the bad guy's possession. The minute they powered things up, everything on the devices would vaporize.

"Okay if I borrow your phone for a second to call somebody?"

The girl had no problem with that. Ali had made her day.

She dialed the DC number she knew by heart. Ali turned away from the associate, whispering as Michael Wright answered the call.

"Michael? Your boys didn't get their new orders. They

tried apprehending me, and a pair of bad guys killed them both."

"Shit."

Michael didn't cuss. Both Ali and Jess considered this one of his shortcomings. Dropping an S-bomb meant there was a fresh dirt clod in his punchbowl.

"Where are you now? Are you OK? Have you contacted Jessica?"

"I'm fine, Michael. Your colleagues relieved me of my technology, so I'm just now getting back on the grid. Do you still want me to go back to my hotel and wait to be rescued?"

"No. Change in plan. Get out of Nashville as soon as you can. I don't care where you go, but don't go back to Paloma. It's not safe for you there. If you have your passport on you, try Cabo or maybe Bermuda. Whatever you do, lie low and don't use any technology with Wi-Fi or cellular data."

"What are you telling me, Michael? You weren't able to call off the good guys?"

"It's not that, Ali. We're not talking about it publicly, but someone has hacked the cellular data network. We can't be certain, but we think the hackers can triangulate where you are the same way we would. Stay off the grid and go underground. If you can figure out a secure Wi-Fi connection and hide your IP address, check your signal messenger when you've found your hideout. I'll contact you when the coast is clear."

Ali's fuse was burning. With all she had seen and experienced, her anger was barely under control. "What the fuck is going on, Michael?"

"The less you know, the better. Now get off this line. If they can read my packets, they might trace them to you. Please trust me on this, Ali. Disappear."

With that, Michael rang off.

It was time to bring Jessica up to speed.

IT RELIEVED ALI TO HEAR JESSICA'S VOICE. SHE TRIED to sound more under control than she felt.

"Hey, partner. How's tricks?"

Jessica sounded breathless. She was walking or running some place.

"An interesting evening in London, partner. My Yelp review of the Wellington Pub won't be all that great."

"Jesus! That's on the news over here. They are saying it's a terrorist thing."

"It may well be. Whoever those guys were, they were professionals."

"Past tense? Are you telling me you discharged a weapon in the United Kingdom without credentials?"

"It was us or them, Ali. And my friend, Lee, is a pretty good shot for not being allowed to carry. What's happening in Music City?"

"There are way too many people playing harps over here. First, the DA. Then the two FBI boys who came after me. There were two bad guys, I think they may have been Russians, who did that deed."

"Let me guess…"

"Yup. I terminated their visas. This is some serious shit, partner. I'm worried about you."

The excitement in Jessica's voice jumped a notch. "I think we're getting close to Culpado's wife. We found intel that suggests she might be taking a train to the continent tonight."

For once, Ali was truly worried about her partner. "If I were you, I'd let her go. Your boyfriend in DC is telling me to blow the country, find some third-world resort, and lie low until he gives the word. Whoever they are dealing with is sophisticated and has lots of resources, including wet teams and hackers who can pinpoint exactly where you are."

Ali could hear Jessica picking up the pace. "I've seen them in action. So, what are your plans, partner? I know you are one of those weird birds who travel with your passport. Heading someplace sunny?"

The Apple girl gave Ali a wave and made a circle in the air with her index finger. "It's ready," she whispered.

"Still thinking about that. Just so you know, Michael says to stop what you're doing and hide out somewhere until the FBI can get the heat under control."

"He's so sexy when he worries about me."

"This is serious, Jessica."

"Are you telling me to give it up after we've come this far?"

"You know I'm not. Just be careful. I'm not there to rescue you."

"Do what Michael advises, Ali. I'm sorry I brought all of this mierda down on top of you. I can handle myself."

The Apple girl produced a white bag with Ali's toys inside.

Her eyes caught something by the front door that made Ali look. A cop was there, scanning the patrons. When he saw Ali, he tensed up.

Time to ring off with Jessica.

"Gotta go, partner. Keep your head down."

———

THERE WAS NO UPSIDE IN TRYING TO BOLT, SO Alexandra Clark walked up to the police officer and smiled her best fake heterosexual smile.

"You look like you could use some companionship."

"Officer Alexandra Clark?"

"See? I knew we were a match made in heaven."

"You're under arrest. Let's step outside of the store."

Damn. Could this get any worse?

Every supposed good guy today who had crossed her path had been killed. Did this cop have a wife? Kids? Ali wanted to ask him. But she began to wonder who was real and who was acting. For now, she would follow orders.

He parked his squad car in the fire lane, the blue lights were flashing, and the motor was running.

"Put down the bag and put your hands on the hood of the vehicle."

Ali complied. "You're not making a very good first impression, Mr. Wonderful."

"I hope I'm making a professional impression, Officer Clark. I'm sure you would extend the same courtesy if I were in your jurisdiction. Hands on the hood, please, and spread your legs."

He was calm and professional. Ali couldn't help but like the guy.

"When a man says, 'spread your legs,' I almost wish I weren't a lesbian."

There was another gunshot. The cop dropped like a stone.

The sound seemed to come from the corner behind the cop. Ali grabbed her bag, dove to the pavement and scampered around to the driver's side of the vehicle. A second shot shattered the right passenger window as she slid into the driver's seat.

"Never leave your keys in the car!" Ali could hear Lou

Harrison screaming the words on her first day on the force.

She was glad her late benefactor didn't follow the rules.

Dropping the tranny into drive, Ali slammed the gas pedal to the floor as another two shots rang out.

Whoever was doing the firing wasn't on his game. She could see collateral damage as a pedestrian on the other side of the street fell to the ground.

The shooter emerged from cover in her rearview mirror. A silver Chevy picked him up, accelerating to catch up with her.

Ali grabbed the microphone and keyed up the radio.

"Dispatch, this is Officer Alexandra Clark of the Paloma, Illinois, Police Department. One of two men, who are pursuing your vehicle in a gray Chevrolet Malibu, license plate unknown, has just shot the officer assigned to it. I am westbound on Abbot Martin Road, crossing Sugar Tree Place. Requesting EMS at the Greenhill's Apple Store and backup."

ST. PANCRAS STATION—LONDON

L ee and Jess made it to St. Pancras with minutes to spare. There was no problem bypassing security. That worried Jess.

"Relationships," Lee said as they moved toward track one, where the sleek train was waiting. "When you've done favors, there is always a return on the investment."

Jess wasn't so sure. Communication was almost instantaneous these days. Maddox had to have connected the dots between the two cops and the Wellington incident by now. By rights, they should be in handcuffs.

The terminal was crawling with police. Either they had been told to leave Jess and Lee alone, or the women must have looked like innocuous tourists. Nobody gave a second glance at Jess and Lee. They slipped into the train just as the doors closed for departure.

The two cops had eluded capture for the moment. Or was something else going on?

The text message ringtone on Jessica's phone sang out. It was about time. Ali was overdue with an update.

She didn't recognize the number. But Lee did. Her boss had found them.

NEW ORDERS: FIND AND PROTECT MARIE CULPADO AT ALL COSTS. USE OF FIREARMS IS APPROVED. EQUIPMENT UNDER SEAT B15— FIRST CARRIAGE. MADDOX.

Jess squinted at Lee. "I feel like I'm naked and your boss is watching me shower."

"Welcome to the 21st century, Jessica. We can't hide as long as we carry our technology in our pockets."

"'Use of firearms is approved.' Is that James Bond for 'license to kill'?"

Lee was already on the move. "Something like that."

"What did he mean when he said, "Equipment under Seat B15?"

Lee smiled. "Come see. I think you're going to like what we find."

NASHVILLE

"**D**ispatch to Officer Clark. Turn right on Estes Road. Units will pick you up at Woodmont Blvd."

Where in the hell was Estes Road? Ali saw the sign in time and swerved right.

The squad car's rear window shattered into thousands of safety glass shards. Ali could see the shooter hanging out of the Malibu's passenger window. The bastard had a shotgun.

He racked another round as she skidded onto Estes Road. Her 45 semi-auto wouldn't be accurate at this speed. But Ali had to make them pay for damaging city property.

"Always shoot the driver." Lou Harrison's voice was yelling at her again from the past. "A snake stops chasing you if you cut the head off."

With her left hand on the steering wheel, Ali turned toward the rear to get a relative aim before squeezing the trigger.

She loved the Smith and Wesson's reassuring kick when it went to work. The weapon provided a wonderful, false sense of security that your aim will be better than the sixty-six percent of cops who miss what they are shooting at.

Ali put a nice hole in the bad guys' windshield, wide to the left of the driver. Wide enough to wing the guy with the shotgun in his left shoulder.

I like it when my screw-ups make me look like I know what I'm doing.

The hollow point's velocity twisted his torso, and he lost his grip on the shotgun. Ali smiled. It felt good to see the weapon bounce like a receding toothpick in the rearview mirror.

At least now they were hopefully pinging each other with equally inaccurate weapons.

Woodmont should be coming up soon, wherever the hell Woodmont was. The two cop cars gave her an idea. One blocking the north, the other blocking the west. They obviously wanted Ali to turn east.

Being relatively compliant when not given a choice, she made the turn on two wheels.

She saw the brother in the unit north of the intersection standing behind his driver's side door with a 12-gauge pump of his own. He had the benefit of solid ground and something stable on which to steady his weapon.

The blast shattered what was left of the Malibu's windshield. Ali watched the scene through her rearview mirror. Shit. The driver had skills and made the turn, anyway.

Without glass between them, both perps started emptying their handguns straight ahead in Ali's direction.

It was hard to speed up when she was weaving back and forth to avoid getting shot. Ali was thankful for the two units that were now giving chase to the Chevy. It forced the driver to follow suit.

She only hoped that the cops who were shooting at

them didn't hit her. Ali had an uncomfortable sense that their orders didn't include her safety.

Two more units had the intersection clear at Woodmont and a road Ali saw by the street sign was called Hillsboro Pike. They were guiding her into the northbound lane.

She could see a sign ahead announcing that Interstate 44 was a mile away. It felt to Ali like the good guys would try to put an end to this soon.

She was right. To her left, a young sheriff's deputy stood at the side of the road as Ali rocketed by him and the green Golf Club Lane intersection sign. With a bowler's body English, he tossed the thorny tool that cops call "stop sticks" onto the road just as the chase vehicle appeared.

She watched the result in her mirrors. The nails did their work, and the driver lost control of the Malibu. Rubber disintegrated. The tire rims bit into the asphalt, flipping the vehicle into a sideways roll.

Ali would never know what ignited the gas tank, but on about the fifth revolution, the entire bucket of bolts burst into a beautiful orange fireball, consuming the two cop killers in a taste of what awaited them on the other side of judgment.

"Dispatch to Officer Clark. Pull over at Stokes Lane. Turn off your vehicle and put your hands on the steering wheel."

Well. That didn't sound friendly.

I deliver the two guys who might well have killed Mr. and Mrs. Yates in cinders, and this is the thanks I get?

Michael Wright's advice was now screaming in her ears. "Disappear."

Ali decided, for once, to follow orders from someone other than her supervisor.

Pressing the gas pedal to the floor, she passed the

gendarmes at the Stokes Lane intersection and hung a right toward a group of townhouses on Lombardi Avenue.

Ali abandoned the vehicle and watched from cover as the cavalry came screaming into the parking lot. An empty vehicle was waiting in the center of the complex driveway. Ali'd left the lights and siren on so it would be easier for them to find.

She was tired of being followed, so Ali also left her brand-spanking-new nine-hundred-dollar cell phone on the front seat.

ST. PANCRAS STATION—LONDON

The 2200 train to Paris pulled out of the station right ·on time. The treasure trove under seat B15 included two Kevlar bulletproof vests and a pair of Glock 21s with enough extra clips and ammo to take down an elephant.

With new orders, the reassuring feeling of protection wrapped around Liyanna Evans's chest and blue steel in her right hand, she and Jessica started forward.

"Now we know why we're not in handcuffs," Jessica said. "The whole idea was for us to get here and take the lead."

Lee zipped her fleece up to the neck to hide the last vestige of the bullet-proof vest from view. "Nobody at the Met knows more about the case than we do. Whoever is running this thing decided we should be the ones to make the identification."

Jessica frowned. "If we don't get killed in the process."

Lee was certain that Marie Culpado was on that train. But she did not know what the woman might look like nearly a decade later, or if any other interested parties were aboard.

Jessica's cell phone vibrated. She handed it to Lee when she recognized a British Telecom caller ID, engaging the external speaker.

"Liyanna Evans."

"Lee, it's Reggie from BT. We've got a GPS fix on that phone number you gave me."

"I owe you, Reggie. Talk to me."

"It's here in London. In fact, it was in St. Pancras Station until a moment ago. We show it northbound at the moment."

"He's on the fucking train?" Jessica said, unable to hide her incredulity.

Lee nodded.

"How granular can you get, Reggie? You've obviously talked with Maddox and are tracking me, too."

"He's 175 feet ahead of you, Lee. Watch yourself."

"I have to call the boss," Lee told Jessica as Reggie rang off. "I need to confirm our orders."

Maddox must have recognized the number because he answered without pleasantries. "Are you on the train, DI Evans?"

"Yes, sir."

"And you have your equipment."

"Yes, sir. What are my orders?"

"No additional changes. Approach with caution and apprehend the subject. I authorize you to use whatever force is necessary to neutralize any threats. Is that clear?"

"Yes, sir."

Lee felt like she should have said something about the Wellington and her failure to follow the spirit of Maddox's orders to keep Jessica out of the game. But she was a little angry that her boss had sent an officer to spy on them without telling her. And Maddox didn't give her the opportunity.

"Officers are working their way back toward you from the front of the train. Powell and Byrnes. You'll know them, and they will know you. We'll be stopping it after you make the turn south for the Chunnel. There will be substantial backup there. Find your subject and hold until relieved."

Lee felt the slightest softening of her boss's voice.

"Be careful, DI Evans. These are very bad people."

"One last question, sir. I found weapons and vests for two persons. Is Detective Ramirez still considered in my custody?"

"No. As of now, she is your partner."

40

NASHVILLE INTERNATIONAL
AIRPORT

Officer Alexandra Clark got to BNA an hour ahead of departure.

Apologizing for her lack of technology, Ali pressed a hundred-dollar bill into the fist of one thrilled Uber driver.

"If someone asks you about all of this, tell them the truth."

The East Indian student behind the wheel smiled. "I am glad I had a fare near your residence, ma'am. Thank you for your generosity. And yes, I always tell the truth."

"Do yourself a favor. Find a place to change that bill and tell anyone who asks that I only gave you a twenty."

———

ALI HAD NO TROUBLE WITH THE TICKETS AND ONLY A slight delay at the TSA. That the locals had not blocked what seemed to be an easy exit was disconcerting.

She didn't like ditching her gun under the Uber guy's driver's seat. But Ali bet that when she got where she was going, a kind soul would take pity on her and provide some additional protection.

Anyway, she knew when they tagged the Uber, they would find the Glock. There would be some uncomfortable moments for the poor driver. But ultimately, the news would get back to Michael Wright.

He would deduce Ali's destination and know what to do.

There was just enough time to buy an overpriced disposable cell phone and a briefcase for her MacBook before she boarded for O'Hare.

Ali upgraded her ticket with the gate agent. She was tired and angry. She wanted plenty of room to stretch her legs and all the free drinks she could swallow. A bulkhead seat in first-class felt appropriate for the occasion.

Ali got down two vodkas before liftoff. They failed to take the edge off.

She tried, without success, to get some sleep. Whenever her eyes closed, a kaleidoscope of death appeared. Images of brain matter on an office wall and a pair of black body bags with two bloody FBI corpses inside were welding themselves into Ali's long-term memory.

There was another troubling picture that kept shifting in and out of focus. It looked like Jessica. She was lying on the ground, her limbs contorted in the grotesque pose Ali often found when the medics peeled a suicidal jumper off the pavement. Jess wasn't breathing. Her gaze was vacant, pupils focused on eternity. Red tributaries of blood trickled away from her skull.

Ali pushed the vision back down into her subconscious and thought of her next moves.

With any luck, she would be in London in the morning.

41

ON BOARD CHUNNEL TRAIN 2200

J ess and Lee were four cars up when Jess saw her.

The years had left their marks on Marie Culpado's features. But there was no doubt that they had found the woman they were looking for.

She wore nondescript travel clothing. Her hair was longer and a light brown, with hints of gray at the roots. The balcony that Harry so admired was evident, even under the cover of a brown suede jacket.

Her companion was no longer the bald cue ball in the passport photo. His hair was shoulder length. A thick 1960s hippie mustache framed his angular face.

The stiffness in the way he sat told Jess he was military. His hands rested on top of one another on his lap, covering what she assumed was his own handgun, likely stuffed behind his belt buckle.

What troubled Jess were the two men who sat across from them.

She could only see them from the back. But the pair had the bearing of the professionals who had tried to take the two cops out at the pub. Their attire wasn't identical but shared a common style Jess didn't yet recognize.

Lee put a hand on Jess's arm as they saw the quartet from the rear of the car. It was nearly empty. Perhaps the lateness of the hour and the day of the week made these last departures lightly traveled. Jess followed Lee's lead and slid into forward-facing seats a few rows ahead of the door.

"Let's wait for the reinforcements," Lee said.

They didn't have to wait long.

In what felt like moments, another pair of hard bodies entered the carriage from the front of the train.

They wore Metropolitan police badges on chains around their necks to confirm their status. Jess could see the recognition in their eyes when they identified the targets. The two moved to each side of the four seats, guns drawn. The weapons had silencers.

Jess took her lead from her partner. Lee's eyes narrowed. She didn't move.

"Marie Yates Culpado?" one said.

The woman shook her head. "My name is Blair, and this is my husband. You should know that the two men sitting across from us are carrying weapons and intend to kidnap us when we reach Paris."

The cop who asked the question turned his firearm toward Marie's companion.

"Arthur G. Aldrich, American Central Intelligence?"

"My name is Jonathan Blair. This woman is my wife."

Whoever he was, those ten words were the last he would ever speak. Jess could see the cop's weapon kick three times and recognized the cough of the silencer. Two of the slugs entered Jonathan Blair's chest, a grouping that she knew would tear apart the ventricles of his heart. The third drilled a hole into his forehead, right above his nose. The force of the impact jerked his neck back over the edge of the seat. His arms splayed, and his body convulsed as the confused impulses from his brain sent broken messages to his extremities.

The few other passengers in the car responded with screams and ran toward the rear of the car. Only Jess and Lee remained. Jess knew it was only seconds until they were recognized.

Marie Culpado's eyes widened in horror. The two who sat across from her were still. But Jess could hear an exchange between them and the cops. It was in Russian.

Every instinct was driving Jess to stand and engage, but Lee had a firm hand on her thigh, holding Jess down in her window seat.

"The two with the badges," she whispered. "They aren't Powell and Byrnes."

"The guys Maddox mentioned?"

"Correct. And I'm guessing they met the same fate as Mr. Blair."

Jess couldn't understand why they weren't putting all four bastards out of action. "I don't know any Russian. I wish I knew what they were saying."

Apparently, her new partner did. She spat the words, slowly drawing her weapon from behind her belt.

"Two women will enter the carriage shortly. Kill the black one and bring us the Latina."

THE COILED SNAKE

A ll the bad guys had to do was look at Lee and Jessica and they would know exactly who they were. And how had Jessica made the cultural switch from Spaniard to Latina?

These guys weren't cops, so Lee wondered if they would focus on the door and not on the two women, sitting just a few rows in front of it, who exactly matched the description.

The perfection of their murder of Jonathan Blair told Lee they would pay attention to detail. She was grateful that she hid the Kevlar beneath her outer garments. That might buy something.

Lee processed all of this in less time than it took to tell it. Jessica had her weapon in hand beneath the table that separated the cops from a pair of empty, rear-facing seats. Jessica looked to Lee to be as cool as an ice cube; a coiled snake, ready to strike.

"I've truly enjoyed working with you, Jessica," Lee said, sensing that perhaps this might be the culmination of her career.

"Let's make them pay for this," she answered.

And then the two women were on their feet.

———

THERE WERE TWELVE BULLETS IN LEE'S CLIP, PLUS ONE in the chamber. She spent six instantly as she moved ahead of Jess and directed fire at the bloody bastards Lee knew had killed her colleagues.

The thump of the first two rounds against the chest told her they were packing Kevlar, too, so she unloaded the other four at their bobbing heads.

Luck was with Lee, and one round took the man who killed Jonathan Blair out of the fight.

A series of explosions quickly overpowered the screams as Jess entered the fray, firing every round at the other man's face. Jessica's aim was perfect. Lee watched her follow the second man's body trajectory to the floor of the carriage, filling his melon with hot lead. Exit wounds shattered the back of his skull, spraying both Marie and her two kidnappers with his blood.

One of the Russians stood and faced them. He held an RSH-12 revolver, the most powerful production handgun in the world. Lee saw him point it at her chest.

The women fired what they had left but couldn't hit a thing. Their adversary's eyes focused on the barrels of their guns, and he seemed to drift casually away from the lines of fire. The moves were beautiful, almost ballet-like in their simplicity. When Lee's and Jessica's clips were empty, he pulled the trigger.

The vest might have saved her life for the moment, but the sledgehammer blow from the huge projectile knocked Lee onto her back, winded and nearly unconscious. She thought about what the next shot might do to her skull.

Out of the corner of an upward-facing eye, Lee could see the second man drag Marie Culpado into the aisle, a 6P35 Yarygin semi-auto pressed against her temple.

She imagined that Jessica must have practiced the reload procedure so many times that her execution was all muscle memory. As Lee heard the familiar clatter of Jessica chambering a round, the man holding Marie spoke.

"Drop the weapon, Detective Ramirez, or the woman dies."

Lee could sense the train slowing, just as Maddox had said it would. Jessica dropped her gun, raised her arms and stepped forward to shield Lee from the enemy.

"What do you want, boys? And how do you know my name?"

Lee was still playing dead and couldn't see their movements. But she could hear the swoosh of the carriage door as the four exited toward the front of the still decelerating train.

THE RUSSIANS' MISTAKE

Marie Culpado and Jessica Ramirez were cuffed and under their captor's complete control. The handgun pressed against Marie's spine kept Jess quiet as the boys moved them toward the front of the next carriage.

There was an interchange in Russian that Jess couldn't understand as they stood next to an exit door.

It turned out to be a countdown.

"Raz, dva, tri."

One man pressed a red button. An alarm sounded for fifteen seconds before the door opened and the kidnappers shoved Marie and Jess into the darkness.

Their captors' planning must have been meticulous. No sooner had the women rolled clear of the tracks and onto what felt like wet grass than fresh pairs of hands gripped them.

Blindfolds obscured their vision as strong arms shoved Jess and Marie into a delivery van.

"Idti!" someone yelled through an open driver's side window, and the vehicle picked up speed.

———

It took a few minutes for Jess to realize that they were alone, with the driver as their only other companion.

She wrestled her body into a sitting position and slid, blindly, toward the sound of Marie's heavy breathing.

The other woman was already upright, leaning against the thin aluminum side panel.

"Marie?" Jess whispered.

"My name is Blair," she barked back.

"It's all right. I'm Jessica Ramirez. I know most of the story. They sent my partner and me to protect you. We've done a piss-poor job so far."

"Are you CIA?"

"Nope. I'm just a local cop from Illinois who is in way over her head."

"No shit, Ms. Ramirez. I won't be sending a love letter to your boss."

"Where do you think they are taking us?"

Marie sounded wary. "I don't know if I should even say anything to you. They put plants into situations like these to get people to talk."

"Oh, I promise you. I don't know a word of Russian, and less than a week ago, I was handing out speeding tickets. Here, press your forehead against mine, and perhaps we can get these blindfolds off."

It was an interesting dance, but the tightly applied fabric eventually weakened enough where Jess and Marie could slide the coverings up and over the top of their heads.

Her eyes adjusted to the darkness, and she assessed her fellow captive. Jess reckoned there were only a few minutes to strategize.

Marie broke the silence. "Giovanni. They are probably taking us to see Giovanni."

"Who is Giovanni?"

"My first husband. Giovanni de Triste. Does the name mean anything to you?"

Jess flipped through her mental Rolodex. "Mob boss. Life sentence. Escaped prison about six years ago. Disappeared."

"Well, he's reappeared. The plastic surgery didn't fool me when I finally saw him. By then, it was too late."

The van lurched into a right turn, knocking Jess on her side. By now, she knew how to move with the cuffs on and could sit back up quickly.

"Vincent didn't know who he was. But the FBI did. They wanted Giovanni, and I became the bait… again."

"Maria Elena de Triste." The story was coming back to Jess now. "The wife of the head of a New York crime family turns on her husband and provides the testimony that puts him away for life. You disappeared soon after the verdict. The rumor was you were dead."

Maria Elena de Triste shrugged her shoulders. "Do I look dead? Witness protection program. I don't know why they decided on Nashville, but that's where I went. New parents, new life, and eventually, a new love."

"Vincent Culpado."

"Yes. I loved Vincent with all my heart. When I learned that Giovanni had insinuated himself into Vince's confidence, it broke me. I told my handlers, and they came up with a plan to smoke Giovanni out."

"Faking your death."

"Vincent confronted me about this so-called affair. Of course, it never happened. But by then, the FBI saw it as another escape route."

"Did Vincent Culpado push you into the river like the DA alleged?"

"Yes. I knew I might die, but it was a chance I was willing to take."

"So, the Feds found someplace else for you to hide."

"And someone found me and brought Giovanni with her."

The revelation was devastating. They had played Jess. She was just as much of a sucker as was the man she saw burned in a Tennessee electric chair. Taking the next leap required little in the way of brains.

"So, Giovanni de Triste is now Jack Crawford?"

"Of course, he is. The FBI only just figured that one out. Giovanni has been on the Most Wanted list for years. Now they have a new face and a new name to chase. So, he's done what he did before. He vanished."

Jess's head was spinning. How could a mob boss build a new empire with no connection to his old life? She remembered the daring prison break. It was said that de Triste had help.

The van was slowing down. The architecture that loomed out of the lone front window of the vehicle told the tale. They were in downtown London again.

Marie Culpado, AKA Maria Elena de Triste, slumped back against the side of the van.

"Who is the money behind this man, Maria? And if Giovanni wants you dead, why are we both still alive?"

"I think we're about to find out."

That's when Jess felt it. A single vibration beneath the Kevlar vest, between her sports bra and her chest.

The two Russian pros had made a mistake.

They hadn't taken her cell phone.

HEATHROW AIRPORT – LONDON – UNITED KINGDOM

Alexandra Clark hit the text send button on her burner phone.

Just left a brand new iPhone with the Nashville Blues. It's getting boring here, so I'm heading your way. Use this number for the time being.

The quiet confirmational beep did nothing to quell the feeling of dread she fought.

Even the toughest constitutions have to process stress.

Alexandra Clark gave it up after a couple of glasses of wine, a business class meal, and a Xanax. She slept without dreams as her silver bird crossed the Atlantic. A flight attendant had to awaken Ali when the aircraft was on final approach for Heathrow.

She was going to London with no plan, no contact with her partner, no weapons, a warrant for her arrest likely processing back in Nashville and hardly any headroom left on her credit cards.

Life was good!

Too good.

The ease with which Ali could purchase her tickets, navigated TSA at BNA, and breezed through passport control at O'Hare whispered warnings. When she flipped open her credentials for the kid at immigration at Heathrow, the picture came into focus.

"One moment, please, Miss Clark."

All he did was raise a hand and four burly uniforms surrounded Ali. They wore anti-terror regalia, right down to the hard hats and automatic weapons.

The one who seemed to be in charge spoke to her softly but firmly.

"Come with us, please."

They knew everything. The tone of his voice and the fact that Ali wasn't in handcuffs proved it. They knew she was a sister in the profession. They must have been briefed on her background, her temperament, and her adventures in Nashville. And they knew she wouldn't resist.

Ali reckoned that anyone who saw the quintet walking down the concourse would have thought she was a VIP under government protection, not a freestyler who had shot two men dead, evaded arrest, and blown the country.

About one hundred fifty yards later, the little parade stopped in front of an unmarked gray door. The leader pointed in its direction.

"In here, please."

Ali couldn't be a smartass to these people who were just doing their jobs.

"Thanks very much for your service. Please stay safe," was the best she could come up with.

Ali felt the need to follow the British reserve and knocked on the door, instantly recognizing the person who opened it.

It was Michael Wright.

"Welcome to London, Alexandra. Let me introduce you to Commander Thomas Anastos from MI6. And…" Michael paused for effect. "This is Detective Inspector Liyanna Evans."

4 5

LOVE AT FIRST SIGHT

She was shorter than Lee imagined. Five-foot-nine and maybe fifty-four kilograms. Her hair was prematurely gray. It matched her eyes, tired gray eyes that had seen too much hatred and death. If her experience was like Lee's, just being different was a burden she disguised with audacity.

The men didn't like us because we liked women. But we differed from the first generation of lesbians in law enforcement. We weren't like them, either. We had not paid the price. We weren't tough enough, a little too feminine.

But damn, she was beautiful. The ache in Lee's chest was still there from that Russian cannon shot. But she was feeling something else in that region.

Focus, Liyanna. You are the only one who can describe the two men who kidnapped both your partner and the woman they ordered you to protect.

Thomas was talking. Focus on that.

"The address is a business. I'm afraid you know it well, Agent Wright."

"Come on, out with it. Two people's lives are in danger,

and we've got to get every resource we can over there to rescue them."

"It's The Maitland Corporation."

The way the two men's eyes locked spoke volumes. But Lee couldn't tell what they were.

Officer Clark knew.

"Maitland!" Her tone was incredulous. "The same fucking Maitland Corporation that sent us the spy in Arizona? The same company that's a front for the KGB? One hundred to one, your captain is over there, or there's someone who knows where he is. What the fuck is going on?"

Agent Wright was clearly struggling. "The Captain and Jack Crawford have Jessica and Maria, Ali. We tracked them to Maitland's London Headquarters. This is Commander Anastos from MI6 and Liyanna Evans, Jessica's counterpart at the Met."

Lee saw Officer Clark spring to her feet. "OK, let's go get 'em."

Michael held out a hand. "This is one we have to run up the flagpole, Ali. Some very important people need to weigh in before we go over there and start shooting."

"The fuck they do, Michael. What in the hell is wrong with you? The woman you asked to marry you is in that building. So is your little witness from Nashville. They are both there for a reason. And it isn't for a spa treatment."

Officer Clark turned her vitriol toward Commander Anastos.

"Okay, James Bond. We're in your territory. I don't even know why you're here, but it doesn't take a genius to deduce that you both are trying to keep DI Evans and me from free-styling. Who do I have to blow to get you to do the right thing and send some SWAT over there to pull our girl's chestnuts out of the fire?"

The commander was ice cold. "We all have to serve somebody, Officer Clark. And sometimes that service requires sacrifice."

Lee was instantly in love. The sound of Officer Clark's voice was tantalizing. The fire in her eyes was like a flamethrower. The woman turned that weapon toward Lee. "What are your orders, DI Evans? They allow you to speak, don't they?"

Lee was tongue-tied by the sheer power of Officer Clark's personality. "My last orders were to protect Ms. Blair."

"And you've fucked that one up pretty badly."

Lee reckoned later that she saw the print of the handgun under her shirt. Since Lee had no reason to believe the American might go for it, she wasn't ready. Her moves were lightning fast. She had the weapon in her hands, racked and pointed at Commander Anastos's head before she finished the sentence.

"Okay, Commander. Get permission and get the troops over there now. Or I'll help you make a sacrifice for your country."

Agent Wright now had his weapon at the ready. He pointed it at Officer Clark.

"Don't do this, Ali. We'll make the calls, but you must understand that it may take some time to get the permissions we need."

Officer Clark didn't take her eyes off her target.

"DI Evans, go relieve Agent Wright of his weapon and cover his ass while James Bond here gets us some permission."

Agent Wright didn't move. And Lee wasn't about to take orders from outside the chain of command.

"Ali," Agent Wright was talking softly, almost pleading, "you know I'll kill you if I have to."

"No, you won't, Mr. Big Stuff. Because then you'll have to explain it to her. And I don't think even your PTSD could stand to see your two favorite women in the world die on the same day."

Officer Clark slipped her index finger from the safe position, circling the trigger.

"Make the call, Jimmy. Do it now."

Then she gave Lee another order.

"If you won't take Michael's gun, DI Evans, then take his damn cell phone and call your boss."

There was an uncomfortable moment where Lee thought there might be gunfire.

Then Agent Wright blinked. He didn't lower his weapon, but he glanced in her direction.

"Okay, Lee. My cell is there on the table. Commander, we're more likely to get a faster answer from your boss than from mine. Our girl will not put down the gun until we update the committee with what we know about that damn location."

Commander Anastos shrugged and dialed.

So did Lee.

46

THE MAITLAND CORPORATION UK
HEADQUARTERS—LONDON

There were at least four men that Jess could count in the darkness as the van's doors opened. Two held Marie and Jess from behind, switching the traditional handcuffs for zip ties. The other two men put virtual reality headsets over their eyes, cinching the straps so there was no way Marie and Jess could see. Then Jess felt a pair of headphones cover her ears. The cool whisper of the noise-canceling circuitry cut out every other sound.

A half dozen hands pulled them out of the van, dragging the pair inside of an office building. The odor of janitorial cleaning solution told Jess that. She could also sense the upward movement of an elevator. The place must have had a ton of floors because it took a while before the doors opened, and the apes guided Jess toward wherever it was they were going.

Two of the bozos picked Jess up as if she were a rag doll and deposited her in some sort of special chair. The zip ties came off. Jess was only unrestrained for a few seconds before leather straps bound her arms and legs. She could feel something sharp and metallic pressing upward against her forearms from what felt like the leather arms of the chair.

Jess had a vision of Vincent Culpado in the electric chair, and, for a moment, she was terrified.

There was a painful poke in her left arm. Jess knew from personal experience what that sensation was.

Somebody was installing an IV line.

———

THE HEADSETS CAME TO LIFE, AND JESS SAW TWO avatars standing at the edge of a placid ocean. The images were a poorly rendered 3D animation. The one on the left spoke.

"Good evening, Detective Ramirez. I've been waiting for this meeting for a long time."

"I don't like playing video games," Jess barked. "Take these toys off and be a man so I can see you."

That's when she felt the jolt. The sharp things under her forearms were electrodes. They were connected to what must have been one heavy-duty taser. Jess's body stiffened, and she couldn't suppress a groan.

"You'll be told when you can talk, Detective." The avatar put an arm on the shoulder of his animated counterpart.

"Mrs. Blair. May I introduce you to your husband? Your first husband. The one you betrayed."

Jess could barely hear Marie's terrified squeak.

"Giovanni," was all she could say before she felt the shock of the taser.

The first anime continued.

"You have both caused us extreme inconvenience. Detective Ramirez, you instigated significant delays in a client project very near to my heart. Your only saving grace was that you killed the incompetent woman who failed me."

Vega! Jess was speaking to The Captain. Was he in the room? Or was he pulling the puppet strings from Moscow?

"Mrs. Blair," The Captain said the words as if they tasted sour. "Or should I say, Mrs. De Triste? By bringing you and Detective Ramirez to me, your husband satisfied his part of a little bargain we made when I helped him escape from prison and become someone else. Encouraging Detective Ramirez to help us find you was a masterstroke. And I am not a man who is easily impressed."

The picture Jess saw suddenly changed. It was a mirror image showing Marie and Jess, bound to a pair of what looked like old-school dental chairs. And she was right about the IV. A clear plastic bag filled with liquid hung from a steel hook next to each chair. A man clad completely in black, including a mask that obscured his face, stood between them. A silver tray with syringes on it lay on a table in front of him.

"And now it's time for me to deliver on my commitment. Mr. de Triste had hoped that that long fall into the river didn't kill you. He wanted to watch you die. He will now have that privilege."

Marie squirmed in her chair. It was useless.

"Vega's obsession with killing had one productive dimension," The Captain continued. "She provided me with a small recipe. You women can be such excellent cooks when properly motivated. It's the same mixture of medications that worked so well to incapacitate her victims before she tossed them into the river. Detective Ramirez is very familiar with its contents, but for Mrs. De Triste's edification, it is a potent muscle relaxant. Its properties strip you of the power to move or breathe. Death comes from brain asphyxiation in ten minutes or less. And it's virtually untraceable. I don't know why Vega had to add such drama. The fall into the canyon would have killed her victims without suspicion."

Jess had seen the Bergulon do its work. The drug was effective and deadly. She and Marie would still have complete feeling but couldn't do anything about it.

"Mr. De Triste," The Captain continued, "do you have any last words you would like to say to your wife?"

Something switched in the headphones. There was no auditory disguise in the voice Jess heard.

"Well, first, I'd like to thank Detective Ramirez. It was so easy to get you to find Marie for me. You notice how I let you turn me down and you still took on the chase? That psychological trick was another gift from my benefactor. But I admit to a small amount of invention on my part. To get you both in the same place at the same time required some creativity."

"The flat." Jess couldn't help saying it.

"Yes, Detective, the flat. Marie never lived there. I knew they were headed to Paris. But I needed you on that train. My benefactor was kind enough to provide a stage on which you could act out your little deductive game. I planted the train schedule. It's unfortunate that the building was damaged, but I'm sure the owner's insurance will more than cover construction of a much newer and more valuable property."

Lee and Jess had been played. Now Jess was too pissed off to keep her mouth shut.

"Those pros at the pub would never have missed. We should already be dead. You sacrificed their lives for misdirection. It was the same at the apartment. Good men were killed, just to get me on that damn train. Why didn't you just grab us at Lee's flat?"

The taser shot her again. That time she was expecting it. The thing still hurt like hell.

The crackle in Jess's headset told her they turned on the scrambler again. The Captain's cool voice circled around her.

"That realization made every expense worthwhile, Detective. I knew I could lure you here if I pressed the right buttons. Approving the execution of your father was all it took."

Jess strained against the leather straps. She expected another taser shot. But it didn't come.

"As you die, I want you to think about how you failed him, as a police officer and as a daughter."

Jess hated to cry. It was the ultimate act of submission. But she couldn't stop the tears of anger and frustration that flowed down her cheeks.

"Just like a woman," The Captain said. "If you want to get a job done, give it to a man."

The headphones clicked, and the whisper of the noise-canceling circuitry returned.

The man in black who stood between Marie and Jess nodded, as if in answer to a command, and picked up one syringe. He was turning to the IV port. She could barely hear Jack Crawford's voice above the hiss of the headphones.

"No. Marie first. And I want to do it."

There was another voice. Very different from what she'd heard. But the accent was unmistakable. The Captain was in the room with them.

"Let the professional do his job. You can watch."

———

Even with the headphones on, the sound of the "flash-bang" was unmistakable. The device cops used to shock perps before overwhelming them turned everything white. There were gunshots everywhere.

And then the screen went blank.

47

SO, I HAVE TO SAVE YOU AGAIN?

"So, I have to save you again?"

Jessica Ramirez knew the voice as well as she knew her own. How did Ali end up in London?

A hand ripped the VR headset and headphones off, and Jess could see.

The place was windowless but large, capable of purposing as a private conference room. A long table lay on its side, ten yards from where she sat. The chairs and a small desk with a pile of electronic gear on top were the only other furniture. Wires snaked from the back of the equipment racks to the two dental chairs that restrained them. A green screen like the meteorologists used to display weather graphics hung on a wall. A camera and tripod pointed at it.

"Behind the table!" The voice belonged to Liyanna Evans.

"I saw them when we came in," Ali yelled back.

Their repartee was like rifle fire.

Lee: "Then why are there still four of them shooting at us?"

Ali: "I'm just off an eight-hour overseas flight after forty-eight hours of zero sleep."

Lee: "And you think I've had any rest the last two days?"

Ali: "I held two uncooperative boys at bay for you…"

Lee: "While I called Maddox and got the permissions we needed to come save your partner's arse."

More gunfire.

Jess knew what was happening. Ali and Lee were flirting. She needed them to focus.

"If you two would let me out of this chair, I might add some value."

Jess could feel the proximity of a bullet close to her left ear. It was too close.

Lee ran behind Ali's covering fire and unstrapped her American partner.

Marie was motionless. Jess could see the two syringes jammed into her IV port. The plungers were fully depressed.

Lee did a barrel roll to get closer to the conference table. She continued firing as Ali dropped her clip and reloaded.

Jess was on her feet. Her eyes scanned both girls to see if they had any additional weapons. "The entire London Met is on this case and all they send me are you two?"

Ali was firing again. "There are others here, including your boyfriend. We've been going room-to-room for the last ten minutes. A pretty fast response time."

The distinctive sound of an AK47 erupted from behind the conference table. They aimed the hail of lead in Lee's direction.

"A little help here," Lee said.

Ali tapped the guy in black that was guarding the syringes. His head snapped backward, and he dropped his gun. Jess recognized it. The RSH-12 cannon that shot Lee on the train.

"Thank you," Lee sang out, knocking over the equipment table for protection and moving ever closer to the bad guys.

Jess dove for the cannon.

"Looks like Ali took out that fucker who tried to pop your Kevlar," Jess said to her British partner as she grabbed the hot iron. There were four shots left in the chambers.

Ali sounded impatient. "Do I have to save everyone's life here?"

The door behind them burst open again, and the cavalry arrived, led by a sexy FBI hard body and some Greek-looking dude Jess didn't recognize.

"We want them alive," Michael yelled.

Lee looked at Jess. The two shook their heads and charged the table.

Crawford and another man bolted for the far door, leaving one soldier with an AK to take on the advancing horde.

Weapons unloaded on him. He danced in death like a piñata, but not before knocking several SWAT types backward, the full force of his bursts slamming into their vests.

Crawford and the man Jess now knew to be The Captain made it through the door.

"Let them go," Lee commanded. "There are sure to be friendlies on the other side of that door."

Jess was on a dead run. "But what if there aren't?"

"Wait, Jess," Michael barked.

Ali was laughing. "Go get 'em, partner," she yelled. "You're all clear."

48

SHOT

Ali wondered how four men could shoot over a hundred rounds each and not hit anything.

Well, not hit anything important. Except for the SWAT boys who were on their backs catching their breath. Michael, Commander Anastos and Ali emerged from the firefight unscathed.

Or so she thought. As the adrenaline tapered off, she felt a sting in her left shoulder. There was blood coming out of it. Ali could see a red boot print that tracked toward the back exit, too. Lee must have taken a round in the leg.

She didn't like that at all. Liyanna Evans was growing on her.

"Follow them," the MI6 agent commanded. What seemed like an unending stream of guys with guns poured in one door and out the other.

When these people got permission, they got permission.

"What's this," Commander Anastos said, looking at the one remaining chair with somebody still in it. "No bullet wounds, but this one isn't breathing."

Ali saw the two syringes. Arizona memories came

rushing back. Michael Wright, lying naked on his condo bed, loaded to the gills with Bergulon. Total sensation, but no ability to move or breathe.

Ali ripped off the headset. Marie's dilated corneas looked beyond her into the next world.

Just like my nightmare. It wasn't Jessica's face that I saw, after all.

"One hundred to one, you'll find Jack Crawford's prints on those needles," Ali said. "There's enough poison in her to stop a horse's heart."

She felt a pair of firm hands on her shoulders.

"You're a little unsteady, Alexandra. Looks like you're leaking."

It was Michael. Ali stopped long enough to scan her body. But her eyes wouldn't focus. The voices seemed farther and farther away.

Michael Wright's arms slid beneath her own.

Was that boy trying to feel me up?

"Breathe," he said. "You're in shock. You're going to pass out if you don't."

Darkness was enveloping Ali. The last thing she saw was Liyanna. The scene was her apartment back home. Lee's naked body straddled Ali. It was not an unpleasant sensation.

49

LEE ON THE ROOF

Lee was having trouble keeping up with Detective Ramirez. It felt as if her own reserves of energy were deserting her.

But she wasn't stopping. That one man was Jack Crawford. Just as Jessica had described him. The other man could only be one person. And Lee couldn't let that person escape.

Why are there always stairs?

Jessica had no problem scaling them two at a time, the big Russian revolver dangling in her right hand. Lee was finding it harder and harder to put one foot in front of another.

Out of the darkness, she could see a light appear and disappear ahead of her. The sound of a turbine whined. That had to be the exit to the roof and a helio pad.

Lee stumbled through in time to see the chopper lifting off. Jessica ran toward the edge of the building after it. It made little sense. She had no way of catching up to it before the helicopter cleared the roof and was airborne.

But, again, Lee discovered how little she knew about this Latina spitfire.

Jessica jammed the revolver down the rear of her pants and lunged for the left landing skid, snaking an arm around it as the helicopter drifted clear of the rooftop.

She gripped a long steel stanchion like a vice, swinging back and forth until she could get a leg on top of it.

The skids were just wide enough to provide an excellent view of the cabin and the churning blades above it.

Lee could see Jessica reach for the cannon with her left hand. She pointed it toward the motor and pulled the trigger.

The recoil alone should have ripped the weapon from her single grip. But whatever was flowing through Jessica's veins must have been rocket fuel. The gun pulled her arm backward, slamming it against the skid.

She didn't drop it.

Lee's bullet-proof vest might have stopped one of those huge lead rounds, but the aluminum engine cover didn't. She could hear the turbines scream in protest, smoke instantly billowing out of the exhaust port.

Lee realized she was standing on the large white *H* that marked the dead center of the helipad. There was a widening pool of red at the base of her left leg.

Bloody hell. They shot me.

She could see the entry and exit points. It must have just missed the femoral artery, or she would be dead. Lee ripped off her shirt and made a makeshift tourniquet, cinching it tightly above the wound as she sat on the cement.

She looked at the departing helicopter. It was fighting to gain altitude as it dipped toward the Thames.

THE LONDON EYE

"Damn, that hurt," Jess muttered to herself. "Remind me never to fire an RSH-12 revolver with one hand ever again."

And what was wrong with her? Jumping onto a moving helicopter at the edge of a damn skyscraper? Jess's mind was in full fear-of-heights terror. Dropping 557 feet with a rappelling rope felt like an elementary school playground compared to this insanity.

But the man who ordered her father's murder and the man who contributed to Vincent Culpado's death were inside that cabin.

Jess intended to make them pay.

Her shooting hand was still numb but managed to slide the cannon back into her pants. She intertwined her arms and legs around the skid, holding on for dear life.

It occurred to Jess at this moment that putting a bullet into the engine of the only thing keeping her from falling to her death might not have been the wisest move. She didn't like the sounds of shattering metal and the black smoke that vomited out of the back of the enclosure.

And what if the bad guys knew she was right below them? Jess was a sitting duck.

One poor decision after another, Jess. When you make it personal, you make mistakes.

As the terror swirled around Jess's insides, the outside world snapped into focus and she beheld the sight below.

London at night was a picture postcard on its worst days. A carpet of stars painted a ceiling above the city lights. The full moon cast the dark concrete silhouettes below into stark relief. It was breathtaking. Whatever building Jess had been in was perched on the edge of the Thames. She didn't know enough of the city yet to pick out landmarks, except one.

The London Eye was dead ahead.

"Don't call it a 'Ferris wheel,'" Lee had warned her. "You'll make the locals think you're a tourist for sure."

The gargantuan trademark stopped taking passengers at 9pm. LED lighting covered its spokes in blinking dot matrix, painting pixilated scenes throughout the night that resolve into pictures at a distance.

Jess could see a colorful depiction of the Union Jack as the aircraft approached it.

They were losing altitude.

Jess's consciousness flipped back to survival mode. The distraction of the scenery vanished into what she tried to imagine were possible landing sights.

Jess didn't like any of the options.

The uppermost gondola pods of the London Eye drew ever closer. There was some question in her mind if the chopper could clear them. Above the piercing whine of the turbines, she heard a door swinging open above her. Voices were yelling.

"She's here. She's right below."

A fist appeared with an AK47 in it. The prop wash

caught the shower of bullets, throwing them back behind Jess as she clung to the skid below. She knew the shooter would adjust for the slipstream the next time.

An idea came to her, and Jess calculated the odds. They weren't good, but she couldn't think of anything else to do.

The hand with the rifle appeared again, and Jess made her decision.

A pod loomed large directly below. It was now or never.

Jess unhooked her legs. A single appendage was all that separated her from a five hundred foot plunge to the unforgiving concrete below. Jess's right hand gripped the landing skid. The cannon was in her left.

The helio cleared the London Eye with ten feet to spare. Jess fired a single shot at one of the pod's skylight windows. It shattered into a million safety glass shards that littered the floor of the gondola.

Jess let go of the chopper and thought of her father.

ON THE ROOF

Alexandra Clark was thoroughly enjoying her dirty dream when somebody stuck the smelling salts under her nose. Seeing Commander Anastos's face was a big disappointment.

"The medics are on their way, Officer Clark."

"The roof," Ali croaked. "Get me vertical and point me toward the roof."

"They shot you. You need to wait here until ambulance services arrive."

She was still unsteady, but Ali was angry. She channeled her anger toward her legs and stood. "Are you going to help me get up there, or am I going alone?"

———

A PHALANX OF SWAT BOYS SURROUNDED LEE IN THE center of the helipad. Michael was with them, attending to her. Ali didn't like the red pool Lee was sitting in. She knew what that kind of blood loss could do.

"She'll be all right, Ali." Michael was trying to soothe her. She hated it when he did that.

Lee was breathing hard. Ali deduced that the blood loss made her metabolism speed up to keep things functioning.

"Over there." Lee's voice was hoarse but still strong.

Ali was falling for her more by the minute.

They turned toward the Thames and saw the chopper barely clear the top of the London Eye. Ali could see a flash just beneath it but nothing more.

"There was a machine-gun burst," Lee said. "I could see it. I hope they missed her."

Moments later, the SWAT radios came alive. "Shots fired at the London Eye."

Ali's cell phone rang. She knew the number by heart.

Her own ticker was pounding, but Ali tried to sound calm when she answered the call. It didn't work.

"I guess you must still be alive, partner."

Jessica's voice was faint but sturdy. "You want to send somebody to this fucking Ferris wheel to get me down?"

5 2

YEAH, IT HURT

Yeah, it hurt. And thanks, Dad. You still look out for me, no matter how many bad decisions I make.

The pod was dark; Jessica Ramirez sat in a pile of safety glass debris. Her ass hurt like hell.

But she was alive.

The silence and the starry night outside were a strange contrast to buffeting downdrafts of the helicopter blades, the scream of the dying engines and the cacophony of point-blank AK47 gunfire.

Anyone else would have been a messy puddle after barely escaping a half-dozen methods of death, all gruesome.

But after a decade in law enforcement, Jess knew cops' minds work differently. She was already past it all, thinking about how to catch the two men who had so profoundly changed the direction of her life.

For the moment, she didn't have the strength to stand and see if the bad guys got away or crashed and burned. She remembered her ride along with the Life Flight team at Paloma General and the pilot's description of what happens when a helicopter loses power. It was in what he called auto-rotation when Jess let go. No lift power. Only the sweep of the rotors to bring the crippled aircraft down to earth with any semblance of safety. Jess couldn't see any place where they could have landed the thing. But pilots train for this all the time. They likely had one of the better ones.

Jess assumed that Crawford and the second pocked face she barely glimpsed were still alive.

And at last, she had seen The Captain face to face.

Beyond the bad complexion, he was a square-shouldered fireplug of a man. Jess's height, all muscle, exuding an intimidating visage that she imagined had frightened much taller, more terrifying men. He obviously knew technology and had resources. What he was doing and why was still unclear.

Whatever it was, it was bad.

Jess' iWatch told her it took an hour to roust someone who could fire up the London Eye. And even then, its glacial pace couldn't be sped up.

A dozen cops ringed the entry queues. Fifty feet away, the remains of the chopper curled tendrils of smoke into the night sky. It was still relatively intact and empty.

Besides a uniformed London Eye employee, only one other man waited to greet Jess.

Michael Wright.

The doors to the pod slid open. Michael was just standing there, hands on his hips, shaking his head. "You, Ms. Ramirez, are a lot of trouble."

"If that's a romantic opening, it isn't working."

Michael took a step forward. He fingered the golden star that still hung from her neck. "Are you okay?"

Jess stepped back, keeping her distance. "Yes. Did you get the two bad guys in that helicopter?"

"Nope. Long gone. Just a dead pilot with a single bullet in his brain. I guess the Russians have little patience for failure." Michael cocked his head toward the still-smoking wreckage. "But we know who they are. Hopefully, between MI6 and the Met, they will be caught."

Jess was instantly disappointed. "I wouldn't count on it."

Michael pointed to a couple of suits standing next to a jet-black government vehicle. "The Brits want to debrief you. I told them it traumatized you, and they would have to wait until morning."

"Oh no, you don't, Michael. You, sir, have not been very helpful so far. Your colleagues almost got Ali killed. And besides, I have my own flat."

"Not tonight, you don't. Alexandra and Liyanna stayed at the hospital just long enough to get a pint of blood each and a patch. They checked themselves out and are healing at Lee's place."

"'Healing,' eh?"

Michael held out a bent elbow, his escort pose.

"I think you could benefit from some *healing*, too."

Jess sniffed and took the arm. But she was still mad at him.

"We will not play cat and mouse like you did in Arizona, big boy. You tell me everything, or I will continue to cause trouble."

The subtext was clear. Michael was genuinely glad Jess was alive. And both were so physically hot for each other that if they didn't find a quiet bed soon, Jess reckoned she would have her way with him in the parking lot.

Michael tried to stay in character. The two were standing by his vehicle now. It was dark, and the cops were out of sight behind it. "You're sexy when you play tough," he said.

"One of those guys had my father killed. I'm not giving up until he pays for that. I'm not fucking around, Michael."

"You will be soon," he whispered.

Then Michael Wright and Jessica Ramirez kissed like two horny teenagers, about to lose their virginity after the high school prom.

ALI AND LEE

Ｂy all rights, Lee and Ali should have both spent
the night in hospital. The surgeons said they were
lucky that the hollow point rounds didn't do more
damage. But Liyanna Evans learned that Alexandra Clark
played by a different set of rules.

"I'm not spending my first night in London in a
hospital bed," she barked.

A profane stream of consciousness ultimately sprung
them. The docs shrugged, pressed release forms in Lee's
and Ali's hands along with bottles of narcotics, and sent
them home.

———

A COPPER GAVE THE TWO WOMEN A RIDE. THEY SAT IN
the back seat like a pair of criminals, eyeing each other in
silence, their gazes speaking volumes.

Lee was never a believer in love at first sight. But whatever magic Ali was exuding as she was bitching out the
boys at the airport was unraveling. When Lee and Ali

found that room where Mrs. Culpado and Jessica were being held, the adrenaline addiction they shared was a powerful aphrodisiac. Years of training kicked in. The two were in the zone. Ali was suddenly more attractive and desirable than Lee had ever imagined. The danger and the proximity of instant death was an incredible turn-on.

Now they were standing in the doorway at Lee's place. Ali wasn't wearing any cologne. But her scent was irresistible. That athletic body was delectable. And the sexual tension between the two was so magnetic, they could both feel it pulling them toward one another.

————

"SO, THIS IS WHAT YOU GUYS CALL 'A FLAT,'" ALI murmured as they entered. "You have good taste."

Ali scanned the layout with a practiced eye, commenting on the little things others missed, the invisible signs that pointed the way to Lee's sexual preference.

Ali noticed the couch, still covered with ruffled blankets where Jessica had slept.

"And this is how you entertain out-of-town guests?" she said.

Lee nodded toward her bedroom. "Good friends join me in there."

Ali unbuttoned her shirt, letting it drift to the floor. She pulled the sports bra beneath it up over her head, cursing as she agitated the bandages on her shoulder. She raised an eyebrow, crossing her arms to highlight her gifts. "How good a friend am I?"

————

THE WOUND IN LIYANNA EVANS' LEFT LEG THROBBED. She popped a Percocet and followed suit.

There is that moment when you know you've found the one when you've both revealed everything, and the thunderbolt hits you between the eyes. Lee was there right now. The pain vanished. The surrounding room drifted out of focus. She felt the lightning strike. Jessica had told her there was someone she needed to meet. Now Lee knew who and why.

"Follow me," she said in her sexiest voice, "and I'll show you how good a friend you are."

There was a soft buzz emanating from the cell phone in Ali's pants pocket.

"Do you need to answer that?"

Ali began unhooking Lee's belt. "It can wait."

AT THE HOTEL

Michael did it again. Jess thought that government guys booking expensive hotel rooms with panoramic views should annoy every taxpayer.

The two behaved as they walked through the lobby. He was all over her in the elevator. And the minute the door to his suite clicked shut, Jess was all over him.

Perhaps both underestimated the trauma they still had not processed from chasing Vega. Michael had asked Jess to marry him in that Phoenix hospital after nearly dying. And Jess didn't even respond. She owed him an explanation. She owed him her life. But there was no way Jess was going to tell him.

Michael tried being a good boy afterward, and Jess was suddenly too busy burying her father and helping Mamacita and her sister find a new place to live. Michael only inhabited the corners of her subconscious.

She thought about their night of passion in Washington and the beautiful necklace that appeared at the dinner table. She shouldn't have accepted it. Things were becoming more complicated by the moment. Jess needed no more complications now.

But seeing Michael's face at the base of the London Eye triggered Jess. Perhaps the proximity of death burned away any remaining shields that protected them from the raw, erupting passion they now felt.

Where Jess got the energy after her experiences over the prior forty-eight hours was a mystery. But it wasn't one she cared about resolving.

She started negotiating the minute she had him naked. They argued with an intensity that matched their lovemaking.

Jess had Michael pinned down on the huge king-size bed. She wanted to control every dimension of this experience. "You know I'm going after those bastards."

Michael responded in perfect time with her moves. It was pure heaven. "Don't do this, Jess. This is the second time I've almost lost you. I'm not losing you again."

She broke a passionate kiss just long enough to chide her lover. "The man in that helicopter did not murder your father."

Michael tilted Jess's head, exposing a delectable neck. "My father got shot when I was in high school. Gang members." He was playing for her sympathy.

"And what did you do?" She whispered the words as if she were a dominatrix, a command dripping with desire.

Michael snarled as he bit her neck. "I tracked each one down, beat the shit out of them, and dragged their bloody bodies to the precinct. They are all doing life now."

That aroused Jess even more. She moaned, instantly angry with herself for showing the emotion. "Then you know how I feel," she growled. "And you've described the minimum of what I'm going to do to Crawford and The Captain when I find them."

Jess's anger increased her rhythm. Michael kept up. He was turning out to be a better lover than he was in Arizona. Jess wondered if he had been practicing with someone else.

"The word is your Russian blew the country for Moscow," Michael panted, "and took Crawford with him."

Jess took his face in her hands and devoured his mouth. "Then I know exactly where I'm going next."

Michael must have felt that he needed control. He rolled Jess onto her back and turned up the intensity.

He was trying to distract her. It wouldn't work.

Michael's kisses began a downward path toward Jess's chest. "When the president discovered I knew you, the director himself put me in the back seat of a fighter jet to get here fast. My sole mission is to keep you out of the game so that clearer heads can manage this. It's way bigger than both of us, Jess."

Jess thrust Michael onto his back again. "Do you always talk this much? You are diminishing my sex drive. Keep arguing and I'll leave you forever."

They both knew that Jess was lying.

Michael grabbed Jess's hips, increasing her grind. "Sometimes we have to let other people do their jobs, Jessica. When it gets personal, we become vulnerable."

He was right, but Jess didn't care. She was going.

"So how do I get to Moscow? Is there still an Orient Express?"

"Jessica!" Now he was moaning. Was he frustrated with Jess or just simply as close to losing total control as she was? "Isn't there anything I can do to calm you down about this, baby?"

Baby? When did I become his baby?
I don't think so.

"You need to learn when you've lost an argument," Jess

said as their heart rates crossed one hundred and thirty beats a minute. "And you've lost this one."

That was when they both burst. Jess and Michael froze, two statues at the summit. Below the surface, it felt like an earthquake.

This was exactly like the graphic love stories Jess's grandmother used to read aloud to her in Spanish when she was in high school: Fireworks, "The Rockets' Red Glare," the most intense and satisfying culmination of her life.

Michael groaned. His eyes rolled into the back of his head. "I love you, Jess."

Victory. Jess knew she had won.

And so went the night.

Jess and Michael made love with the desperate intensity of two people who thought that this moment together might be their last. It was a swirling tornado of insatiable, frantic lust, wrapped in a genuine mutual affection that neither could now deny.

When both were finally spent, Jess lay atop her man's panting body, her head resting on palms, elbows pinning Michael's shoulders to the mattress.

Michael gasped for breath like a marathoner at the finish line. Jess wrapped a hand around the base of his chin and turned his face so she could look directly into his devastating eyes.

"So, are you gonna help me, or what, cowboy?"

ANDY IN TROUBLE

A dull ache in Ali's shoulder woke her up. Bright sunlight filtered through Lee's curtains. She could hear the sounds of morning traffic building on the street below.

Lee must have reloaded on the Narco. She slept peacefully, spooned against Ali's back. Strong arms wrapped around Ali's waist. Lee's head rested on Ali's good shoulder.

The last twelve hours were among the most exquisite she had ever experienced.

Things had to go downhill from here.

Ali's phone vibrated on the nightstand. It was her Proton Mail account. Andy Milluzzi's icon flashed in the inbox.

Officer Clark,

You were right about the other interested parties. We had a visit from their representatives tonight at the lab. Twelve of them for the six of us. We all got handcuffed, and they tore the place apart. There were warrants for all our gear, the servers, our backpacks, our phones, keys to our apartments, the works.

They herded us into several black, unmarked SUVs. The radios gave them away. Feds, probably the NSA guys you warned me about.

Before they could get my cell, I hit the speed dial text number you gave me to call if we had any trouble. We had a bit of luck. I guess the only place they could book us was at police headquarters.

Attorney Hammersmith was waiting. He received the message just like you said he would and talked his way into getting me alone for a few moments before it was my turn with the fingerprints and cameraman. Mr. Hammersmith let me use his phone to send this to you.

If I'm not released by midnight, a cron job on the cloud server will dump all our stuff into your secure folder. We were about done anyway. It is interesting.

I'm not sure what happens next to us. But thank you for another fun project.

I think you'll be pleased with our results.

Best,

Andy

Good old Andy. The shit storm comes down on him, and he's as cool as a cucumber. Attorney Hammersmith would have his work cut out for him. But Ali's favorite public defender knew people. She hoped her nerds would survive the adventure with few lasting side effects and some fun stories to tell.

Ali slid out from under Lee's embrace. Her laptop was charged up. She had some reading to do.

56

HEADQUARTERS—BRITISH SECRET INTELLIGENCE SERVICES / MI6— LONDON

"**A**bsolutely not." Commander Anastos was livid. "This is a huge operation involving a half dozen different governments. It's been years in the making, costing millions of pounds. No college town copper is going to inject a personal vendetta into the mix."

Michael slid his tongue between his teeth and the inside of his lower lip. That was how Jess knew his brain was engaged.

"Detective Ramirez is the only one who can point out Crawford on sight and one of the few who has seen The Captain up close. Yes, there is a personal dimension to this, but I can vouch for her ability to compartmentalize that. She can be as tenacious as a bulldog when she's on the scent. This one is still fresh. Put her on it."

The phone on the oversized desk that took up most of the space in Commander Anastos's cramped office at MI6 rang. After looking at the screen, his back stiffened as if he were at attention .

"Commander Anastos speaking... Yes sir. I understand, sir. Why the change in plan? Yes, sir. No questions, just get it done." Anastos fidgeted in his chair. "It will be two mammoth operations, executed in parallel, sir. It stretches some pretty thin resources. Recent information? Your conference room in fifteen minutes. Yes, sir. We will be there. All of us."

The commander cradled the phone. His eyes bore into Jess's. "You're getting your wish."

Michael's expression morphed into worry. *The bastard was expecting to lose this fight,* she thought. She had suddenly won the argument, and he didn't like it.

Jess didn't break the gaze. She could be tough, too. "What happened?"

"You are now the key to the success of this operation. The prime minister and the president agree we can't do it without you."

Michael was ahead of Jess. She hated that. "No. You can't let them do this, Tom."

"It's done. She's the bait."

57

GERHARDT'S PLAN

Ali had seen way too many spy movies. She expected an enormous conference room with fifty agents and a huge world map like they had in *Thunderball*.

Reality wasn't nearly as interesting. The room needed painting. The table looked like it came from a secondhand office furniture shop. No windows. No maps. Just a boring whiteboard and a projector.

There were fifteen. Jess, Lee, Michael, and Commander Anastos were the faces she knew. Lee's boss was there, along with people who must have been MI6 section heads, military liaisons, and the United States government's requisite representation. Associate Director Terry Taylor's image flickered on a laptop screen, connected to his office in Washington.

After reading Andy's material, Ali told Lee to pull the fire alarm. Ten minutes on the phone with the right person had gotten them both invited to this gathering. Ali had a bad feeling about what that meant.

The man who apparently headed up the project looked nothing like what she expected. He was short, dressed more like a bureaucrat than a spy. There was something else unique about him. He sat in a wheelchair.

His voice was firm, and his eyes exuded authority. Ali wanted to slap herself for stereotyping him.

"I'm Associate Director Gerhardt. Thank you all for coming on such brief notice."

His fingers tweaked the joystick that controlled his electric wheels, spinning the chair to face the whiteboard. A thumb pressed a remote control, and the projector came to life. Two blurry photos appeared on the screen.

"These are our two subjects. Giovanni de Triste and Vladimir Prokofiev. Some of you know de Triste as Jack Crawford, the individual responsible for the murder of Marie Culpado. He is in Prokofiev's employ, a quid pro quo for assistance provided to create a new identity for de Triste after he escaped from prison."

"Prokofiev is a former captain in the KGB, hence his preferred moniker. He's a private businessperson now, with vast real estate holdings here in the UK and a half-dozen projects involving governments who enjoy less than cordial relationships with the west."

Gerhardt craned his neck to look at Jessica. "Detective Ramirez and Agent Wright came into contact with one of his associates last year in Arizona."

Jessica and Michael exchanged glances. Hers telegraphed disgust. Once again, Michael had known more about all of this and had kept it from everyone. Ali could imagine the argument ahead.

"For political reasons, our two governments cooperated on a plan to 'smoke out' Crawford, as you Americans like to say. It involved great sacrifice, which we deeply regret.

But it was successful in proving the connection between Crawford and The Captain, giving us legal avenues to seize the Russian's holdings and seek a warrant to arrest him for a half-dozen capital offenses."

Gerhardt glanced at two of the men Ali didn't recognize. She assumed they were intelligence people.

"The information de Triste could provide to us in exchange for his life is of inestimable value to both our governments. This influenced our decision to allow the Culpado drama to take its course in Nashville."

He turned again to Jessica.

"What we didn't expect was the depth of The Captain's desire to exact revenge on Detective Ramirez for her part in the neutralization of his planned attack in New York. That became clear when Crawford surfaced at the prison in Nashville."

Gerhardt grunted as if what came next tasted sour.

"We allowed Detective Ramirez and Officer Clark to play out their little dramas. When the unfortunate incidents at the Wellington and in Covent Garden occurred, we knew we were on the right track.

"Marie Culpado became less important. Detective Ramirez emerged as a more crucial asset."

Asset? Ali thought. *More like an expendable pawn. Did these people have any compassion for human life?*

The picture on the screen flipped. There was the *Thunderball* map. Way too small and insignificant.

"This is the City of Moscow. We have information that Crawford and The Captain are there now. Legal proceedings are underway to relieve The Captain of his real estate empire and the associated cash flow. International warrants are being processed for his arrest. Of course, they are meaningless in Russia."

Gerhardt fingered the joystick. The wheelchair rotated so he could face the group. He looked directly at Jessica.

"He wants you, Detective Ramirez. It is clouding his judgment and gives us an advantage. The PM and the president agree that we should involve you in efforts to capture him."

Gerhardt nodded to an assistant. The man circulated briefing papers.

"Which brings us to our other problem. The Captain's operatives have created a method to breach the worldwide cellular data network and perhaps the Internet itself. They have cataloged crucial devices carried by intelligence and governmental assets and know their exact whereabouts. An agent in Seoul alerted us to this possibility at the cost of his life. Our American partners reported at least two incidents where The Captain's command and control applications caused havoc. One at an automotive test track in Michigan. And the second, a more high profile incident resulting in the crash of an aircraft in the American Air Force 2 inventory. The hacks kept our enemies one step ahead of us until a low-level member of their organization forgot to search Detective Ramirez after her capture. By retaining her cellular phone, we could triangulate her location and attempt arrests."

Gerhardt's cheek twitched. His dark expression targeted Michael and Commander Anastos.

"Our attempt failed. Crawford and The Captain are now thousands of miles away in an enemy nation under the protection of an adversarial government."

The associate director spun his wheelchair back toward the screen. "Our mission, ladies and gentlemen, is to find and destroy the infrastructure that breached the cellular network, to identify the location of Crawford and The

Captain and to take them into custody, returning them to England for prosecution and trial."

Ali scanned the documents neatly organized on the table. Andy's stuff was among them. Ali hoped that the associate director had acted on her demand to get her friend and his buddies sprung from jail. She would need them.

Two names appeared on the screen. Ali felt her stomach sink.

"Commander Anastos will take the lead on the extraction activity in Moscow," Gerhardt said. The joystick tweaked, and he looked directly at Ali. "Officer Clark will lead the team that will find and neutralize the security breach."

Associate Director Gerhardt swung his wheelchair back to face the group. He nodded to Taylor's image on the laptop. "Anything to add, Director Taylor?"

The visage shook his head. Speak up, and you can become a target if the plan craters. Stay quiet, and you can deflect the blame.

Gerhardt made eye contact with each individual in the room.

"Questions?"

Yeah, Ali had questions. Andy and his crew had figured out how to trace the cell network hack. They could plug the leak in days, and it was just a matter of time until they could pinpoint The Captain's location. This wasn't world-shattering stuff. There had to be more that Gerhardt wasn't sharing. What the hell was it? Why was finding The Captain so quickly so important? Why were they so willing to put her best friend's life in danger?

The tone of Gerhardt's voice told everyone there he didn't want to hear any questions. The meeting concluded.

Ali touched Jessica's elbow as the rest of the attendees

left the room. Even though she towered over Gerhardt's wheelchair, Ali felt small and vulnerable in comparison.

But Ali was Ali. She had questions and wouldn't be leaving until Gerhardt answered them.

"A moment, sir?"

58

ALI GETS AN ASSIGNMENT

Michael Wright and Tom Anastos stood in the doorway. Ali imagined they were waiting for some sign from the director to drag her and Jessica from the room.

Gerhardt shot a glance in their direction. Anastos must have recognized the non-verbal command. He touched Michael's shoulder, and the two departed, closing the door behind them.

The director studied the two women. Ali wondered if Jessica felt that this diminutive, yet powerful man could see through her, too.

"What is it, Officer Clark?"

"What is he planning? Why is this so important?"

Gerhardt sighed, as if he knew all about Alexandra Clark and her obsession with knowing things. He touched a button on the remote that controlled the projector. A map of the United States appeared with dozens of red dots on it.

"Does this projection mean anything to you, Officer Clark?"

It did. Ali walked toward the screen, pointing at the dots as she spoke. "It's a map of every intercontinental ballistic missile location in America," she said. "The ground-based nuclear arsenal of the United States."

The edges of Gerhardt's mouth bent upward, almost imperceptibly. Ali figured this was the closest he came to a smile.

"A correct guess, Officer Clark. Part of the allied deterrent that has kept the Russians and us from attacking one another for half a century."

Gerhardt's palm maneuvered the joystick, turning his wheelchair so he could face the map.

"Outdated, antiquated, and vulnerable. There are real men and women in each of those silos. They take orders directly from the US Commander in Chief via a system that is easily compromised."

Ali's eyes widened. She could see that Jessica's did, too.

"Can The Captain initiate a missile launch?"

Gerhardt kept his gaze on the screen.

"He can. And he will. Your government is already aware of the threat and is rushing to mitigate it. But there are too many locations, and all that is needed is one successful launch to provoke a Russian response."

"Armageddon," Jessica muttered. "The end of the world."

"Not quite," Gerhardt answered. "Prokofiev has given the Russians an advantage. Minutes are all that are needed. The Star Wars research that President Regan funded is one of the many things that Prokofiev's people have stolen and provided to the enemy. We believe that they have developed a system that can defend against mutually assured destruction."

"Why?" Jessica exclaimed. "Why do this? It makes no

sense economically or politically to vaporize the largest market in the world."

Gerhardt's wheelchair purred as it turned him to face Jessica and Ali. "That world is changing, Detective Ramirez. China, India, and Russia combine to create the largest consumer market on earth. The United States is considered politically unstable, no longer a reliable ally…" Gerhardt paused.

"And expendable."

"Are the leaders of those nations in agreement on this?" Ali asked.

Gerhardt nodded. "There are more powerful interests than politicians. We believe that a trio of oligarchs is behind the operation. The politicians have the luxury of using the private sector as cover. Plausible denial sounds incredible. But if the last four years have taught us anything, it's that anything can happen."

The director's eyes darted between the two police officers. "It is essential that we destroy Prokofiev's command-and-control system. We are close to successfully testing our own Star Wars deterrent. NATO has set a public demonstration for next week. We need to buy just enough time for our enemies to see that the United States and Great Britain again have the power… and the will to protect ourselves. Equilibrium will return. The uneasy peace that is the insurance policy of mutually assured destruction will prevail."

Gerhardt's eyes drilled into Ali's. "Officer Clark. Can your team disarm The Captain?"

Ali was silent. She didn't know.

Gerhardt turned to Jessica. "Detective Ramirez. You want retribution for your father's murder. Can you control your desire for revenge to help us neutralize Vladimir Prokofiev?"

Ali saw the look in Jessica's eyes that she knew so well.

"Yes, sir. I can. And I will."

Ali couldn't hide her excitement. The fun was about to begin.

59

AEROFLOT FLIGHT 2251 -
SOMEWHERE OVER RUSSIA

When Jessica Ramirez was sixteen, her church youth group went camping. Jess had never been outside of Paloma and only knew the comfort of sleeping in her own bed.

The days in the wild end with the sunset and begin well before dawn. The forest awakens before you can see. The ground was an unforgiving mattress. Primal instincts pulsate beneath a phalanx of trees, reaching upward in search of nourishment from the sky. Existence was reduced to the basics: food, rest, and surviving the day. You miss the perceived tranquility of your bed, realizing that the walls that protect you are thin.

It was a lesson Jess remembered during a decade of broken dreams, lying perps and chauvinistic cops who lived Voltaire's maxim: "Those who can make you believe absurdities, can make you commit atrocities."

The rules are simple in the wild. The universe unconcerned. It had no opinion. Success was survival. Each morning was a new beginning, each evening an achievement.

These things were on Jess's mind as she sat between Commander Anastos and Michael Wright in the cramped coach section of Aeroflot Flight 2251 to Sheremetyevo—AS Pushkin international airport, Moscow.

They were going in above the radar. The Embassy arranged a public appearance, promoting Jess as "The Local Police Officer Who Crushed a Hacker." Russian intelligence knew they were coming. That meant The Captain knew, too.

That was the plan. Beyond that, they had nothing. "Put her out there and hope The Captain tries to grab her," was how the associate director had phrased it.

Three people against a vast oligarchy and the entire Russian security infrastructure.

Just the odds Jess loved.

———

RUSSIAN CUSTOMS WENT THROUGH THEIR BAGS LIKE hunting dogs on a scent. The only thing they couldn't touch was the diplomatic pouch Michael carried.

"Are you visiting for business or pleasure?" a foreboding customs officer asked. He was a mountain of a man, better suited to be a lineman for the Chicago Bears than a low-level government service job.

"Business at the United States Embassy," Michael said, flashing a diplomatic passport and his megawatt smile.

"And her?" The lineman sniffed, nodding in Jessica's direction. "Your wife?"

Michael chuckled. "Not yet. But a guy can hope."

"What sports do you play?" Jess asked, going against the conventional wisdom that the less said to a Russian official, the better.

"Football. Hockey," he rumbled.

"You're still in great shape," she added. "How do you do it? Stay so... healthy?"

The linebacker stuck his tongue against a perfect row of front teeth, popping his upper denture out of his mouth. "I still play when I am not arresting curious American girls."

Jess shot a glance at Michael. He and the commander didn't like her friendliness. "You can play with me anytime, handsome," she said, running her own tongue across her lower lip.

The customs agent allowed a gurgling laugh to erupt from deep within. "Is this how all American policewomen behave?"

Jess didn't reveal her profession. But he knew. She guessed they all knew. "Only the good ones," she answered. "If you ever get to Illinois, I'll treat you to some real football."

The linebacker shook his head and stamped their passports, waving a hand to his minions to zip the suitcases and let them pass.

"There is a problem with your transportation. The government will supply," he said.

"What problem?" Commander Anastos asked.

"Who knows? I was told to make arrangements. My associate will take you to meet your driver."

The associate was a third the linebacker's size and half his height. Jess guessed he recently graduated from what passed for a high school in Moscow. He was learning the ropes.

"This way," the kid said, pointing toward the ground transportation center.

The group walked through the airport maze, noticing many heavily armed soldiers patrolling the concourses. Putin didn't tolerate dissent. These were his enforcers.

A door opened, and a black Mercedes-Benz V-Class minivan sat purring at the curb.

"This is Leo," the kid said. "He takes you to the embassy."

Michael scoped out the road that paralleled international arrivals. "It's not very busy," he muttered. "I wonder what 'the problem' was?"

Leo turned out to be short, slim, and wiry, probably KGB, assigned to monitor and report. He wore blue jeans, a white shirt, and a sport coat with a folded handkerchief in his breast pocket.

"Would the lady care to enter?" he asked, pointing to the passenger door handle.

"In America, we still have gentlemen," Commander Anastos said, sliding it open for Jess.

Leo took a step back, shaking his head before loading the luggage into the back. "As you wish."

Jess ended up with the center seat all to herself. Michael and the commander took the back seat. Leo buckled up, turned on the stereo and pulled into the sparse traffic.

"We have dinner with the embassy staff tonight and a meeting tomorrow morning with the security chief," the commander said, thumbing through a notepad he pulled from his breast pocket. "Your speech is tomorrow night at the American Center. It's in the Embassy complex, open to the public. If your friends want to find you, it should be easy."

He said the words loud enough so Leo could hear. Jess was certain that Leo already knew.

"How many times have you been to Russia?" Michael asked.

Commander Anastos put an elbow on the armrest, balancing his chin in a half-circle he made with his thumb and index finger. "Hmm... The first time was when I was a boy. My grandparents were Greek immigrants. We had family in the country. I spent one year during primary school here before the family moved to London."

Anastos paused. Jess thought she could detect a wince. "We attended the American Center dedication in 1993. Between work and pleasure, I've been to Moscow nearly a dozen times over the years."

All of this was common knowledge. Leo could report it if he wanted to. But everyone knew better than to converse about anything other than pleasantries and the weather.

The Mercedes navigated the M-11 highway between the airport and the embassy in one hour and thirty-seven minutes. The trio was silent most of the way.

When she saw the signs for the Tversky District, Jess sensed that something was amiss. The commander's breathing labored. As the limo pulled into the compound, she noticed his sweat-drenched body. His corneas contracted into pinpricks.

Michael must have noticed it, too. He had the door open when the van rolled to a stop. A memory came into focus in Jess's brain. A Russian dissident and a deadly poison. She shouted a command to the Marine by the entrance.

"Draw your weapon, corporal. Cover the driver. And don't touch the doors. We'll need medical help right now."

Within seconds, a pair of strong arms were helping Commander Anastos into the Embassy. He could barely walk.

Michael must have come to the same conclusion. He drew a set of keys from his pocket and opened the diplomatic pouch. Among its contents were three handguns. He passed one to Jess, taking another into his fist, pressing the muzzle against Leo's temple through the open driver's side window.

"Where did you put it, Leo?"

The chauffeur feigned ignorance, shrugging, suddenly unclear about the English language.

Michael racked a round in the semi's chamber.

"Tell me, Leo. You're on US soil, and nobody will give a shit if I blow your brains all over the dashboard."

Jess replayed the airport events in her brain.

"Would the lady care to enter?"

"It's on the door handle, Michael."

Michael motioned to the Marine. The corporal opened the driver's door with a white-gloved hand and pulled Leo out. Michael and Jess were next to him.

With the corporal's help, Michael dragged Leo toward Jess. "What do you know about this, comrade?"

Leo relaxed in Michael's grasp, just enough for the FBI agent to loosen his own grip. That's all it took. The driver shot a palm toward the passenger door, swiping it across the top of the handle.

He tried to slap Michael across the face, but there were two sets of fists controlling his arm.

In seconds, the Marine had the handcuffs out, securing Leo's hands behind him.

"Watch that left hand," Michael said. "My guess is that there is enough Novichok there to kill all of us."

He was right. The commander must have had a tough constitution to keep the symptoms at bay for an hour. The driver convulsed against the powerful arms that held him up. His lungs contracted against his will. His face morphed into a cyanotic blue Jess recognized from too many strangulation crime scenes.

In minutes, he was dead.

60

CORNWALL—UK

A trio of Land Rovers converged on the innocuous farm, south of St. Ives in Cornwall. It was a place nobody paid attention to. With protected access to the beach and a straight shot westward across the Atlantic, toward New York, it was an ideal spot for UK Undersea Communications to launch a subaqueous fiber optic cable.

Each strand of glass could transmit the entire contents of the Internet back and forth in less than an hour. Alexandra Clark thought it ironic that Cornwall was home to this amazing on-ramp to the information superhighway. Data speeds for the locals here were little better than obsolete dial-up connections.

What focused her attention on this place was a minority investor in UKUC: The Maitland Corporation.

SIS Technical analyst CJ Riemer led a team of agents toward a nondescript cinderblock building, out of place and out of sight behind the 18th-century farmhouse at the end of the winding driveway. An explosive expert's eyes and the noses of a pair of bomb-sniffing dogs confirmed the facility was safe to enter.

Ali could hear the rotors of a Royal Navy helicopter in the distance. She hoped it carried the human cargo she had asked for.

The security team framed a landing zone in the neatly manicured side-yard. Moments later, a Commando Wildcat AH1 was discharging its single passenger.

Ali recognized the smile instantly.

"Hey, Officer Clark. Thanks for busting me out of jail."

Andy Milluzzi's five-foot-ten frame took a moment to watch the chopper spin up and ascend into the late afternoon sky. The backpack he carried looked out of place, so far away from the Paloma University campus. Ali knew its contents were worth their weight in gold.

"Sorry to put you right to work, Andy, but we need to know if there are countermeasures inside the building so we don't unintentionally alert the bad guys."

Andy grinned. "No worries." He gave the grounds a cursory inspection. "There's your fire alarm," he said, pointing to the tiny satellite dish on the roof. "No reason for that old technology when you've got a zillion other safety systems reporting in real-time. Somebody wants to keep watch on this place with no one else knowing."

Unzipping the backpack, Andy removed a laptop and what looked like a single small jumper cable connected to his computer's USB port.

CJ Riemer materialized from the crowd of uniformed agents and shook Andy's hand. "I thought the dish was out of place, too. Let me get you a ladder so you can take a closer look."

Ali smiled. Andy knew a kindred spirit when he saw one. "It sounds like you and I have been parallel processing. Any more infected 'Friedas' out there?"

"Too many, my friend. Let's figure out how to get them well."

CJ motioned to a team member who quickly produced a ladder. Andy scaled it with ease to examine the small circular disk and clasp the jumper cable to its coaxial connection.

As the laptop screen scrolled row after row of data, Andy pulled a short piece of coax from his backpack, studying the N-connector to make sure it would fit the back of the dish.

After about a minute, he nodded in satisfaction, typed a command on the keyboard and plugged the coaxial adapter into the computer's thunderbolt port.

"Yup," he said. "That's the handshake signal, all right. These older devices are easy to fool. Now, if I can just time the switch right."

With Ali watching from the ground, the ones and zeros streamed across the screen. Andy waited for the five-second silence interval, first loosening the N-connector at the back of the dish and then quickly swapping cables to connect his laptop directly to the antenna.

It was only when a broad smile creased Andy's features that Ali realized she was holding her breath.

"Good to go," he said. "As far as the other side knows, nothing is amiss. We can play to our heart's content now."

Ali nodded to CJ, who gave a sign to a pair of agents standing by the door. Seconds later, it was open, revealing blinking lights and racks filled with laser gear and network connections.

The cop patted her friend on the back. "Impressive," Ali said. "But can you tell me the one thing I want to know?"

Andy pulled an Iridium Extreme 9575 Satellite Phone from his pocket. "Modified," he said, "It doesn't use the compromised cell network. But it does everything else a cell phone does."

He opened an app on the tiny screen. A map appeared with a red hammer and sickle icon blinking smack dab in the middle of the City of Moscow.

"There's your Captain," Andy said. "And he has no idea that we know his exact location."

61

MOSCOW

Govyadiny Moscava translates as "Beef Russia." That's all that patrons see on the dim sign in front of the tiny restaurant located south of the Moscow River and less than a mile from the Kremlin. Beef Russia had the perfect mix of anonymity and access—a hole in the wall, hidden in plain sight with access to a high-capacity fiberoptic cable that ran northwest, through Estonia and across the Baltic Sea to Stockholm. The roof of the building obscured satellite dishes from the street, but not from the CIA's spy satellites.

The agency could not connect the place with anything particularly sinister, considering that "sinister" was associated with just about everything and everyone in Russia's capital city.

Now, there was a connection, and Govyadiny Moscava was about to get a lot of attention.

Vladimir Prokofiev sat at his private table, a circular red-leather booth with a complete view of everyone who came in and out of his restaurant. On the wall to the rear of his booth, a large, thick pane of mirrored, one-way, bullet-proof glass made the place seem bigger than it was. Prokofiev's office was behind the glass. But he liked how the smell of the applewood bar mixed with the aroma of grilled red meat and retreated to the sterile silence of precise furnishing only when privacy was a necessity.

Besides the attraction of its beef, the chefs at Govyadiny Moscava cooked everything in plain sight. Half of the place was an open kitchen. Steaks sizzled atop gas-fired grills. Breaded chicken bubbled in deep fryers, boiling in canola oil. Salads were tossed with the dexterity of a pizza chef. And it was all within view of the customers.

The place had a wide-open feel.

Not that security was an issue among the patrons. Every employee, from the burly bartender to the husky East German waitress, had KGB credentials and weapons. Any malcontent who made the mistake of coming in the front door and confronting the wrong person disappeared out the back door into eternity.

———

THE CAPTAIN WASN'T ALONE. JACK CRAWFORD, AKA Giovanni De Triste, sat in the booth with him, maintaining his distance, his right arm pressed against his chest in a sling and a plaster cast.

Despite some excellent Russian narcotics, Crawford felt the throbbing pain of his fractured humerus and two taped ribs. He felt lucky to have survived the chopper crash in London.

"Why did you shoot the pilot?"

One did not ask The Captain those kinds of questions. But the meds gave Jack Crawford a precarious shot of courage.

The Captain grunted. "Broken legs. The man couldn't

get away and allowing him to be interrogated by British Intelligence was an unacceptable option."

Crawford considered the hulks behind the bar. "I sometimes wonder what you might do if I outlived my usefulness."

Prokofiev sniffed. "You are a long-term investment, my friend. And you still have one significant task to perform for me."

Crawford instantly knew what the menacing man was talking about. "I delivered the two women into your hands. We are even."

"Jessica Ramirez still lives. Yes, we know she is currently barely a mile away, but while she breathes, you have failed. Your attempt at the airport was another failure."

"We neutralized a British agent who has long been a problem for your country. On my ledger, that counts as a success."

The Captain brushed a bit of dust from the tablecloth. At the bar, Crawford saw an employee flinch. Prokofiev terrified even his closest associates. "We know that he still breathes. And as we've seen, the SIS puts damaged men into wheelchairs and continues to utilize their wisdom and experience against us."

Crawford's voice belied incredulity. "No normal human being recovers from the dosage Commander Anastos received."

Prokofiev grunted. "The commander is anything but normal. Do you know his history?"

"I know he will live the rest of his brief life on a ventilator. If your plan executes as you expect, his existence won't matter."

The Captain continued to focus on his vodka. "Death

is the ultimate arbiter. Anastos is a resilient and resourceful man. If he survives, he will exact vengeance."

Crawford ignored the warning. "What's so important about one small-town police officer? If you left her alone, she would probably have spent the rest of her life arresting college kids for smoking dope. You've killed the girl's father, and she's not one who will let that go."

The Captain considered the top-shelf vodka that gleamed in a crystal glass on the table before him. "You of all people should know that the snake remains deadly until you cut off its head."

"This snake is part of a nest. She has imaginative friends."

"Then we shall kill them all."

Crawford sipped his bottle of Baltika. He'd had better beer but could understand how the brew was second only to vodka in popularity here. "You have a plan?"

Prokofiev continued to study the glass. Crawford watched him move his thumb to trace a droplet of condensation.

"The British have assembled a team that will attempt to abduct or kill me. Detective Ramirez's associate is among them. I have a trusted operative in their midst. Our little snake is about to lose her closest friend. And MI6 will know the extent of our power over them."

Crawford narrowed his eyes in concern. "Why do this when you are so close to victory? We are within forty-eight hours of executing your plan."

"The assassins will be here in twenty-four. Detective Ramirez speaks tomorrow night. We will soon have her in our grasp. If all goes as I contemplate, witnessing the deaths of her associates will be her last living act."

Crawford pondered this new information. His mind

was unchanged. "Eventually, someone will come for you, too."

The Captain lifted his glass, sniffed the contents and drank. "I don't expect to die in my bed. We all serve someone. I failed my client because of that 'small-town police officer.' I have convinced them that what I now propose is worth a second chance. If I fail again, the entire national security apparatus won't be able to protect me."

He said this without emotion. Empty gray eyes scanned the restaurant and the street on the other side of the front windows. Crawford wondered if the man had any feelings at all.

"And yet, you have no fear."

Prokofiev turned those gray eyes to consider the American. "Fear is weakness. It can be a tool to control a man, a flaw to exploit."

Crawford didn't break the gaze. Everything with The Captain was a test. "And if someone channels the desire for revenge to banish fear?"

"Then," The Captain said, "they become dangerous beyond measure."

62

THE AMERICAN EMBASSY
INFIRMARY—MOSCOW

Tom Anastos fought to breathe. Every beat of his heart was an exercise in will. The commander knew the symptoms of Novichok poisoning well. Now, as he lay intubated in a makeshift hospital bed at the American Embassy, he felt a curious detachment from it all.

He thought back to his boyhood in Greece and how a love for ice hockey in a country with hardly any ice first brought him to Russia.

His teenage teammates were all bigger, stronger, and more experienced. They saw the boy with the strange accent and the trusting smile as the perfect target, a disposable plaything for a group of thugs who enjoyed covering dogs in gasoline, lighting a match and watching the helpless animals run themselves to death, engulfed in flames.

Tom learned his lesson when his hockey "teachers" sent him toward thin ice after a puck. He heard it crack and couldn't turn back before what held him above the dark, icy water gave way.

The force of his forward progress sent his body below a

hard, shimmering shield. It soaked his clothing, dragging him deeper into the freezing darkness. Tom felt as if his lungs might explode. His fingers were instantly numb, and he felt the icy grip of death encircling him.

He imagined his parents interrogating his teammates and the shrugs they would give in return. His bloated body would not appear until the ice melted in late spring, if at all.

Kids disappeared here all the time. Parents mourned. Everyone else moved on.

Fear morphed into anger. Tom brought his legs together and undulated like a mermaid. The movement, along with the slight buoyancy of the oxygen in his body, slowly lifted him toward the glassy surface.

Frozen fingers felt their way along the thickness until he sensed a break. Grabbing the edge of the shelf of ice, he pulled himself into the open air, gasping for breath.

Nobody offered him help. Life and death were his two options. Only his desire to survive gave him the will to persevere past the searing muscle pain and the hypoxia, dragging his body back onto a thicker foundation.

Naturally, his teammates laughed. The show was over. They dispersed, leaving Tom, wet and shivering, to walk home alone.

But Tom Anastos learned a lesson that day. And he remembered every face. Over the next few years, each disappeared, one by one. The manner and timing did not attract attention. Everyone knew bad boys had a way of self-destructing.

That Tom Anastos exacted his revenge in ways that made his victims' final horrific moments the stuff of nightmares didn't bother him. He did not kill for sport. But he was not afraid to kill for a purpose.

The ideal profile for an MI6 field officer.

Tom Anastos understood how the world worked and how to survive. Hockey didn't kill him. There was no way that Novichok would, either.

63

I NEED DISTANCE

J essica Ramirez and Michael Wright stood next to the commander's bedside. Jess couldn't know what was going on inside of Tom's head.

All she could feel was anger.

"Now, do you see why I'm terrified that they involved you in this thing?" Michael asked.

Jess nodded. Her iron expression did not change.

"Now, do you see why I have to be? This has become more than just a personal vendetta. Phoenix. New York. They are all connected to this man, Prokofiev. We set him back a step. What he intends to do will kill hundreds of millions of innocent people. But I'm his weakness. By drawing me into the game, he's revealed enough for us to find him."

Michael interrupted her narrative, his voice unusually cold. "He tricked you into the game, Jessica. And you delivered Marie Culpado into his hands, almost losing your own life in the process. That was a fail, Jess. You're in over your head."

Jess turned to face her lover, taking a tiny step backward as she did so.

Distance. She needed distance.

"You're right, Michael. Rule number one in our world is that when it gets personal, you make mistakes. I know that now. But it's personal for Prokofiev, too. Anastos said I'm the 'bait.' So, let's dangle that bait in front of this asshole's face. Put me up on that stage tonight as planned. Invite the public. Put your agents all around me if you have to. But let's grab whoever he sends to dispatch me and squeeze him until we know exactly where The Captain is.

"With any luck, they will succeed in abducting me tonight. The Captain wants to take me out with his own hands. Like Crawford did to Marie." Jess's expression turned ice cold. "Get me in the same room with that bastard, and I'll kill him myself."

"Excuse me, Agent Wright." It was the measured tones of the US Ambassador, who had silently entered the room. "There's a message for Detective Ramirez from Officer Alexandra Clark."

64

CORNWALL

Andy Milluzzi grinned. "Message received. And nobody knows what it is or where it came from."

Apparently, the comms system Alexandra Clark's students at Paloma University crafted had done the job.

Ali returned her young mentee's smile. "You're pretty damn good, kiddo. How in the hell did your team figure this thing out?"

Andy looked to his SIS counterpart. CJ Riemer grinned back. This was heaven for nerds and hell for everyone else. "No offense, Officer Clark," Andy said, without a bit of arrogance in his voice, "but it's beyond your level of experience."

"Then dumb it down for me."

"Every communications protocol includes a 'hand-shake.' When it connects with the server that controls it, it transmits the same bit of code every time. In amateur radio, we call these 'packets.' They contain identifying information about the device and other stuff that the system needs to know to do what it needs to do. I don't know how this Captain of yours did it, but he's infected every server, every cell phone, every smart device with this tiny bit of software that spits out everything the device knows to his servers."

CJ jumped in when Andy took a breath. "Using other information he already somehow possesses, he's able to extrapolate where we are, read our mail and, in some very scary cases, give commands to our technology that can do some pretty ugly stuff."

Ali knew what that last bit meant. A rash of minor news stories about tiny failures in rural power grids, smart cars that suddenly swerved into oncoming traffic, text messages and social posts that could influence malleable minds to do bad things. This was the currency Ali traded in. And there had been more of it lately.

Was it all connected?

She saw Andy watch her process what he was saying. "Right before your NSA friends arrested us, my team hacked into the MSPC, the Midwest Power Cooperative. That's the central authority that balances electricity demand for ten states, including Illinois. Guess what we found in the command-and-control data stream?"

"Shit," Ali muttered. "How universal is this thing?"

Andy shrugged. "Who knows? But my guess is that your Russian friend is working for some entity that would benefit, either politically or financially, from social upheaval and economic chaos."

An agent interrupted the conversation. "Excuse me, Mr. Riemer. We think we've found the device they are using to connect their servers to the fiber cable. Do we have your permission to remove it?"

Ali saw CJ and Andy exchange wordless communication.

"Are you sure that dish is still out of commission?" CJ finally asked.

Andy tilted his head. "Only one way to find out."

CJ nodded to his associate. The agent disappeared back into the building.

"How many more of these nodes do you think have this little technological gem in their equipment racks?" Ali asked.

Andy pointed to his laptop, still chugging away on the roof. "That guy should be able to tell us. A network is a network, and now that we know enough about how your friend has set his up, we should be able to get a list of devices, perhaps even locations."

At that point, a klaxon sound effect from *Star Trek—The Next Generation* wailed from the speakers on Andy's computer.

"Uh oh," Andy said, scampering up the ladder.

Ali watched his eyes scan the screen. "Yup. I was afraid of that. The box in the rack phones home via the fiber, too. They know we're here."

Ali barked a command. "Out of the building, everyone. Now!"

Andy disconnected his laptop from the dish and scampered down the ladder.

The SIS vehicles faced away from the structure, drivers already behind the wheel with engines running. The group piled in. Wheels spun, tossing dirt clod rooster tails in their wake as the team put distance between themselves and the blockhouse.

"Did you get the box?" Ali asked, shooting a glance into the back seat of her SUV, where Andy and CJ sat.

CJ held up a nineteen-inch by two-inch object. "Hopefully, this thing isn't full of explosives, too."

Ali didn't want to take the chance. She grabbed the device, tossing it out the passenger window.

Andy Milluzzi's eyes were glued to his laptop screen. He spoke like a NASA flight controller, counting down to liftoff.

"Seven. Six. Five. Four. Three. Two. One."

As Ali looked out the back window. The building and everything in it exploded.

65

THE AMERICAN CENTER—MOSCOW

The American Center was the ideal venue to dangle some tasty bait in front of Vladimir Prokofiev's nose. It was located at the Embassy and was the one place in Moscow where American Culture could be publicly celebrated.

Jessica Ramirez stood behind the podium in what might have passed for a quiet library back home.

The title of her talk, "The Local Police Officer Who Crushed a Hacker," was titillating enough to draw a capacity crowd.

She could see Michael standing at the back of the room, arms crossed, unsmiling. She also recognized several Embassy security people dressed in casual clothes that did nothing to make them blend into the mix of ex-pats and locals who filled the room.

Jess was not a natural public speaker. Somewhere along the line, she had learned to lock on to a friendly face in the crowd and pretend she was talking one on one with that individual. Here, about as far from Paloma as one could get, everyone looked like a criminal.

Tonight, Jess knew that, at last, the good guys had a competitive edge. Ali's message had reported that she knew Prokofiev's exact location, a restaurant less than two miles from the American Center.

Despite the explosive incident in Cornwall, Andy's trackers still had The Captain in their crosshairs. MI6 had a strike team en route to take Prokofiev into custody.

Jess's job was to keep his attention focused on her until that team could steal into the country.

"I'm Jess Ramirez. I'm a first-generation American-born US citizen, the first in my family to go to college and the only one crazy enough to become a cop."

That line always drew a smattering of laughter and broke some tension.

"I live and work in a place called Paloma, Illinois. It's a river town on the Mississippi. Author Mark Twain passed through several times, and some say he got the idea to write *Huckleberry Finn* while fishing on the banks of what is now the Paloma University campus."

Jess motioned to a staffer who dimmed the lights slightly. A tiny projector flashed her slides on a screen behind her. Dim, but not dark. Bad things could happen in the dark.

"Last year, I got into a little trouble at work and earned a bit of a vacation, something you all might call a 'suspension with pay.'"

More laughter. The crowd was connecting with her.

The image on the screen changed to show the sprawling magnificence of the Grand Canyon.

"I decided to visit my uncle. He's the sheriff who shares jurisdiction with the National Park Service over this beauty. He was dealing with a serial killer, and being a nosy girl, I got involved."

A couple of people in the audience nodded, possibly

remembering the news coverage of what became an international headline.

Jess looked for that one friendly face and saw one that was familiar. It would take a moment for her to conjure up its identity. Her focus was on the speech, not on the man. But Jess decided he would get her constant eye contact.

"It turned out that our bad girl was also a computer genius with designs on doing some pretty bad things. Tonight, I'll share that story and how we could stop her."

Jess told Vega's story in as much detail as she was allowed, how the woman dispatched her murder victims by tossing them off the canyon's rim, how she created a computer virus that infected the statewide police computer network and how she nearly destroyed the New York Financial District.

The audience seemed mesmerized. Tears appeared when Jess talked about her father's murder. And there was applause when she concluded her narrative with the stunning single combat that had taken place in the Arizona whitewater in the dead of night.

The burly male face Jess had picked as her personal connection wore the hint of a smile. His open-collared shirt and blue jeans didn't seem part of the memory she was trying to bring back to the front of her mind.

"So what did we learn, ladies and gentlemen?" Jess concluded. "Danger often dresses in casual clothing and looks like the girl next door. We can protect our tech with complicated passwords, virtual private networks, and vigilance, but the bad guys keep getting smarter, and we need to keep getting smarter, too. Like putting more weight on the barbells at the gym, it's about continuously building our strength, increasing our knowledge and developing a strong situational awareness."

Jess pressed a remote control to bring up her last slide. It was a picture of children playing in a park.

"These kids will ultimately know more about technology than any previous generation. It's our job to create a world where they can use it responsibly and safely. Thank you all for coming tonight!"

The wave of applause felt good. Once she had launched into her tale, Jess forgot about where she was and her dislike for being the center of attention. She was a woman on a mission. This was just a necessary tactic to hopefully get the job done. Affirmation for her work was icing on the cake, a brief sugar high she knew would quickly evaporate, but still, a moment worth savoring.

The Center's director stood and turned to the audience.

"Are there any questions for Detective Ramirez?"

That was when the lights went out.

————

MICHAEL WRIGHT KNEW THAT THE BUILDING HAD emergency generators. Despite Russia's copious natural gas reserves, power outages in the country were still a thing.

A glance out the windows told him that the streetlights still worked. There was power feeding the adjoining buildings. This darkness was deliberate.

The security team spread out like spiders, weapons drawn, flashlights on.

"Breaker box," one shouted to the director. "Where is it?"

Beams of luminescence danced around the room. The crowd wasn't hysterical. This was Russia. Things like this happened. They calmly stood, pressing toward the exits.

A moment later, the lights came back on. The room was nearly empty, except for a smattering of guests and armed embassy men pointing handguns and flashlights in every direction.

Michael looked at the empty podium area. Fear grabbed at his throat as his eyes darted around the venue, and realization dawned.

Jessica's cell phone and ID badge rested on top of the podium. But she was gone.

66

TALLINN INTERNATIONAL
AIRPORT—ESTONIA

The 1960s era Antonov AN-12 transport plane lumbered off the single concrete runway at Tallinn Airport on the outskirts of the Estonian capital city. The aircraft usually required a crew of five, but tonight only two were flying her, carefully selected local contractors who wouldn't attract attention when they filed a cargo flight plan to Moscow.

Alexandra Clark and Liyanna Evans looked exactly like their MI6 wet team counterparts, dressed in black paratrooper garb, strapped into the hard plastic seats that lined the outer bulkhead of the aging cargo plane.

"What are the chances that the Russians will figure out what we are trying to do?" Lee asked Ali.

"Cargo flights from Estonia to Russia are not uncommon," Ali answered, checking to make sure that the special satellite phone Andy had built for her was in working order. "If we suddenly see a couple of MiGs on either side, we'll know that things are about to get interesting." She checked her watch. "Just give us two hours, Lord."

Ali replayed Director Gerhardt's personal briefing at Heathrow.

"You will depart Tallinn for Moscow, where the wet team will parachute into the outskirts of the city, retrieve the subject and depart on a Boeing CH-47 Chinook transport helicopter that already has take-off clearance to return from an airshow that took place earlier this month.

"We purposely delayed its departure on the chance that an operation like this might develop and your only challenge will be to elude airport security and board the aircraft undetected."

Gerhardt made it sound easy. Ali knew that this would be the most dangerous part of the extraction plan.

"An RAF aircraft carrier will await you in the Baltic. The Russians don't like it, but we run exercises there this time of year, so a re-fueling stop won't draw undue attention.

"Under no circumstances are any of you to fall into enemy hands. You all have self-destruct devices that will vaporize your body and anything within fifteen feet into virtually undetectable particles. If that eventuality occurs, make sure you take as many of the enemy with you as you can."

Gerhardt turned his wheelchair to face Lee and Ali.

"You are all aware that this is a voluntary assignment. If you're having any second thoughts, now is the time to voice them."

Ali remembered stealing a glance at Lee and exchanging shrugs.

"Fine. Board your aircraft, and good luck."

————

ALEXANDRA CLARK PATTED LEE'S KNEE. "ANY regrets?"

Lee smiled and shook her head. "None. My life became a lot more interesting the moment you walked into it. I don't know a single detective inspector who's visited Russia, let alone with a device that can turn us both into sand through an hourglass in a nanosecond."

"I always focus on the future in situations like these. It keeps the fear at bay," Ali said. "What do you want to do when we get back?"

It was Lee's turn to touch Ali's leg. "The same thing we did before we left."

————

Moscow

Now Jess remembered the face that she focused on during her speech. It was the customs guy from the airport. Michael had interacted with him, too. Why didn't he make the ID?

Perhaps he did. The goal was to put her in harm's way. That had worked out perfectly.

This time, metal handcuffs secured her wrists to the wall of the van. Her captor had manacled Jess's ankles and knees. Gray duct tape covered her mouth, leaving her nose as the only airway.

The burly Russian sat in the driver's seat at the front of the unmarked van that Jess knew would take her to The Captain.

"No cell phone this time, shlyukha," he said, looking back at her handcuffed form. "I could have killed you myself at your little speech. You will wish I had after we get to our destination."

Jess ran the calculations in her head. If everything went as planned, she wouldn't be the only American greeting The Captain tonight.

A voice she knew well whispered into her ear.

Things like apologies and affection do not come easily to me. But I hope that in your heart, you know how proud I am of you and how much I love you.

Her father's phone message, recorded in the moments before his death, echoed from that part of her brain that held every suppressed memory from a lifetime of compartmentalization.

She pictured her mother, sister and grandmother, relaxing on the beach in Cancun, Secret Service agents discretely watching over them.

She thought of Ali and the decade of friendship they shared. She wondered if her partner were on board the aircraft she knew was wending its way toward Moscow with the elite team on board who would either take Vladimir Prokofiev back to London for trial or kill him on the spot.

And she thought of Michael Wright. Of Jess's many suitors, Michael was clearly above and beyond. She replayed his drug-addled marriage proposal in that Phoenix hospital bed and the two very different nights of passion they had shared.

The physical attraction wasn't the issue. Could she ever give her heart to one man? Jess could feel the chain around her neck and pictured the beautiful golden star with its three blue stones woven inside, swinging back and forth as the van bounced Jess toward her destiny.

Was what she felt for Michael true love?

Jesus, Jess. Focus! The game is just beginning. Where is your professional discipline?

Then another voice from the past spoke to her. The vision of her father's face morphed into an innocent man strapped to an electric chair.

God, forgive me for my sins. I surrender myself to His will.

RESEARCH LAB—BRITISH SECRET INTELLIGENCE SERVICES / MI6— LONDON

In the bowels of MI6 headquarters, CJ Riemer and Andy Milluzzi looked at the eviscerated black box they retrieved from the wreckage of the fiber node in Cornwall.

CJ squinted at the circuit boards. "This is way too simple, Andy. It's just a control interface, addressable to one or more devices."

Andy Milluzzi scratched his chin. "The brains must be in the server. If only we could break into that CPU."

"It could be anywhere," CJ mused, looking at a visual depiction of the worldwide Internet on one of the lab's flat screens. "A true needle in an enormous haystack."

Andy studied a second screen. The Captain's cell phone icon blinked at the same location in Moscow. "Could it be that simple?" he murmured.

CJ focused on his American counterpart. "What do you mean?"

"Is The Captain stupid enough to have the brains of this whole thing that close by?"

He punched a couple of keys to change the visual from a graphic representation to the latest spy satellite scan, hitting the enlarge command again and again to zoom in on the roof of Govyadiny Moscava. "See the satellite dishes? We know that the place is dead center on the fiber path that winds from the Kremlin toward the Baltic. Is the server in that little restaurant?"

CJ lit up like a sparkler. His fingers flew across the keyboard. "We've identified the other node locations. There are only four. If I ping them with the same bogus packets, they should phone home."

A red dot appeared at four points on the Mercator projection of the world. A series of crimson lines flowed from the nodes toward one central location, illuminating **Govyadiny Moscava** with a pulsing yellow circle of light.

"Bingo," CJ whispered. "That's the nerve center. Take that facility out and we negate the threat."

Andy held up a palm. "Before we do that, how about trying to hack the place and grab as much code as we can?"

CJ continued to bang the keys. "Way ahead of you, mate. We had better work fast. Looks like things are about to heat up at Moscow Beef."

Andy focused on the video depiction of the city, zooming out to visualize the location of the blue arrow at the top of the screen. A tiny aircraft icon appeared, heading straight for Moscow.

Between the American Embassy and Prokofiev's flashing icon, another image was moving inexorably toward the restaurant.

"That's Officer Clark's team," Andy said, pointing to the plane. "But what's this other icon?"

CJ glanced up from his work only long enough to confirm the ID. "Your friend, Detective Ramirez, seems to be converging on Comrade Prokofiev, too. I'd say she's about five minutes out."

Andy wiggled a finger. "And the blue icon behind her?"

"That's Agent Wright."

MOSCOW

A discrete distance behind the battered van that held Jessica Ramirez captive, a Russian UAZ Hunter tailed an American Embassy vehicle that followed in pursuit.

A plainclothes security guard was behind the wheel. Michael Wright's eyes were on his cell phone screen.

"Yup. She's headed to the lion's den."

The driver concentrated on dodging traffic without losing his target. "I'm sorry about the personal vehicle. Director Taylor insisted on..." he paused to get the words right. "Discretion where his friend, Agent Wright, was concerned."

"No problem here," Michael said. The agility and speed of what felt like a 1970s Jeep clone were impressive. "We're more careful with our own cars in traffic."

The driver nodded in acknowledgment. "If they discarded Detective Ramirez's smartphone, how are you able to track her?"

Michael smiled and thought of his sister. "That extra little blue chromosome," he said. "Jessica is going to slap me silly when I tell her that the necklace I gave her has a GPS beacon embedded in it."

The FBI agent closed his eyes and imagined the loving smile and the bear hugs he got whenever his sister saw him walk in the door.

You truly are a star, Juliette.

Jessica's icon veered to the right.

"Looks like they turned right up ahead," Michael said. "Do you think the other guys still have a visual?"

A Ural Typhoon seemed to appear out of nowhere. The twenty-four-ton armored vehicle sideswiped the embassy car in front of Michael, pressing it to the left and into oncoming traffic. The Chevrolet SUV tried to correct to the right, but it was no match for the battle-hardened military vehicle.

Oncoming cars careened out of the way as the Typhoon continued to press the SUV toward the guardrail that separated the road from the Moscow River. Michael could see a flash at one of the truck's windows. The rear passenger glass on the Chevy shattered, followed almost instantaneously by a thunderous explosion.

The SUV crashed head-on into an oncoming vehicle, becoming an airborne fireball that only extinguished when it splashed into the still-icy water.

AIRBORNE—NORTH OF MOSCOW

2 00 kilometers to go and on schedule.

Alexandra Clark checked the Antonov's progress on the screen of her GPS. She ran through the checklist in her head for the hundredth time.

Fifty kilometers before landing, the aircraft would be at the altitude for the jump. The jump master would emerge from the flight deck and open the long rear ramp. The six of them would debark at roughly eight thousand feet above ground level, higher than the twelve hundred fifty feet required to pass paratrooper jump training but low enough not to require oxygen during descent.

There would be a moment of free-fall before the chutes would automatically deploy.

If all went according to plan, they would land in a field thirty kilometers from the outskirts of Moscow. The embassy would have transportation waiting nearby.

———

ALI STUDIED THE FOUR TEAM MEMBERS GERHARDT had hand-picked for the mission himself.

Check that, the director selected only three. A fourth fell ill hours before departure, and the military hastily provided a replacement.

Ali didn't like that. Cops hated strangers. He didn't know the team's culture and chemistry. But they said he was one of the best. The man was a Russian refugee named Garin, who spoke the language flawlessly and had the same elite skills as his three counterparts.

She studied him in the dim glow of the Antonov's cabin night-lighting. Six feet tall. One hundred ninety-five pounds. All muscle, sinew and bone. Prime beef.

Garin, Ali thought. Her grasp of Russian was minimal. But she knew that Garin translated to the word guardian. But whose guardian was this man?

Garin supposedly knew the area well enough to fill the role of the team geographer. It would be his job to take them directly to The Captain without being detected.

She hoped Garin was up to it.

The public address system in the cargo bay crackled to life. "Five minutes to drop zone."

All six stood at once. Four men who had been sleeping as peacefully as if it were nap time on a Sunday afternoon were fully alert. They turned in pairs to inspect one another's gear.

Ali did the same with Lee. When it was her partner's turn to check Ali out, it impressed her how quickly her UK counterpart had memorized the drill.

Ali resisted the urge to look at the face of her lover. This was a mission that required attention to detail. Ali turned hers to the pros across the cabin. She wanted to make sure she didn't forget something.

As Garin's jump partner tilted his head upward to aid in the inspection, Ali saw the move.

Garin briskly drew his handgun. Placing it under his partner's chin, he pulled the trigger.

Even amid the noise of an uninsulated cabin, the blast stunned Ali. Garin's victim crumpled to the floor, giving him a clear shot at the two other operatives.

He knew the exact locations of exposure where bullet-proof vests met helmets. Garin positioned a pair of slugs in the center of the two other men's necks, shattering the C3 vertebra, killing them almost instantly.

Then, the Russian calmly swung his weapon toward the two women.

By now, both Lee and Ali had deduced the truth. Someone had compromised their mission.

The pair dropped to the deck, rolling away from one another, weapons blazing in Garin's direction.

There was only so much detail a human mind can commit to memory in a short period. The soft spots in Garin's Kevlar were not part of that detail.

Tiny flashes reflected in the darkness as the rounds bounced off the traitor's protective vest.

The flight deck door opened, and the jumpmaster emerged. Unprotected, Garin killed him with a single shot.

Then he turned his attention to Ali, dropping a spent clip and reloading his weapon in one smooth movement.

As if in response to her thoughts, Garin aimed a single round of covering fire in Lee's direction. The detective inspector ducked as the shot flew over her head.

Garin had slowly shifted his position to the back of the aircraft. He leveled a sidekick to the heavy-duty switch that activated the jump ramp, continuing to fire in Ali's direction.

Garin ran toward its edge even before the ramp fully deployed into the buffeting three hundred kilometers slipstream.

Ali could see something in his left hand. His thumb pressed its center, and a tiny orange LED flashed. With the acumen of a major league pitcher, he rocketed the device toward the open door to the flight deck and jumped into the night.

The wind noise was deafening, but there was no need for verbal communication. Ali and Lee sprinted for the ramp, launching their bodies clear of the Antonov seconds before Garin's device detonated.

The aircraft burst into a fiery comet. A trail of red and orange flame consumed the Antonov's flight deck before igniting the kerosine in the wing fuel tanks. The fireball lit up the sky like the midday sun.

Ali imagined the Moscow flight controllers were wondering why the blip on their screens suddenly disappeared. That alone would bring them unwelcome company.

———

LIYANNA EVANS LOOKED AT THE ALTIMETER ON HER right wrist. Her chute would deploy automatically at twelve hundred fifty feet AGL.

The night was clear, and the wind cut through her layers of insulation, chilling her to the bone. She strained to pick out the small LED lights that illuminated the top of Ali's and Garin's helmets. The flashing red dots seemed to converge.

———

Alexandra Clark was furious. Somehow The Captain had inserted a man into the team. His job was to ensure that Ali was killed, another calculated psychological blow to Jessica.

You're pissing me off, tovarishch.

Ali determined that this mission would be Garin's last.

Pressing her arms against her sides, she tilted her body toward the blinking projectile that seemed to get closer with every passing second. Garin was descending spread eagle, preparing for his chute to open.

Her target was slowing. Ali was accelerating.

She found the plunger that disengaged the auto-deploy sequence and hit it. Above the hurricane-force winds, she could hear its squeal.

Ali found the M2 paratroopers switchblade in her vest, pressed the button to flip open the razor-sharp blade and held the weapon in a death grip in her right hand.

She spread her arms seconds before her body collided with Garin's.

The two grappled like a pair of weightless wrestlers. But Garin was stronger. He held Ali in a single-arm bear hug, slamming his left elbow into the soft tissue surrounding her face and neck again and again.

Blood poured from Ali's nose and forehead. She could feel herself losing consciousness.

"Do svidaniya predatel," she barked, thrusting the razor-sharp M2's blade into Garin's carotid artery. She jerked it forward to slice open his windpipe.

So long, traitor.

Garin's grasp softened. Ali pressed a fist against the plunger on his chest to disengage the automatic deployment of his parachute, gently pressing his inert body away from her own.

At exactly twelve hundred fifty feet, Ali pulled her ripcord. The jet-black silk of her own chute blossomed into the night as Ali scanned the vicinity for Lee.

70

FOR THE FIRST TIME IN MY LIFE, I'M TERRIFIED OF LOSING SOMEONE.

Ali felt grateful for the instructor who had taught her how to control a parachute at the Paloma University Skydiving Club. She and Lee landed within fifty meters of one another in the center of a wheat field.

To the south, the lights of the capital city were visible in the distance.

Ali checked her watch. Right on schedule. She pressed a button on the sat phone Andy had given her until she heard a reassuring beep.

"Bollox, girl. What happened to your face?"

Hearing Lee's voice triggered something inside of Ali. Her cop composure crumbled, and she embraced her lover in a viselike hug.

"Just a minor disagreement with that traitor, Garin."

Lee cocked her head to the right. "What's left of him is hanging upside down in that tree over there. Should be an interesting sight for the farmer who runs this place in the morning."

Ali took a breath.

Composure, Alexandra. There was work to do.

She still couldn't bring herself to let go of Lee.

"Our ride should be on its way. Sure hope they get here soon."

Lee pressed Ali back to look her over. "Are you okay?"

Ali contemplated the beautiful brown face, the whites of those exceptional eyes that seemed to light up the night like stars, the warm smile that disarmed Ali and the delicious lips she so wanted to kiss.

"Being in love really sucks."

Lee's eyebrows bent downward in confusion. "Why?"

"For the first time in my life, I'm terrified of losing someone. It's clouding my judgment, big time."

Lee gripped Ali's chin with her hand, shaking it gently. "Rubbish. You're thinking with your twat instead of your head, Alexandra. We're cops. Something bad could happen to either of us any day we go to work. You've lived that life for ten years. So have I. It's what we know, and it's what we both love."

"This is different," Ali said. "They know we're coming. We've lost the advantage of surprise."

Lee could see a single pair of headlights in the distance. Their ride was approaching.

"Maybe not. Those aerial fireworks lit things up for miles around. A little finesse and we might make that short Russian bastard think he killed everyone on board."

Ali could see a flashlight next to the vehicle, now stopped about 200 meters away. Its beam ticked on and off, flashing Morse code for "USA."

Lee put a hand behind Ali's head, pulling their mouths together for one last passionate kiss. "Let's go do that job," Lee said when she finally let her lover go. "And when we're done, we can go back to my flat and ravish the PTSD out of both of us."

71

GOVYADINY MOSCAVA—MOSCOW

Another fucking dental chair? Jessica Ramirez squirmed under the leather straps that bound her arms and legs. *What is it with these Russians? Don't they floss?*

Her eyes adjusted to the dim confines. A row of computer racks surrounded her in a half-circle, filled with CPUs, blinking lights and a whole lot of technology she didn't understand. A tropical beach scene looped on a wall of video monitors that made up a mosaic of color above the racks. The cooling fans and the vast ceiling-mounted air-conditioning unit drowned out most of the ambient noise. But Jess thought she could make out the sounds of people talking behind her. Plates and silverware jangled. Was that a jazz trio playing, too?

She tried to remember the setup at The Maitland Corporation's London headquarters. Something was different. There was no IV. No bag of saline.

"You cost me 500 thousand pounds and one accomplished pilot, Detective."

The voice belonged to the same diminutive man Jess

remembered from London. The tall countenance of Jack Crawford circled within her field of view behind The Captain.

"Vladimir Prokofiev, I presume," Jess said with a bravado she didn't feel. "You know, you could have simply sent me an invitation, and I would have come."

The Captain extended a hand to encompass his computers. "I thought it fitting to show you my little playroom, before I snuff out your insignificant life."

"Strapping a defenseless woman to a dentist's chair isn't exactly good manners, Captain. And do you always monologue before you kill somebody? How well did that work for you in London?"

Prokofiev turned to Crawford. "Was she like this in Nashville?"

Crawford shook his head. "Not quite. But overconfidence is definitely one of her weaknesses."

Jess pressed on. She needed to buy time. "You know why I'm here, guys. Every law enforcement agency in the free world knows you're here, too. If something happens to me, there will be others."

The Captain approached her. He studied Jess's face with the precision of a surgeon, deciding where to make his incision. "I doubt it, Detective. My protectors include the highest political authorities in three countries. I'm surrounded by trusted associates who have sworn to give their own lives to protect mine. And the little restaurant you can hear whispering behind you is simply the public face of an impregnable fortress."

"Overconfidence," Jess said. "You were overconfident with Vega, and you are overestimating yourself again now."

"Am I?" The Captain asked, moving his face close enough so Jess could smell his cologne. "You assume you are not alone. Let me share a little entertainment with you."

The picture on the video wall dissolved into a telephoto shot of a cargo plane flying through the night. "Estonian Air Cargo, Flight 27. Does that mean anything to you?"

Jess was silent, but her eyes were riveted to the scene.

"Your friends Alexandra and Liyanna were aboard that flight tonight."

As Prokofiev said Ali's and Lee's names, the front of the aircraft burst into flames. The headwinds pressed the conflagration toward the rear of the aircraft, igniting the fuel tanks. The entire screen became an orange and red fireball.

The Captain's face took on a mock sadness. "I can confirm that there were no survivors on board."

"Anybody can create a scene like that," Jess challenged. "Your special effects geeks are very good."

The Captain ignored her. "And a certain agent of the Federal Bureau of Investigation attempted to follow you here tonight. You must recognize the American Embassy vehicle."

The screen dissolved into a shot of a flaming Chevrolet that Jess instantly recognized, slowly spinning through the air before smashing, nose first, into the Moscow River.

The Captain shook his head sadly. "I'm afraid that Agent Michael Wright's body will require dental records to confirm his identification."

NORTH OF MOSCOW

our imposing military vehicles passed the Chevrolet SUV, lumbering toward the farm that was Garin's temporary mausoleum.

"Interesting," the Embassy security man behind the wheel murmured. "Those guys are usually more observant, especially when they see a beautiful American-made car with diplomatic plates."

The Chevy felt empty without the four other team members in it. Under other circumstances, Ali and Lee might have been VIP guests.

Ali's mind was clear of the emotion that bubbled over just minutes before. She began reworking the extraction scenario.

"We won't have coverage at the front and back of the building like we thought," she said. "Just two of us against whatever army The Captain has for his personal security."

Lee spoke to the driver. "Any chance we can recruit some Marines to help us out?"

"Sorry, ma'am," he answered. "Our mission is to protect Embassy personnel. It would cause an international incident if American military personnel were found to be involved in violent action in a country with whom we are at peace."

"At peace," Ali muttered. "Another Pearl Harbor is twenty-four hours away. We know it's going to happen. And our own government won't raise a finger to assist."

Lee tried to mitigate the tension. "You're right, sir. We can't ask you to violate orders. But you can give us the benefit of your experience. Our training is primarily responsive. We're trying to break into a highly secure facility with elite forces protecting it. Pulling it off with just six people didn't feel right. Now it's just us two. If you were in our boots, what would you recommend?"

The driver thought for a moment, glancing in his rearview mirror to make sure the Russians weren't following them. A smile slowly creased his face.

"I'm Lance Corporal Todd Mireles, United States Marine Corps. I was a skinny kid. Small for my age. I endured a lot of bullying until I caught up with the rest of my class. You ladies probably know the feeling. Picked on for being perceived as a weakling."

Ali could relate.

"The one thing that kept me going was my comic book collection. Graphic novels were just becoming a thing, and I had a ton of them. Well, you can imagine what happened when the gang found that out. One day I came home from school and they were gone. It was a warm one and we couldn't afford air conditioning, so I left my bedroom window open. The little bastards slipped in, grabbed my stuff, and slipped out."

Ali could see the Marine's cheek twitch. She imagined this was what passed for an emotional reaction in his mind.

"I thought about asking my dad to intervene but knew that would only make things worse. I needed to make the other kids understand I was not someone to be fucked with."

He punctuated the last sentence by pounding a fist on the SUV's dashboard.

"We lived in South Carolina. Fireworks are legal there. The really good ones that make a lot of noise. I broke into my piggy bank and took what amounted to my life savings and bought a big box of M-80s."

The Marine glanced into the mirror to see if this registered with his passengers. It didn't.

"M-80s are basically micro sticks of dynamite. One in every eight kids back home lost fingers to those little jewels. And I had enough to blow up a good-sized building."

Mireles swung the SUV off the highway and onto a dirt road. "We avoid the checkpoints this way. Sorry in advance about the bumpy ride."

He returned to his story.

"Anyway, this gang had a clubhouse. It was a trashed house trailer at an automotive graveyard. You know, the place where you search for junk parts for your car? They slowly built up a mound of abandoned iron and rubber that hid the place pretty well from view. I think the owner knew they were there but decided it was better to placate the little hornets than to rile them up.

"I was certain that this was where they took my stuff. And I hatched a plan. I started blabbing around the school that I just got a super rare Batman comic worth over a hundred bucks from some poor sucker who didn't know its value in a trade. I sprinkled the story with complaints about how we still didn't have AC and how grateful I was that I could leave my windows open. And damn! That day I had forgotten to hide it, and it was just sitting on my bed, asking to be stolen.

"'You should have kept your mouth shut,' one girl told me that afternoon. 'I heard Donnie say that the gang is heading to your house after school to steal your comic book.'

"That was music to my young ears. I told her I had chess club after school. And, of course, she told the other boys about it. That gave me the opening I needed."

Another right turn and the SUV was back on the blacktop, weaving through the matrix of streets toward the target.

"I took my box of fireworks to the junkyard, and damn if there was not a single soul at their clubhouse. Yup, my comic books were there. I dumped my M-80s inside the box. Then I tied everything together, so the stuff connected to a single long fuse. I lit the sucker and ran for my life.

"I still remember the sight. The whole place went up like you see in the cartoons, car parts flying every which way. The concussion broke windows for a block on all sides of the junkyard, and the poor owner's house was on fire."

The driver turned to look at his passengers for a split second. "I made sure nobody was around before I lit the damn thing.

"You know how people love to watch dumpster fires. The boys heard the explosion and came back to see their headquarters and everything they had ever stolen going up in flames. The firetrucks came. So did the cops. And the owner of the place was quick to point out every one of those little shits and signed a complaint for trespassing, theft, you name it.

"Of course, they thought about me and came looking. But I had a few allies who had suffered the bullies' wrath, and when the cops arrived at the school, they all swore that I was there playing chess the whole time."

Ali was growing impatient. They were nearing their target. "Is there a point to this reminiscence, sir?"

"A diversion, ma'am. You need something to draw Comrade Prokofiev's men away from him."

The Marine's face broke into a grin. "And that, my dears, is something I can help you with."

GOVYADINY MOSCAVA—MOSCOW

S*o, this was it. The Captain wanted her to see what else he could take away from her before he took her life.*

Rage flowed through every pore of Jessica Ramirez's body. Everything, every plan, every instinct had gone horribly wrong. First her father, then her best friend, and now the man that might well have been the love of her life.

That box in her mind where she shoved a lifetime of suffering was bursting at the seams. The little girl in Jess wanted to let it blow open. Crying felt good back then. It was a healthy release. Jess knew the reason women lived longer than men was because culture dictated that it was okay to cry.

Women cried. Got their shit together and kept on living the realities of second-class citizens. Jess had fought that stereotype her entire life. Men, like her father, had to sublimate it all. Never show weakness or get exploited. All of that repression eventually had to find an outlet. Heart attacks and alcoholism were the most common in the cop ranks. But suicide statistics were also on the rise.

Jess always wondered what could possess a person to end it all. Despite her training and her reflexive ability to talk anyone off the ledge, she could never fathom going willingly into the darkness.

Until now.

"Oh." The Captain raised a finger as if he had forgotten something trivial. "One more thing, Detective. I have associates in Cancun. I expect news shortly about the fates of three women there who you know well."

Jess saw Crawford's eyebrows raise. She couldn't tell if it was surprise or admiration for how Prokofiev had carefully played his systematic destruction of everything Jess held dear.

"You bastard," Jess growled. "Does it feel good to step on one small fish who destroyed your big plans in New York?"

The bravado tied a string around the edges of that bulging box of PTSD in her head.

"And Vega. That was a good recruit. Sure, she had some skills, but all it took was a couple of undergrad gamers and a small-town computer nerd cop to smash your big plan to bits."

She noticed the tiniest flinch on The Captain's face after that last remark.

Focus, Jess. You're buying time for the good guys to get here… if there are any good guys left.

Jess widened her gaze to include Jack Crawford.

"What is it with guys like you? Were you abused children? Didn't get enough love from daddy? Something to prove to the schoolyard bullies and a world that constantly reminds you how weak you truly are?"

Her eyes drilled into Crawford's. "De Triste. Italian for 'a man of sadness.' More likely a man of weakness. What true Italian would betray his wife's trust to the point where she wants to send him to jail?"

Jess bit off each word. She spat them at Crawford and The Captain. "You two aren't heroes. You're not even men. Your people don't respect you. The thin threads of fear you use to control them will snap the moment they can betray you."

The slap across the face that Jess expected came, but not from Crawford. It was Prokofiev. His palm was a large, callused piece of plywood connected to a tiny body.

Jess's head snapped to the left as the blow came. She could feel the tiny necklace jump. "Small man syndrome," Jess growled. "Does hitting a girl make you feel powerful?" The sting felt good. Jess had long since learned to transform the daily slights and outright hatred she received from her fellow officers into the fuel that fired her desire to win.

She'd delayed whatever The Captain had planned for her. Could she keep it up?

———

THE TALL AMERICAN SMILED AT THE HOSTESS. "How many?" she asked in flawless English.

"There will be two of us. I'm meeting someone. Is it possible to sit near the cooking area? She likes the show."

The hostess nodded. Her customer knew she could tell he was with the Embassy. That was good. She would assume he had real money. And the Americans tipped well.

Lance Corporal Todd Mireles settled into a booth with a perfect view of the proceedings. A burly waitress materialized. Her command of his language wasn't as good. "A drink for the gentleman while he waits for his companion?" she asked.

The Marine could easily make out the print of a handgun behind her apron. Her smile seemed genuine. Her eyes told a different story. She was assessing the threat.

"Kvasya, please," he said, ordering the oldest and most famous Russian cocktail. Thirty-five milliliters of kvass, ten milliliters of vodka and five milliliters of cinnamon syrup. Even for a man who preferred a Dos Equis, this was a treat. "And one for my lady. I expect her momentarily."

The waitress nodded. She would report his presence to her boss.

———

DESPITE ALI'S PROTESTS, LIYANNA EVANS HAD WON the argument. Alexandra's bruised face would attract attention, even in the low light of the restaurant. Sure, Lee was black and black people were still relatively rare in Moscow. But the American Embassy was like everything else back home. Diversity and inclusion were part of the culture at every American outpost. She would draw stares, but everyone would conclude that she fit the profile.

Lee waved at her date, gesturing to the hostess that she knew where to go. The woman behind the podium smiled, gesturing toward the man seated and smiling by the open kitchen.

"Don't you look lovely, Ms. Evans," Mireles said. "Where on earth did you find that beautiful coat?"

Lee grinned at the Marine who knew about M-80s and diversions.

"Oh… It's just something I found lying around," Lee answered, fingering the full-length garment that fully obscured her black-ops uniform. She picked up the cocktail and leaned in for a toast. "Did you have to kill the guy to get it?"

Mireles shook his head. "Not quite. He'll wake up with quite the headache. Did Officer Clark disconnect the fire control systems in the alley?"

Lee nodded as glasses clinked, and she took a sip of the drink. "What made you change your mind? For a soldier who follows orders, you're a little too deeply involved in this diversion thing?"

"The guy with your FBI friend out back? He's my gunnery sergeant. I guess he must have gotten new orders."

MI6—London

Two thousand eight hundred seventy-seven miles away, CJ Riemer grinned at the blue flat screen on the wall of his lab at MI6.

"Got it all. Every last data byte is locked in our own little secure sandbox for future analysis… And I made one tiny modification."

Andy Milluzzi cocked his head. "Which is?"

CJ twirled a finger, pointing at a set of numbers on the screen. "I changed a few IP addresses and injected a couple of new commands into the system. If The Captain pulls the trigger, he'll get a little surprise."

Govyadiny Moscava—Moscow

Lee drained the Kvasya with a second gulp.

"Let's not keep Detective Ramirez waiting," she said.

The Marine produced a classic Zippo. He held it out of sight next to the long granite island that separated the diners from the culinary show on the other side. "I've never smoked a cigarette in my life," he said, "but there's no telling when you might need a reliable flame to light a fuse."

His thumb twirled the black flint wheel, creating a spark that ignited the lighter-fluid-soaked wick. "I'll miss this old girl. She's the longest relationship I've ever had."

Lance Corporal Todd Mireles winked at Lee. "Showtime?"

Lee liked this guy. She hoped he wouldn't be dead in the next few minutes.

"Showtime," she repeated.

The Marine tossed the flaming lighter toward the deep fryer and studied the two men guarding the door at the back of the restaurant.

———

Behind that door, Vladimir Prokofiev approached his prey. "In time, science provides an antidote to every poison, a worm that can defang any technology."

His eyes were ice cold, his face expressionless. "The way to be sure you have destroyed the threat is to do it with your own hands."

The Captain produced a revolver. It was a twin of the gargantuan RSH-12 Jess used to shoot out the helicopter turbines in the skies over London.

The Captain placed the long barrel of the gun against Jess's temple. "Your usefulness is at an end," he whispered. Spinning around, Prokofiev aimed the weapon at Jack Crawford's chest. "Say hello to your wife, Signor De Triste."

The concussion from the revolver deafened Jess. Crawford didn't have time to react before the slug pierced the upper right quadrant of his chest, mushrooming on entry, ripping a heart--long devoid of compassion--apart.

Giovanni de Triste pressed his hands against the wound. His eyes widened as the oxygenated blood no longer flowed to his brain. The man Jess knew as Jack Crawford fell backward. He was dead before he hit the floor.

The Captain put the smoking weapon on the small circular table module that was the control center for his server farm, returning his focus to Jess.

The powerful hand that slapped Jess's face had a brother. Jess could feel thick fingers encircle her neck.

"The best revenge is suffocation," Prokofiev said, slowly tightening his vise-like grasp. "The best death is dispatched with bare hands."

Alarms wailed in the restaurant. The door to the server room opened, and a bodyguard shouted something in Russian.

"Ogon!"

Even without knowing a word of the language, Jess could smell the translation.

"Fire!"

74

I ALMOST SHOT YOUR ASS.

Alexandra Clark pressed open the restaurant door, firing at anyone who remotely looked like they were carrying a weapon.

Lee took out the waitress and the bartenders, ducking as the two bodyguards by the rear door to Prokofiev's lair unloaded their clips in her direction.

The Marine's aim had the practiced reflexiveness of a professional. He double-tapped the two guards. Lee noted his surprise to discover that neither wore bulletproof vests.

The flames from the burning fryer oil licked the ceiling tiles. Without the automated extinguishers, the entire building was at risk of becoming an inferno.

Diners surged toward the exits. Ali could feel the sting return to her injured shoulder. Spinning around to find the threat, she saw the diminutive hostess standing in a firing stance, a tiny semi-auto in her hand.

"Everywhere I go, there are guns," Ali exclaimed, shooting the attractive brunette between the eyes.

She was grateful for the small caliber of the weapon

and the hostess's poor aim. The slug only grazed her shoulder. She was still in the fight.

———

The C5 plastic explosive that Michael Wright attached to the back door of Govyadiny Moscava detonated. The concussion echoed down the alleyway.

Michael and his Marine partner shouldered through the door and ran down the hallway toward the gunfire at the front of the building.

Michael found Lee and Ali undoing the leather straps from around Jessica's arms and legs. At that moment, he wanted only to embrace Jessica and never let her go.

But Jessica was already on the run toward a hole in the ground surrounded by uprooted computer-floor tiles. "He's down there," she shouted as she disappeared into the escape hatch.

Michael wanted to follow. Ali stopped him.

"We don't know how much time we have, Michael. Help us rig this server room for demolition."

Michael hesitated.

"Let her do this," Ali commanded, pulling Gerhardt's suicide detonator from behind her Kevlar. "It has to be her."

———

Jessica Ramirez slid down the long steel ladder that seemed to have no end. The darkness that enveloped her slowly merged into light as a cement platform came into view below.

Jess found herself at one end of a long subway platform. A nearly deserted metro train was pulling out of the station. Inside, she could see the dark countenance of Vladimir Prokofiev staring back at her.

Jess ran to the far end of the platform, launching her body toward the last car. She snagged a handrail and hung on as the train gained speed.

Before wrapping her other arm around the support, she felt for the reassuring bulk of the RSH-12 pressed between her belt and her back. It surprised her that her abductor did not take it with him.

Never leave your weapon unattended, Captain. Bad things can happen.

The door to the last car was locked. Not a soul was inside. No amount of effort on Jess's part could budge the damn thing.

Jess mentally computed the distance from her location to the car that held her target. She climbed toward the roof of the train and began crawling forward.

———

GOVYADINY MOSCAVA ERUPTED IN A BRILLIANT RED mushroom cloud. Ali and Lee watched the drive-in movie scene through the back window of the Embassy's Chevrolet SUV as the heat consumed several other parked cars nearby. "That's the last time I use my personal vehicle at work," the gunnery sergeant muttered as his UAZ Hunter exploded.

Michael Wright grinned. "You needed an upgrade, anyway. I'll speak to my superiors about it. You only have to do one more thing for me to earn it."

The senior Marine waited for orders. "The Metro runs under that building," Michael said. "Where is the next stop?"

———

VLADIMIR PROKOFIEV WAS ALREADY PLANNING HIS next project. He may have lost this server farm, but he could build others. The software lived in the cloud. Perhaps his servers should, too. Much harder to disable and easy to move if discovered.

The Group of Three would not be pleased with this second failure. But The Captain was more than just a survivor. He was a visionary. Every attempt bracketed his fire. The next time, he would hit the target.

The gun blast made The Captain flinch. Glass across from his seat shattered, and a body vaulted into the carriage. He recognized the face and ran toward the rear of the train.

———

DESPITE HER DESIRE TO KILL VLADIMIR PROKOFIEV, Jess entertained the idea of bringing him in alive. Her single combat with Vega in the Colorado River had revealed the unexpected emptiness of revenge. And perhaps what was in The Captain's brain would be valuable to Director Gerhardt and his team of inquisitors in London.

She thought of all of this as she sprinted behind her quarry. His legs were shorter, which made him a faster runner. But Jess knew there would be another station ahead, and the train was only so long.

Their own single combat was inevitable.

———

"WE'RE NOT GOING TO THE EMBASSY?"

Ali knew her directions from studying the maps. The SUV's abrupt turn to the right confused her.

"You're getting out of the country now," Michael said. "Armed, no passports, no visas. If you're caught, you'll end up in some gulag for the rest of your lives."

"I suddenly prefer the peaceful life of a detective inspector in London," Lee said.

"There are fresh clothes and documents in the back of the vehicle," Michael said as the young Marine who knew about M-80s and revenge accelerated toward the airport. "You'll have to change on the fly. I hope you're not modest."

"You better hope the authorities haven't connected any dots," Ali barked as she ripped off her Kevlar. "Or we'll all be shot."

Michael was glued to his cell phone. "Okay, guys. Let me out at the Metro stop up ahead. Time to go rescue the love of my life."

Ali guffawed. "Watch yourself, cowboy. Or you'll be the one to need rescuing."

———

THE LENGTH OF THE METRO TRAIN TURNED OUT TO be longer than Jess had calculated. She also expected it to stop, but the carriages only slowed as they lumbered through what looked like a deserted station.

Prokofiev still had about a thirty-foot lead, giving him valuable seconds to press the emergency release for the rear car door.

As it slid open, Jess dove to tackle him.

The detective and her prey tumbled out of the train and onto the tracks next to the abandoned Troitse-Lykovo Metro Station. Originally meant to be a fully functional terminal, they altered construction plans when the structure above was deemed a historic landmark. Jess and The Captain found themselves between the rails, next to the twenty-six-meter platform, the shortest in the Moscow Metro System.

The fall knocked the wind out of both adversaries but only for a moment. Jess was first on her feet. Shaking the cobwebs from her consciousness, she reached for the revolver beneath her belt when she felt the upper-cut.

The gun flew from her hand and bounced out of the field of play. The Captain's powerful fist sent her reeling within inches of the dangerous yellow third rail and its deadly eight hundred twenty-five volts of direct current.

Jess found her footing and grabbed a turpentine can painters had left on the platform, smashing it against The Captain's face. The chemical drenched him. She could see tears form in his burning eyes. The stench from the fumes permeated the tunnel.

It did nothing to diminish Prokofiev's fury.

A flailing backspin kick caught Jess in the face, and she went down again.

She knew that The Captain would press his advantage. He was on top of Jess in an instant. His thick fists were again encircling her throat. "This is the last time you will interfere with my plans," he snarled.

Jess could feel her consciousness slipping away. The lack of oxygen sapped her strength. As the veil of death descended, she again heard her father's voice, talking to a sixteen-year-old girl about to go on her first date.

"A man's weakness is between his legs. If you ever feel in danger, kick him so hard that he will remember it for the rest of his life."

With the last of her strength, she thrust a knee upward. The Captain screamed. His hands let go, and he tried to stand, but the shock of the blow put him off balance. He stumbled, catching a heel in the station side rail. He tumbled toward the platform. His head scored a direct hit on the yellow power conduit.

The Captain's body completed the circuit. It stiffened as the electricity coursed from head to toe. Blood vessels ruptured. He froze in mid-scream. Red rivulets flowed from terrified eyes. A flame spurted from the connection point on The Captain's skull, igniting the turpentine fumes. All that was mortal of Vladimir Prokofiev was consumed in smoke and fire, leaving a charred human hulk that no doctor or dentist would ever decipher.

Jess's mind flickered back to Nashville's death chamber and the innocent man who had suffered a similar fate. But once again, there was no victory in vengeance. The Captain's death couldn't bring Vincent and Marie Culpado back to life. Nor could it resurrect Jess's father. Her only consolation was that each had made their own bargain with fate. Nothing she did could protect them.

In the end, we alone are responsible for the choices that lead us toward destiny.

She thought about the grief counselor's callous admonition that, "We can never go back to what was. We can build a life with what remains."

There were footsteps in the stairwell. Jess limped toward the revolver as the crescendo of sound grew. Despite the pain, she spread her legs into a shooting stance, raising the weapon into firing position.

"Jessica?" Michael Wright was smart enough to call her name before popping his head from behind the safety of the thick tiled stairwell.

Jess rolled her eyes and lowered the gun. "Jesus, Michael, I almost shot your ass."

———

MICHAEL STUDIED JESSICA'S BRUISED AND BATTERED body. He noted the short bursts of breath and exhaustion in her eyes.

He broke into a grin, shaking his head as he noted the smoke rising from the blackened corpse that had once been Vladimir Prokofiev. "You, my love, are the most beautiful thing I have ever seen."

Jessica exhaled, rolling her eyes. "Men. Let's get the hell out of here before I throw up."

75

SHEREMETYEVO—A.S. PUSHKIN
INTERNATIONAL AIRPORT,
MOSCOW

T he American Ambassador met the two travelers as the Embassy SUV pulled up to the airport. Two men in Marine flight suits stood on either side of the diplomat. Armed Russian security guards stood at a distance, watching.

"Ladies!" he said with amplified enthusiasm. "I'm so glad I could be here to see you off. Are you ready for some adventure?"

Alexandra Clark and Liyanna Evans could have passed for two embassy staffers. The pantsuits they wore fit perfectly. Matching backpacks were filled with a second set of civilian clothing, hiking maps, and a few gift-wrapped trinkets.

The bruises on Ali's face were the only thing that drew unwanted attention.

The ambassador put a hand on her shoulder. "When you return from vacation, I want to hear more about that nasty fall. They did not make those steps at the museum for stiletto shoes, young lady."

Ali shot a glance at Lee. "But it was so worth it, sir. I

wish you could have seen what we've seen during our time in Moscow."

The ambassador stifled a chuckle. "Perhaps I will."

He turned to the two Marine pilots. "Now, gentlemen, do you think you can still fly that helicopter after all the free time you've had since the end of the air show?"

A Marine who had the bearing of a flight captain saluted. "Yes, sir, she's all fueled up and ready." He turned to the women. "Ladies. Let's move through passport control and board. We are approaching departure time."

—————

"WHAT HAPPENED TO YOUR FACE?"

The muscular Russian at passport control frowned at the black and blue marks on the American woman's forehead and neck. There was something familiar about her, but he couldn't place it.

"I'm such a ditz!" she said, "I wore high heels to the museum and fell down those one hundred and eighteen steps when we left. My mother is going to give me the dickens when I get home."

The Russian studied her passport, "Rachel Hermann. Jewish?" The tone in his voice was not flattering.

"Kosher in every way, sir." Ali slipped her arm around Lee's back. "All are welcome in the Land of the Free. We have weekly presentations at the American Center if you would like to learn more about our inclusive culture."

The Russian handed the woman her passport and shook his head. "I've been to one. Unimpressive."

"Excuse me, ladies," the man in the Marine flight suit said. "We have an aircraft carrier to meet in the Baltic, and we'll need to depart on time if we're to catch her."

The Russian waved them through, and the four travelers walked toward the metal detectors. His mind returned to the report about an explosion near the river. He knew the address and wondered if the woman they assigned him to abduct and deliver was inside the building when it went up.

THE AMERICAN EMBASSY— MOSCOW

Tom Anastos was sitting up. The Embassy physician stood by, stunned and confused. Nobody recovered from Novichok poisoning that quickly.

Anastos wasn't about to tell him about the searing pain that still wracked his body, the effort it still took to breathe, and the heart palpitations that would set off looks of concern at every physical examination he would have for the rest of his life.

The morning sun streamed through the windows. It truly felt like a new day dawning.

Tom Anastos would prevail. He always had, since that day on the ice. And he always would.

"Can the patient have visitors?"

Tom recognized the feminine voice and grinned as Michael and Jessica entered his makeshift hospital room.

"Well," Jessica said, putting her hands on her hips, "I guess you're harder to kill than Jack Crawford thought."

Tom's voice still bore the weight of the proximity with which he had come to death. "That was Crawford's idea?"

Jessica nodded. "Yeah. I was hoping to keep him alive so you could have the pleasure of returning the favor, but The Captain shot him dead before I could intervene."

Anastos considered the detective. Freshly showered and dressed in casual clothing, she was a beauty. But he knew her story. Behind the mask was a survivor. It was likely her quick thinking that had saved his life. And Tom Anastos always paid his debts.

"I guess that makes two things I owe you for," he said.

Jessica looked perplexed.

"You diagnosed the poison on the spot. That probably helped me live to fight another day. And I know that, in your own way, you contributed to the retribution that Mr. Crawford so richly deserved. How can I return the favor?"

Jessica approached the bed, kissing the commander on the forehead. "Unnecessary. My playtime is over. There's a small-time crime boss still running around in Illinois, and I'm ready to go hook him up to some steel bracelets."

Agent Michael Wright held up a hand. "That might not be as easy as you think, Jessica. Director Taylor tells me that Crouch bolted for Brazil. He's working on citizenship there, and they never extradite their own."

Jessica kept her gaze on the commander. "Well then. Perhaps a trip south is in order. We Latinas can handle Portuguese with ease." She looked at her iWatch. "Gotta go, Commander. It's gonna take two weeks and some diplomatic tap dancing to get out of this damn country. Thanks for everything."

––––––––

THIS TIME SHE KISSED ANASTOS ON THE MOUTH, A long probing kiss that reminded him of a fitness fanatic he knew back in London. He would have to do something about that relationship when he got home.

Anastos could sense that the kiss had its intended effect on Michael Wright. His face said he didn't like it one bit.

Jess whispered in Tom Anastos's ear. It was purposely loud enough for Michael to hear. "I know you were always looking out for my best interests."

Tom Anastos nodded as she backed away, waving as her exquisite form bounced ahead of Michael and toward her future.

"I always will," he called after her, idea forming in his mind.

77

GUILIN—CHINA: TWO WEEKS LATER

The Group of Three sat together in the lobby of the Banyan Tree, Guilin's most sought-after five-star hotel. The low mountains of Yangzhou looked like black soap bubbles, cast against the orange sunset in the west.

Whenever the group met there, the resort canceled all other bookings. Only the massive security detail inhabited the sumptuous accommodations. The resort, set in a rural area of China, was easy to guard. It was a coveted assignment.

News channels from around the world whispered on the large screens placed with Feng Shui care in the lobby. But the three men barely paid attention.

To an untrained eye, they looked like tourists, casually dressed, cocktails in hand.

The Chinese oligarch host sighed. He thought about his comments to the governors at the G8 summit. Today's news reported the American economy would, in fact, exceed expectations this year.

"Another failure for Prokofiev," he murmured.

"His last," the Russian grunted.

The Indian billionaire took off his Ray-Ban sunglasses, folding them behind the top button of a Hawaiian shirt that would have better suited a Western tourist than a short, thin businessman.

"The Americans are more resourceful than we expected," he said. "When their children can neutralize weaponized technology, that bodes well for their future."

"Perhaps stability is the best policy," said the host. His compatriots nodded in affirmation. "For now…"

As he said the words, the power at the resort flickered. When the half-dozen flat screens came back on, they broadcast a single image. It was a video of Whitney Houston singing the final stanza of the American National Anthem at the 1991 Super Bowl.

"Oh, say does that star-spangled banner yet wave? O'er the land of the free and the home of the brave."

"MI6," the Russian scowled.

The Indian smiled. "Well played, CJ. Well played."

78

RIO DE JANEIRO—BRAZIL: THE
NEXT DAY

The Hilton Rio de Janeiro Copacabana, Crouch concluded, wasn't an awful place to hide out until his Brazilian Citizenship and protection from extradition back to the United States came through.

He didn't have his usual bodyguards, but the small-time, Midwestern crime lord felt safe and sound. As far as anyone knew, he was still somewhere in Illinois. And he still had soldiers there, sworn to do his bidding. It would be a matter of time until they carried out his orders regarding Detectives Harrison and Ramirez and that damned district attorney.

Crouch surveyed the target-rich environment at the hotel pool. Which beautiful young lady would be his guest for dinner and rough sex tonight?

Damn, he wanted a cigarette. They only allowed vaping at the pool, and his nicotine addiction was strangling him. Perhaps that was what drew his attention to the sun-drenched man, stretched out on the reclining chair next to his.

Mirrored sunglasses hid the guy's eyes. He was probably counting the number of boob jobs languishing in the sunshine. A broad hat protected his head from the sunshine, almost covering his face. A thin white bathrobe, surfer swim trunks, and flip-flops completed the ensemble of someone who was clearly another American tourist.

But what held Crouch's attention was the vaporizer the man was inhaling. The bouquet was irresistible. Crouch's keen sense of smell detected menthol, cinnamon, and a hint of THC in the blend.

"Smells great," Crouch said to his neighbor.

"The best," the man said, not moving a muscle, except to take another long pull off the vape pen.

"No cigs allowed out here," Crouch griped. "I guess I have to find a smoke shop and get me one of those."

The other man snaked a hand into the pocket of his robe. "Your lucky day. My wife was supposed to join me down here. But she decided to go spend my money instead. This is hers. Loaded and ready. It would make her angry if I gave it away."

The man held out an identical vaporizer, exhaling another bouquet of nicotine toward Crouch's flaring nostrils.

"You sure it won't get you in trouble?" Crouch didn't care. But decorum required one more question.

The man was still motionless. Relaxed. It must be the THC. "It absolutely will, which is why I make the offer."

Crouch proffered a hand, and the man passed the vape over. "They say this stuff can kill you," the man said, at last turning his mirrored sunglasses toward his neighbor. "But sometimes a short life is better than a long life."

Crouch thought about the many lives he had shortened. He adjusted the pen and inhaled its contents. The mixture of nicotine and the active ingredient in cannabis gave him a warm glow.

Crouch held up his cocktail. "Here's to a short life."

The man in the reflective glasses smiled, taking another pull off his pen. "To a short life."

Crouch wanted more. He sucked on the vaporizer, again and again, slowly feeling a nap coming on. His arms felt limp, and Crouch found it harder and harder to inhale the mixture.

The other man stood and surveyed his neighbor's diminishing breath sounds. "Perhaps a snooze before I pick out a babe for tonight," Crouch slurred. "Maybe I'll see you at the bar."

The vape pen fell from Crouch's hand. The gentle rhythm of his heartbeat against his carotid artery slowed.

His neighbor pocketed the device, turning toward the hotel.

"No, Mr. Crouch. You won't."

———

COMMANDER THOMAS ANASTOS FELT THE VIBRATION and scanned the screen on his cell phone.

LAST OF C'S NETWORK ARRESTED. HOPE YOU ARE ENJOYING RIO. HARRISON.

That would be Lou Harrison, the portly detective from Paloma, Illinois. Tom had heard that the guy could be pretty vindictive when someone made him angry.

The commander tossed both vaporizers into the mechanical trash compactor by the entrance to the hotel. He looked up at the sunny afternoon sky.

"Thanks for the Bergulon, Vega. You did something good, after all."

OVER THE BALTIC SEA—28,000 FEET AGL

The flat-screen GPS in the passenger cabin of the Gulfstream G650 pinged as the jet cleared Russian airspace. Gerhardt had worked his magic. Jess and Michael's ride home belonged to one of America's richest dot com zillionaires: outfitted with satellite communications, a fully stocked bar, even a queen-size bed at the back of the sumptuous cabin.

The detective and the FBI agent sat across from one another in Corinthian leather seats. Besides the two-man crew, they were the only passengers on a flight that would take them non-stop from Moscow to Washington.

Directors Gerhardt and Taylor had pulled every string to get the pair out of the country. "The opulence of the transportation," Gerhardt said, "was the least we could do for all you have done for us."

The pilot's voice crackled on the intercom. "Incoming call for you, Detective Ramirez."

The video screen morphed from displaying the flight's position to the interior of Detective Inspector Liyanna

Evans's flat in London. She and Ali were there, wine glasses in hands, grinning at the extravagance.

"I save humanity and get fish and chips," Ali laughed. "You two take a Russian vacation and get the royal treatment. There's something wrong with the world."

Jess pursed her lips. "What are you still doing there, Alexandra? Play time's over. We're supposed to report back to work on Monday."

Ali shot a prurient glance at Lee. "I decided to burn a little more vacation and check out the UK job market." She pinched her partner in the ribs. "I kinda like the scenery."

"Any blowback from your boss, DI Evans?" Michael asked.

Liyanna blushed. "A commendation from the queen. But no promotion and no raise. When an American freestyles outside of her jurisdiction, she gets a private jet. I'm back in the research section on Monday."

Jess chuckled. "Thanks for everything, Lee. I wish you two could be here with us now."

Ali choked on her wine. "No, you don't. I can see that bed behind you. Four is definitely a crowd up there." Jess's partner glanced away from the screen for an instant. "The clock says we'll lose the satellite connection in about a minute. Come see us the next time you're in London."

"I'll see you in Paloma next week, Alexandra. Who else can I trust to pull my chestnuts out of the fire?"

The connection flickered. The moving map returned to the screen, nine hours and fifty-five minutes until touchdown.

"That wine looks pretty good," Jess said, rising from her chair and inspecting the alcohol inventory. "Want some?"

Michael joined Jess at the bar. "I think we've seen

enough red for three lifetimes," he said. "How about some Pinot Grigio?"

When the glasses were full, the FBI agent sat on the edge of the bed, an overt invitation that appealed to Jess. She settled next to him. "A toast," she said, "to building with what remains."

Michael clinked his glass with hers and drank. "I've been thinking. The last time we were alone like this, I was in the hospital asking you to marry me. Why didn't you answer?"

Jess rolled her eyes. "You were stoned out of your mind, Michael Wright. We both knew the timing wasn't right."

Michael's smile was disarming. Jess could feel its warmth surround her. He slipped a hand in his pocket, retrieving a small square box.

"How about now?" Gliding down on one knee, Michael flipped it open to reveal a glittering diamond ring. "Jessica Ramirez, you can live the rest of your life in Paloma, Illinois, Washington, London, or Timbuktu. But I can't live the rest of my life without you in it."

Jess's eyes widened. She started to speak, but Michael held up a hand. "I wasn't in my right mind in that hospital in Phoenix. But I am now. Neither one of us knows what the future may bring. But whatever that future is, let's live it as husband and wife."

Michael placed the open box in the palm of his hand and held it up. The rays of the afternoon sun reflected off the diamond's facets, painting prisms on Jess' face.

Jess put a hand on each side of the collar of Michael 's shirt, drawing him toward her. She probed his mouth with a delectable kiss that made them both hungry for more.

"Marry me, Jess," Michael said, his voice just above a whisper.

Jess responded in her sexiest voice. But her answer was anything but alluring. "You saved my life, Michael. But you also put both Ali and me in danger. As usual, you knew more than you told us. You were ahead of me every step of the way. And the necklace," she fingered the beautiful star that still hung from her neck. "Even that had a secret you didn't share. Did you think I'd ditch it if I knew it was a GPS locator?"

"You probably would have," Michael admitted.

"If this is going to work, we can't have secrets."

Michael's expression darkened. "Secrets come with the job. There are some things I can never share. You know that."

"It's all or nothing, Michael. If we are going to link our two families, the best interest of the team must come first. I'm not a pawn on your chess board. If we do this thing, I have to be your Queen."

"Queen before country?" Michael asked.

Jess shook her head. "Family First."

She watched as Michael pondered all she had said. The wheels were turning, but this time, he wasn't a step ahead of her. She began to wonder if her demands were fair to this man who was willing to do whatever it took to win her love.

Michael's eyes narrowed. She knew that meant he had made a decision.

"Perhaps a test drive is in order. Tell you what. Let's do what we did that night in DC. Let's act the part before we commit to it. Wear my ring. Try me out as a husband and I'll try you out as a wife. Do Catholics still go to hell if they live in sin before marriage?"

Jess couldn't surprise a smile. "We're both already headed in that direction, cowboy. And by the way, you'll have to convert."

"Who said I wasn't Catholic?"

This surprised Jess. "You are? What about the divorce."

"Annulled. I took my sister to the Vatican to help me get it approved. Juliette loves The Pope."

Jess felt a tiny twinge of excitement. *Another sister in the family. Maria and Mamacita will love that.*

Michael stroked her cheek. "Maybe you're right, Jessica. There are a lot of things we'll only discover about each other if we try this out first. I'll commit to your.." She thought he was going to say "demands," but he didn't.

"Your priorities. And you'll have the chance to better understand mine. If it doesn't work, we walk away with broken hearts. If there's a consensus that is the true love we both think it is, we'll do it up right. A wedding that celebrates two individuals, two cultures, coming together to create a new entity, stronger and more amazing than we could ever build alone."

Michael took Jess' left hand and slid the diamond on her ring finger. She didn't stop him.

"Whadaya say, Jess? Got the cujones to risk it all for love?"

"I'm still a little uncertain." Jessica Ramirez pulled Michael Wright on top of her, their bodies sinking into the plush mattress. She shot a glance at the countdown clock. "You've got nine hours and forty-seven minutes to convince me."

THE END

ACKNOWLEDGMENTS

This one took a long time to write. Between navigating the pandemic and stumbling into several other priority projects, "Jess 2.0" took shape more slowly than I would have liked.

But good things come to those who persevere. It was my fellow author, the talented Kate Anslinger, who challenged me to the daily word count duel that brought the project over the finish line. Kate writes great stuff! Look her up and give it a taste.

Dawn Alexander's sense for my strengths and weaknesses made this a much better story than it was before her magical eyes focused on it. Joan Turner's editor's pen transforms many of my bad habits into something readable.

About the cast…

Mo Gerhardt is a real person. He's not with MI6, but he lives exactly as I've described him. Check out his autobiographical *Perspective From An Electric Chair.* You'll discover what a real hero he truly is.

Same goes for CJ Riemer. We each come into the world with our own set of tools, and CJ always amazes me with how he uses his. I thought he'd love channeling a younger version of Ian Fleming's *Q*.

Andy Milluzzi is a true wizard. We're ham radio buddies, and the thought processes his character exhibits in *Chasing The Captain* are exactly how I'd expect him to react if this tale were real.

Tom Anastos has spent his life pursuing his hockey passion. His accomplishments are too numerous to mention here, but he would make a great MI6 agent, too.

Terry Taylor is also a real person. We played drums together in junior high back in the 1960s. After fifty years of friendship, I reward him with a bit part and not a starring role? What kind of friend am I?

Liyanna Evans is a composite of several women I admire. Author Louise Dawn, a South African by birth, gave me the name and some Lee's spice. Her other inspiring contributors prefer anonymity. But you know who you are.

Alexandra Clark also is a delightful mix of many of awesome people. Shelley Appelbaum gave Ali her name. The courage and love my LGBTQ friends express in a world where so much prejudice against people with differences still exists breaks my heart. They inspire me to contribute to positive change in some small way. I hope Ali's star shines brightly in that direction.

There are many "Easter Eggs" in the story, little nods to people who have been instrumental in my growth as a writer and a person. See if you can find them.

I have been blessed with a plethora of generous advisers within the law enforcement community on both sides of the Atlantic. Research for *Chasing The Captain* deepened friendships and gave me a greater appreciation for the sacrifices these dedicated men and women make to keep us safe.

And then, there are my beta readers and support team. The writing community is filled with cheerleaders, and I'm blessed with the best. Thank you, Dänna Wilberg, Stephie Walls, Danielle Girard, Eve Elliot, Pam Stack, Kerry Schafer, Kay Hutcherson, Heather Graham, Tori Eldridge, Boyd Morrison, D.P. Lyle, Lee Goldberg and many others who have been immensely helpful as I continue to learn the craft.

My kids, Shelby and Brandon, aren't kids anymore. With their soulmates and progeny, they give me faith in the future.

The star necklace that Michael gives Jess in Washington, DC is real. My talented daughter-in-law, Stephanie Vutera Westerman, designed it, and you can buy it as a necklace or lapel pin.

It celebrates my granddaughter, Juliette, who came to us with Down syndrome and reminds me every day of the treasures to be found when you take life on the scenic route. Her brother, Hudson, is exactly the kind of kid that Jess and Michael might create, if they ever quit fooling around and get married.

Finally, every good thing that has happened to me I owe to the two most important women in my life. My sister, Judy Westerman-Silver, died around the time *Chasing Vega* was published. A long-time book nut and respected publicist, my sister is still with me in spirit as I try to channel her gifts as I distill my books into blurbs and sound-bytes.

Anyone who knows us will tell you that my forty-four-year love affair with my beautiful Colleen would make a great romance novel. I marvel at how it's possible to care about someone more with each passing year. I would never have become an author without her constant support.

And most of all, thank you, dear reader, for reading my

stuff. Like many of us in the trade, I began writing fiction to heal. It's opened a world of treasured friendships, evolving from process, to passion and purpose. The if the rest of the world were populated with the kind of people I've met on this journey, many of the challenges we face might well resolve themselves.

Terry Shepherd
    Jacksonville, Florida - August 2021

Made in the USA
Middletown, DE
04 September 2021

47589066R00177